The Templar's Woman

by

Cynthia Breeding

The Templar's Woman

Cover Art by *Debbie Taylor*

The Wild Rose Press, Inc.
PO Box 708
Adams Basin, NY 14410-0708
Visit us at www.thewildrosepress.com

Publishing History
First Edition, 2022
Trade Paperback ISBN 978-1-5092-4340-2
Digital ISBN 978-1-5092-4341-9

Published in the United States of America

Like ghostly wraiths, twelve ships glided silently around the headland of Orkney under the cover of night, tendrils of fog curling around the hulls and obscuring the sound of oars dipping into the flat water. A new moon shed only a sliver of light from its crescent as Adrian de Soules lifted his eyeglass to peer at the closing shore.

"Is the earl waiting, Captain?" Pierre Robillard, his first mate, came to stand beside him on the bow of the flagship.

"Not yet," Adrian answered, lowering his scope.

"He may not have seen our lantern with this thick mist." Pierre swiped at his face. "And it's *cold*. I'm going to miss the south of France."

"Better be cold and alive than dead," Adrian replied. "We were lucky to have enough warning to load the treasure before the king's men found it."

"Or us."

"*Oui*." A muscle clenched in Adrian's jaw. "I just wish we could have gotten Jacques out too."

Pierre grimaced. "You know de Moray would never leave until the last Templar was safe."

Prologue

October, 1307

Like ghostly wraiths, twelve ships glided silently around the headland of Orkney under the cover of night, tendrils of fog curling around the hulls and obscuring the sound of oars dipping into the flat water. A new moon shed only a sliver of light from its crescent as Adrian de Soules lifted his eyeglass to peer at the closing shore.

"Is the earl waiting, Captain?" Pierre Robillard, his first mate, came to stand beside him on the bow of the flagship.

"Not yet," Adrian answered, lowering his scope.

"He may not have seen our lantern with this thick mist." Pierre swiped at his face. "And it's *cold*. I'm going to miss the south of France."

"Better to be cold and alive than dead," Adrian replied. "We were lucky to have enough warning to load the treasure before the king's men found it."

"Or us."

"*Oui*." A muscle clenched in Adrian's jaw. "I just wish we could have gotten Jacques out too."

Pierre grimaced. "You know de Moray would never leave until the last Templar was safe."

Adrian knew that only too well. He'd spent several hours arguing with the Grand Master while the ships were being loaded. Word had been sent to his brethren scattered across France that Pope Clement—the damn fool puppet of King Philippe—had declared all Templars heretics and ordered them to be rounded up. It was only a ploy so the French king wouldn't have to pay the vast debt he owed to them, but they didn't have the numbers to launch a revolt against the entire French army, to say nothing of the Holy Roman Empire.

"I think I see something!"

Adrian raised his eyeglass again. Faintly, he saw a lantern swing in a half arch and then another a small distance from the first. "That's our signal. The entrance to the cove." He lowered the glass. "Give the helmsman the order."

As Pierre hurried away, Adrian turned his thoughts to Jacques once more. The Grand Master stayed because no Templar left his brothers on the battlefield to die. But de Moray was also right that the treasure the original nine men had recovered from the temple of Solomon nearly two hundred years before had to be protected from falling into the hands of the greedy king. Or worse, of the Catholic church. The scrolls themselves would be enough to turn Christianity upside down, to say nothing of the ancient relics. Especially one relic.

He looked to the shoreline where he could now make out a half dozen men waiting with a couple of wagons. He had to have faith that Henri St. Clair, the Earl of Orkney and Baron of Roslin, had chosen trustworthy men for this mission, but *faith* was not one of Adrian's strong suits. He preferred dealing with physical things he could see, touch, and feel.

"Heave ho!" one of the sailors called out as several

lines uncoiled like snakes and slithered through the air.

The men waiting on shore caught them, and Adrian could feel the hull scrape against the sand as the boat was pulled forward. Waiting for the gangplank to be lowered, he wondered which man was Henri St. Clair, since they were all working to secure the ships and no one was standing about like a grand lord. A good thing, in Adrian's estimation. The earl was also a direct descendent of the St. Clair family whose daughter the first Templar, Hugh de Payens, had married, so he simply was the best choice to guard the treasure.

Besides, the Scots were in the middle of rebellion against the English. *That* was something Adrian could understand.

And the Templars could help.

Chapter One

Berwick-on-Tweed
November, 1309

Passing through the city gate, Adrian reined in the feisty black stallion just short of the hill that led to Berwick Castle and looked up at the fortress, wondering for the thousandth time what he was getting himself into. If his Uncle John—who'd been trying to broker peace with Edward II—hadn't died, he'd still be training with his men in the western Highlands.

Fighting he knew how to do. He'd never felt comfortable at the French court, even before Philippe had turned on the Templars. There were too many treacherous men lurking about, eager to put a dagger in someone's back. Not to mention the fawning courtiers greedy for power. He detested the deceitful lies and basic lack of honor amongst them.

And here he was, about to become entangled in the English court.

He nudged the horse forward with a sigh. Robert Bruce had asked him to take over for his uncle John, a request he'd immediately turned down...until Robert had sweetened the offer by asking him to spy as well. The Earl of Pembroke was supposed to be visiting at Berwick. Rumor had it that he, along with several other earls and barons, were not happy with the regulations and taxes imposed by Edward II on the peerage to restrict their power. Bruce wanted to know whether he might be persuaded to ally with Scotland. If he did, Wales would back Bruce as well.

In the three years since the Templars had first landed on Scottish shores, Adrian had come to understand why the Scots were willing to fight so fiercely against the English. Edward I had committed unspeakable atrocities against them—including their women and children—that made even hardened-to-battle Templars cringe.

Scotland's war had become theirs.

****

"Welcome, my lord." The garishly dressed footman bowed as he opened the door to the castle wider for Adrian to step inside.

The loud, raucous clamor emanating from the left of the entryway in what probably was the Grand Hall drowned out any reply Adrian might have made. He managed not to grimace. Lucifer's horns! He'd forgotten how noisy a king's court could be. For a moment he wondered if the footman—dressed in red, bright yellow, and blue—might actually be a jester escaping from whatever was going on in the other room.

A rather ostentatious man, dressed in more somber colors, emerged from another doorway. "Lord de Soules?"

"Just *Monsieur,* not lord," Adrian replied. Robert had decided to make the most of his French background since Philippe had already acknowledged Robert's claim to the Scottish throne. Hopefully, Edward would recognize the subtle reference that France might back

Scotland against England if a truce were not brokered.

"As you wish, Monsieur." He gave a nearly indiscernible sniff. "I am Hubert, the castellan. His Majesty is hearing a dispute at the moment, but you can wait in the hall. Follow me, please."

"*Certainement,*" Adrian replied, not at all certain he wanted to follow the man anywhere. But then, he was here to spy, not criticize the entertainment or whatever it was causing such an uproar.

Hubert left him almost before he'd fully entered the large room, and Adrian had a small inkling of empathy for the man. He'd leave too, if he could. It looked like Edward had travelled with his entire London court.

The crush of people was even worse than in Paris, although the Great Hall of Berwick Castle was nothing like the lavish one in the French court. Berwick's arched roof was wood hammer-beamed, the walls adorned with a collection of weaponry rather than tapestries, the trestle tables absent fancy silver. The massive chandeliers suspended from the ceiling were of pewter, not crystal, and there wasn't a trace of gold gilt anywhere.

But the simplicity of the room contrasted sharply with its inhabitants. Even though it was only late afternoon, the men wore fine, velvet cote-hardies, and the ladies' elegant gowns shone in bright jewel colors from the glow of fires burning in all the hearths along the sides of the room.

His attention was caught as a petite woman with elaborately-coifed raven hair entered the hall at the far end, accompanied by a small party. Her shimmering red satin dress showed more cleavage than he'd seen in a brothel. From the way the people near her suddenly started bowing and curtseying, he assumed she was Queen Isabella.

Even from where he stood, he could tell her eyes were nearly as black as her hair. As she climbed the dais with her entourage, she inclined her head and smiled enticingly at the men nearby. She reminded him of Salome, the seductress who demanded the head of John the Baptist.

Adrian grimaced. For a Templar, she was a female devil incarnate, to say nothing of her being the daughter of King Philippe.

Almost out of habit, he stepped back into the shadows along one wall so he could observe without being noticed. Her lady attendants stood silently about, while the usual courtiers fawned over her, preening like peacocks eager for her attention.

One man stood slightly to the side, however, and made no attempt to approach the queen. Nor, now that Adrian thought about it, had he bowed when she entered. Interesting. Dressed in a dark burgundy surcoat, he was slightly built. Certainly not a warrior, but he didn't act like a courtier, either.

As he continued to watch, a second man joined the first, and Adrian recognized him as the Earl of Pembroke. His target for this mission. He started to breathe a sigh of relief that he hadn't come to Berwick in vain, when his breath caught in his throat.

A young woman walked toward the earl, her stride too long to be considered ladylike, but she moved with the lithe grace of a cat. And with purpose, looking neither to the right or left. Her reddish-blonde hair was loose and straight, fluttering slightly from the swiftness of her walk. Dressed in a simple gown of green-and-brown striped muslin, she looked like a forest nymph.

Adrian stepped out of the shadows for a closer observation just as she turned around. Her green gaze found his and held, intensifying for just a moment before she raised her chin and looked away.

One of his eyebrows rose of its own accord. Not many women turned away from him. This one hadn't even smiled, let alone given him a come-hither look he was used to. There hadn't been even a *subtle* invitation in her eyes, yet she'd held his gaze as steadily as any man. He sensed spirit in her. Independence. Maybe defiance, if the lift of her chin were any indication.

He grinned as he turned to leave. Feisty women were usually passionate in bed, as well.

****

Kendra de Clermont blinked, temporarily forgetting why she walked across the room. Who in the world was that tall, broad-shouldered man standing near the far door? His long, dark hair touched his shoulders, and she'd noticed the unusual color of his eyes. Golden, like a predator's, and just as sharp.

She felt the intensity of his stare. A slight tingle slipped along her spine, a sensation she experienced when something other-worldly was present. Not that she told anyone about those incidents. Men were too likely to label a woman a witch if she had any kind of unexplainable skills. Still, a vision of the man wearing a strange sort of armor had floated through her mind for a mere second before her sight told her he was only wearing a tunic with breeches and a cloak.

He certainly wasn't one of King Edward's pompous-assed fops that floated around the room, dressed in elegant fabrics and drenched in cologne that battled for prominence with the women's perfume. Her nose wrinkled as the heavy scents wafted in her direction. They failed to hide the stench of too many unwashed bodies—especially in a crowded, overheated room—and Kendra wondered why the English nobility didn't bathe as often as her own Welsh people did.

And to think that her aunt Beatrice wanted her to marry an English noble. Pah! She had no intentions of marrying at all and becoming chattel to a man. She valued her freedom to ride across the wild moors, where the wind shrieking from the cliffs sounded like the wails of ghosts that haunted the hills. She'd even seen one a time or two—some might say the white wraiths were only fog, but she had felt their *presence*. Which was all the more reason to remain single.

But she'd sensed the same sort of *presence* coming from the stranger. Not that he was a ghost. He was definitely alive. Kendra had the oddest feeling he probably smelled of the outdoors, of wooded forests and the sea.

She glanced over her shoulder to steal another look and then frowned. He was no longer standing by the door. Quickly, she scanned the room. Even though it was crowded, a man as tall as he was would stand out. She didn't see him anywhere.

He was gone.

****

To Adrian's relief, dinner with the English king was served in a smaller, private dining room instead of the vast hall. The man he'd seen talking to the earl was seated to the left of the king this evening and introduced as Piers Gaveston. It seemed to Adrian that Edward was more interested in conversing with him than with the queen. Not that Adrian blamed him exactly. Women like Queen Isabella were generally only concerned about themselves and their conversation equally limited.

She was appraising him with a sideways glance through lowered lashes. Even if he weren't here to spy—and broker a truce, supposedly—he wasn't about to fall into her trap. Women like her were spiders, weaving a fine web hardly noticeable until a man tried to escape from it. By the devil's horns, he'd nearly gotten arrested in France, *before* Philippe's edict, by making the mistake of believing a seductive female.

Angelique—he didn't miss the irony of her name— had been ever willing to make time for him, to pleasure him however he wanted, to become his mistress. She had spent hours encouraging him to talk, especially about the Templars and the wealth they'd accumulated. It was only when he realized that she was trying to get information about their *real* treasure that he suspected she was in King Philippe's employ.

After that betrayal, he resolved to limit his relationships with the opposite sex to the bedroom only. Give them pleasure, take his own, and be done. All in all, quite simple. His reverie was broken by the arrival of the Earl of Pembroke.

"Forgive me for being late, Your Majesty," the earl said, "but there was a bit of a squabble between your soldiers and mine about the use of the barracks. I thought to end it before it escalated into a brawl."

"Excellent, excellent." Edward waved a dismissive hand, not turning from his conversation with Piers. "Have a seat."

"Thank you, Your Highness."

Even as he spoke, two women entered the room as well. The first, Adrian supposed, was the earl's wife Beatrice, daughter of the former Constable of France. But the second... His breath hitched. The second lady was the wood nymph herself.

He stood at once, fighting the urge to grin at his luck. She hadn't changed out of the striped gown she'd worn earlier, which told him she wasn't obsessed with fashion or the need to change ensembles for every occasion...even if it was dinner with the king of England.

He didn't miss the slight widening of her eyes when she saw him, or how those eyes turned a shade darker, reminding him of the depths of a forest. But why was she with the earl? She'd walked over to him earlier in the hall, as well. Could she possibly be a companion for the countess? That might explain her not needing to change clothes.

Adrian bowed, pulling a chair for her while the earl attended his wife. Before he could ask for an introduction, the earl spoke.

"You must be the new envoy, Adrian de Soules?"

"I am not sure that is my official title, but yes, I am replacing my uncle."

"I knew John de Soules well," the earl said. "I thought I saw you earlier in the hall."

"I had only just arrived." Adrian gave both ladies a diplomatic smile. "May I have the honor of an introduction?"

"Of course. This is my wife, Countess Pembroke." He gestured. "And this is my ward—and niece-by-marriage—Lady Kendra de Clermont."

Adrian managed to keep his smile pasted to his face while he felt he'd just been kicked in the stomach by his horse. The wood nymph was the *niece* of the man he'd come to spy on? Robert would say that a golden opportunity presented itself here. If Adrian got to know her better—and he wanted to, at least in the carnal sense—would she reveal her uncle's plans? Yet he remembered how betrayed he'd felt when Angelique had used him the same way.

The Templars had long ago dropped vows of chastity, but they still upheld honor. Was he being given some divine choice to make?

Chapter Two

"I am so relieved that you did not argue with me about attending this dance tonight," Beatrice said. "With the way the day has gone, I already have quite a headache."

"I would not want to increase your pain, Aunt," Kendra replied and looked around the Great Hall that had been transformed into a dance room this evening by moving the trestle tables to one side. A trio of musicians with flute, mandolin, and drum were arranging themselves on the dais. She briefly wondered if a priest travelled with the court. Probably not, since the Church frowned on public dancing.

She truly had *not* planned to come—the king's London entourage's mannerisms were too affected and artificial—but she hadn't seen Adrian de Soules all day and, for some reason, that kept her from making an excuse not to attend.

She had no idea of what was wrong with her. Or even why she wanted to see the man. At last night's dinner, he had been polite, but he hadn't flirted. Mayhap that was what intrigued her about him. Not that she wanted him to flirt. Lord, in the few days since she'd been here, there had been far too many pretentious sons of nobility fawning over her and offering flowery compliments. One had even called her delicate as a rosebud in a spring rain. She tried to stifle a snort.

Beatrice frowned. "Must you make such unladylike sounds?"

"I'm sorry. I was trying not to sneeze." A white lie, but it seemed to placate her very proper aunt. The falsehood also proved—to herself, at least—precisely why she would never fit in with noble society. Too many rules. Too many restrictions.

"Ladies never sneeze. They pinch their noses behind their fans." Beatrice appraised Kendra. "You do look rather nice tonight."

"Thank you." Coming from her aunt, that was probably a real compliment. Or maybe just a statement of fact, since she preferred wearing simple, utilitarian dresses—and even breeches, when she was riding the Welsh moors. One more reason to get away from Edward's court as soon as possible. She *missed* those trews.

"And you will dance with the gentlemen who ask tonight, won't you?"

Kendra managed—barely—to refrain from rolling her eyes. That was another habit her aunt found irksome. "Yes, I suppose I must."

Beatrice's eyebrows rose. "*Must*? It's an honor to be asked, not a punishment."

She wasn't at all sure about that, but wisely held her counsel. She knew full well why those young men hovered about. She was no English rose—forget about rosebuds—and she wasn't a shrinking violet either, if one wanted to mix metaphors. She was tall and slender, not petite and curvy. Her skin was not the pale alabaster preferred by society, but rather tanned from the sun. She even had a smattering of freckles. And she spoke her mind, another trait her aunt tried desperately to curb.

"Here comes young Lord Turner." Her aunt's fan snapped open. "I prithee, do be pleasant to him."

"Of course." Kendra held back a sigh. Lord Turner wasn't the biggest clout or most boring of the lot, but he was typical. All of them were ambitious. They hoped, since she was both niece and ward of the Earl of Pembroke, that not only would she have a large dower, but—since the earl had no legitimate heirs—that her husband would also gain power and status from such an association.

Not that she planned on procuring a husband.

Her gaze swept the room as Lord Turner led her to join the dancers forming a circle. Still no sight of Adrian de Soules. She frowned slightly. Mayhap he'd not been invited? Then she shook her head, dismissing the idea. He was an envoy, which meant he was an honored guest. But then, the king had not made an appearance either. Maybe they were meeting about the truce her uncle had mentioned last night.

"Have I done something amiss?" Lord Turner asked, his mouth pinched.

Kendra blinked. "No. Why do you ask?"

"Forgive me, but you were frowning, and then you shook your head."

"Oh. I…was just… My aunt had quite a headache over this afternoon's activities. I was thinking about that."

"You should not concern your pretty head about something so trivial as soldiers brawling in the courtyard, my lady."

Kendra bit back a retort. Half of those soldiers had

been her uncle's men. Evidently, what he thought he'd put to rest the evening before had blown up again today. And it was very much her concern, since one of the older soldiers had taught her to ride when she'd first arrived at Pembroke Castle as an orphan. And, after she'd bedeviled them endlessly, another had shown her how to throw a knife and a third how to use a bow. Not that her aunt or uncle were aware of those particular skills.

"Soldiers with too much time on their hands get bored," she said. "Mayhap the king should hold a boxing match for them."

Her companion nearly gaped at her response, but Kendra only smiled sweetly, enjoying goading him. "Would you not agree?"

"I…I am not sure."

Just as the circle started to move, Adrian stepped into the hall, and her breath caught. For a moment, she'd thought he was wearing that strange armor again, but as he moved she realized he wore a black cote-hardie with silver threads and a silver belt. His dark hair was pulled back in a queue this evening, which only accentuated the hard, angular planes of his face.

She caught his gaze just before Lord Turner spun her in a different direction and she lost track of Adrian. When the dance mercifully stopped minutes later and Lord Turner deposited her—probably gratefully—with her aunt, Adrian was no longer by the door. Her eyes swept the room again, and then she frowned.

He was speaking to Queen Isabella. And she was standing *very* close to him.

****

Adrian's eyes trained on Kendra like a hawk spotting a

hare the minute he entered the Great Hall. She was dancing with one of the young English nobles, and she was smiling. Was he one of her suitors?

The afternoon had proved quite interesting. While he and his own two soldiers helped Pembroke subdue the unruly brawlers, he'd heard one of the older ones mention the reason the fight had broken out was because one of the king's men tried to take Lady Kendra's horse. Apparently there had been heated discussion over whether he'd meant to "borrow" the mare or "steal" her. While the Andalusian was certainly of quality blood stock, Adrian had seized the opportunity to ask a few other questions about the woman he couldn't seem to get out of his mind.

He'd soon learned that Kendra had been orphaned several years ago and was now nearing one-and-twenty. Her aunt despaired of finding a suitable match for her, Adrian gathered from words not spoken, since the lass—the Scottish word seemed to fit her—might have a bit of a stubborn streak. And a temper. He'd bitten back a grin, since he much preferred feisty women over tame ones. But still... The earl wanted to marry her off to a suitable nobleman, and Adrian was here to spy for Robert, not secure a wife.

So was the lout pulling her around one of those suitors?

"Lord de Soules," a feminine voice said from slightly behind him. "Why do you look so glum?"

He didn't have to turn around to know who she was. He'd caught glimpses of the queen hovering in the shadows of the courtyard this afternoon while he helped quell the melee, and then he noticed her again when he was practicing swordplay with his own men.

Adrian sighed inwardly. Probably ignoring her at dinner last night had not been the best strategy. How often had he seen women in the French court becoming practically obsessed by his fellow Templars who didn't flatter them? Playing the chivalrous knight might satisfy her need for attention. He bowed.

"Your Majesty. *A quoi dois-je donc cet honneur?*"

She tapped her fan on his sleeve and moved closer. "Mayhap the honor is mine?"

He forced a smile. "You flatter me, Your Majesty, when it is I who should be flattering you."

She gave him a coy look. "I should like that."

He kept his smile in place. "I am no poet, but I am sure you have caught the eye of every man in this room." They'd have to be blind not to notice the décolletage of the silk gown she wore. Her nipples nearly showed.

"How kind, Monsieur." She swept her eyelashes down and gazed up. "I hope you are one of them?"

Thankfully, his Templar training caused him not to start. "It would be an insult not to notice you, Your Majesty."

Whatever her response would have been, it was thwarted by the entrance of the king and Piers Gaveston. Isabella frowned.

"I am afraid you will have to excuse me, Monsieur De Soules."

He bowed again. "*Certainement.*"

She moved away with a regal walk, the only agitation showing in the tight line of her mouth before she transformed it into a smile. Or a baring of teeth.

Adrian turned his attention to another swain bowing low over Kendra's hand. Her expression, even from where he stood, looked like someone about to be led to the guillotine. His mouth quirked as he strode forward.

This was one damsel he didn't mind acting like a gallant knight to save.

****

Out of her peripheral vision, Kendra saw Adrian walking toward her. Of course, she had been pretending *not* to watch him as he flirted with the queen. How he'd bowed and smiled and acted as though he were enjoying every word. Of course, every courtier in the king's entourage did the same thing. It was dangerous not to, given the queen's tendency to feel insulted. Or was he the sort to flirt with every woman? Still, Kendra had let a small smile escape when the king entered the room.

A smile which, apparently, had encouraged the young man bending over her hand at the moment. She tried to remember what his name was. The smile faded, and she barely managed to keep from scowling as she pulled her hand away.

The young man cleared his throat. "I would like to request—"

"*Excusez-moi*, I believe Lady Kendra has promised me this dance."

She had done no such thing. As she looked up at him, she caught a subtle scent of soap and leather about him that was refreshing. She also caught the arrogant lift to his eyebrow. Her emotions warred. Was she the next convenient woman to be flirted with? Or was he rescuing her from whoever this young man was because he didn't think her capable of saying no? What if she didn't want to say no to Mr. Whatever-his-name-was?

Or maybe Adrian de Soules thought himself so attractive that no woman would refuse him, even when another man had gotten to her first. Maybe she should just tell both of the men "no" and leave.

Beside her, her aunt's fan snapped open and closed with a sharp click, a sound that told Kendra, louder than words, there wasn't any way she could leave right now. She put on the smile her aunt had made her practice.

"I am sorry," she said to the anonymous young man. "I must honor Monsieur de Soules' request, since he was of great help to my uncle this afternoon."

He started to protest, but Adrian didn't let him finish. Instead, he took Kendra's hand and lifted her out of the seat with a graceful motion that she was sure he'd used hundreds of times before with probably hundreds of women.

As he led her to the center of the floor where other dancers were forming a circle, she was aware of how large and strong his hand was. Her own was not particularly small, but it felt engulfed by his. And, she noted, his fingers were calloused, as was his palm. It was a hand used to wielding a sword. A hand that spent *hours* practicing. She gave him a sideways glance, almost expecting to see the image of armor appear again. He had not claimed to be a French knight, but he was a warrior. Of that, she had no doubt. He moved with the lithe agility and adeptness of a man used to battle.

Had he fought for King Philippe? The king had recognized Robert the Bruce's claim to the Scottish throne and, according to her uncle, always had an eye on claiming English soil. It wouldn't be the first time France had sided with Scotland against England. Was something nefarious going on?

Was Adrian truly here to broker peace with Edward in place of his late uncle? Or was he using that guise for some other reason?

Chapter Three

"You asked to see me, Monsieur?"

Adrian turned from the window in the small room that functioned as a scriptorium, near the back of the castle, to smile at his fellow Templar, Remy. "There is no need to be formal. We're alone in here."

Remy relaxed his shoulders, but he still took a quick look around the room. Adrian let his smile widen. The French court had taught them never to let their guard down, and their training with the Bruce had only enforced that belief.

"I already made a thorough inspection." He gestured. "There is hardly a place to hide in a room this size."

"That is what we thought about a certain parlor in Paris as well."

Adrian's smile faded. Remy might say "we," but it was he who'd nearly allowed himself to be caught in what he had come to think of as Angelique's net. She'd been trying to draw him out about the Templar treasure. If he hadn't noticed an unusual flutter to the heavy velvet drape, he might never have realized another person was present. The man had taken off running, and Angelique had claimed she'd no idea how an intruder had gotten in. It was only later—and thanks to Remy lingering on the street corner—that they'd discovered the intruder had been a spy for the Crown.

"Mayhap you should do a second check."

"I meant no offense."

"None taken." Adrian ran a hand through his hair. Remy might be posing as one of the personal soldiers who'd accompanied him, as was Pierre, but all three of them had been prepared for the Brotherhood since they were old enough to be pages. And each of them was a member of the secret *Prieuré de Sion* itself, which meant they held equal rank.

"I need for you to take a message to Robert."

"A message that can't be sent through our usual channels?"

By that he meant a seemingly innocuously worded letter sent by public courier to an equally benign coaching inn near Stirling where the proprietor would hold it for one of the Bruce's men to retrieve. Adrian shook his head. "That would be too slow."

Remy lifted a brow. "It must be important if you're willing to keep only one of us here."

"I don't anticipate any major problem in the near future." Adrian paused. "I found out at dinner night before last that Lady Kendra de Clermont is Pembroke's ward and niece—"

"*Crème pour le pouding.*" Remy grinned. "A sweet advantage, *non*? You should have no trouble loosening the girl's tongue to tell all she knows."

The image of "loosening her tongue" with his as his mouth covered hers set an unexpected spike of blood rushing to his groin. Thoughts of kissing those full, pink lips had caused him to get little sleep last night. The one dance they'd shared last night had sent lightning bolts up his arm each time their fingers connected and made him want to keep his hands on her

23

for much longer. Lucifer's horns! He hadn't expected the attraction to be so intense.

Aware that Remy was regarding him curiously, he shook his head again. "Let me finish. She's also the granddaughter of the recently deceased Constable of France." He waited for that statement to make an impact. "Which means she might still have close ties to King Philippe himself."

Remy's grin turned into a frown. "You think she's a spy for France?"

By all that he held holy, Adrian didn't want to think so. But he hadn't thought Angelique a spy, either. His mouth tightened. "I don't know, but I intend to find out."

Remy tilted his head. "If she *is,* that could work *for* us… The Bruce would welcome French forces to back him if Edward won't sign a truce. Is that what you want me to tell him?"

"In part, yes." Adrian hesitated, then drew his hand through his hair once more. "But get word to our brethren also. You know King Philippe has ordered our arrest in Britain as well. If Lady Kendra is a spy and she finds out we are Templars, who knows which king she will inform first?"

****

As she took her seat, Kendra both anticipated—and dreaded—the second evening dinner in the king's private dining room. She looked forward to seeing Adrian, yet knew she'd have to watch the bewitching queen continue to work her charms on him like she'd done at the dance. She'd seen the queen watching him practice his swordplay this afternoon in the courtyard.

Not that Kendra would have noticed otherwise, but

she just *happened* to be taking a stroll through the bailey for exercise and was drawn to the sounds of swords clashing. She had to admit watching Adrian in motion was spectacular. The laces of his tunic were open, its sleeves rolled up, revealing both a broad, tanned chest and well-muscled forearms. He moved like a Roman gladiator, every step measured, every slash calculated. And he hadn't broken a sweat.

All of which confirmed her suspicions. He was no ordinary envoy. So who was he?

Her attention caught when she heard the king telling her uncle that King Philippe now had money to spend on holding the Ottomans in check, since he'd disbanded the Templars and seized their banks.

"Of course, Philippe was a fool to get himself indebted to them in the first place," Edward said.

Pembroke nodded. "Having Pope Clement label them heretics might have been going a bit far."

"I quite agree," Gaveston broke in. "Sometimes the Church is too judgmental."

"That's true." Edward smiled at him. "Which is why We will not allow England to be controlled by Rome."

Kendra put down her spoon. Women weren't supposed to voice opinions, but she didn't agree with that notion. "Well, I'm glad the Templars have been rounded up."

All eyes turned to her. Even Isabella stopped fluttering her lashes at Adrian. He, in turn, stared at Kendra. "Why would you say that?"

"I prithee, Monsieur, to ignore my niece's outburst," Beatrice said. "She should know better than to interfere with the conversation."

Kendra felt her face warm, not out of embarrassment but from anger. Why shouldn't she be allowed to have an opinion? It didn't help that Isabella looked highly amused. She probably *should* offer an apology to the king, since, more than likely, she'd broken a dozen different rules of protocol in his presence, but Piers had leaned over and was whispering something to him.

"Actually, I find ladies' opinions are often much more astute than men's," Adrian said. "I would like to know why Lady Kendra feels as she does."

Kendra bit back a smile at the aggravated look on Isabella's face and the equally astonished look on her aunt's. At least, she couldn't be criticized for answering.

"I think, as a group, they were highly irresponsible."

One of Adrian's eyebrows lifted. "For lending the French king money?"

She waved a hand dismissively. "Not *that*. My father was also in their debt. They lent him money because of who my grandfather was—"

"Kendra." Her aunt frowned. "We do not discuss family matters in public."

"But Monsieur de Soules *asked*."

"That I did," Adrian replied before her uncle could intervene too. "Your grandfather was the Constable of France, *non*?"

"*Oui. Mais mon père...*" Kendra slipped into French, then switched back to English, "but my father should never have been loaned money."

Adrian looked quizzical. "And why not? It allows the merchant class as well as retired knights the chance to be independently successful."

"Mayhap," Kendra replied, "but my father had a weakness for gaming—"

"This is not an appropriate conversation!" Beatrice looked at her husband. "Say something."

"It's not a secret," Kendra went on quickly. "After *Maman* died, Papa's gambling got worse. When he realized he could not repay what he'd borrowed, he committed suicide. That…" She gave her uncle a steady look. "…is how I came to be your burden."

"You are not responsible for your father." Pembroke frowned. "And you are not a burden."

Her aunt didn't look so sure. Kendra would be in for a huge lecture once they were out of earshot. She sighed. She'd had a lot of lectures since she'd arrived. "Well, if it weren't for the Templars thinking my grandfather would cover the loans and kept giving my father money, he might be alive today." She lifted her chin. "So, for whatever reason, I'm glad the Templars were gathered up."

"I see," Adrian said.

****

And he did indeed *see*. Or, Adrian thought as he strode into the courtyard the next afternoon to fence with Pierre, he saw where the line had been drawn. If Kendra de Clermont ever discovered he was a Templar, she would have no qualms in turning him over to the authorities. His men, too. Edward might not send them back to France, since he had refused to honor the edict to look for exiled Templars in Britain, but that didn't mean Kendra didn't have contacts in France who'd be more than willing to sail across the Channel.

Pierre grinned at him as he drew his sword. "You

look rather vexed this afternoon. Does that mean I'm in for a *real* match?"

"It does," Adrian replied, pulling his own sword and advancing without the usual *en garde*. Surprised, Pierre barely managed to parry.

"*Qu'est-ce qui ne va pas, mon ami?*" he asked as their swords clashed.

"Nothing's wrong," Adrian bit out as he disengaged and then lunged once more.

"*Non?*" Pierre feinted left, then stumbled as Adrian's sword came down hard to his right. "*Vous agissez comme un fou!*"

Adrian took a deep breath. He *was* acting like a madman, which could very well get him killed in battle. He made a calculated lunge, pressing his sword against Pierre's. "I cannot tell you here. There are too many ears about."

Pierre disengaged, then reposted. "*Oui.* And some of them are women." He parried a cut, then cut over and grinned again. "I assume one of them is the problem."

Adrian didn't return the grin. Most of the time, when a woman was the problem—for any of them—it was because she was reluctant to leave their beds. He'd already endured good-natured jesting about the queen following him with her eyes whenever they were in the same room together. And he knew she was standing in the shadows of the covered walkway even now.

If only she were the problem. Kendra de Clermont presented a much bigger danger, even if he had trouble keeping at bay the image of a naked Kendra writhing beneath him and begging for more pleasure…

He didn't see the blow coming. Pierre feinted right,

and Adrian automatically struck left, only to realize too late that Pierre had done a double-feint. His momentum was met with nothing but air, and he stumbled two steps before he balanced, but by that time Pierre's sword had come down and he felt a sharp, slicing pain in his arm.

"*Mon Dieu!*" Pierre grounded his sword and gave him a wide-eyed look. "No one has ever drawn blood on you before."

Adrian grimaced and swiped at the thin line of red seeping through his shirt. "It's nothing." At least it wasn't his sword arm. And it served him right for being distracted. He raised his sword and assumed the first guard position. "Let us start over, shall we?"

As their swords engaged once more, Adrian decided that Lady Kendra de Clermont was a threat even if she didn't know who he was.

And then he forced thoughts of her from his mind.

****

From the safe confines of the stable, Kendra watched in horror as one of Adrian's soldiers slashed his arm. It took all of her will power not to run to him when she saw the blood color his shirt. He was wounded! But how badly? The other soldier had grounded his sword. No doubt he would help him from the courtyard. Mayhap she could nonchalantly stroll from the stables across the yard and intercept them?

She saw a shadow move along the covered walkway by the side of the castle. Isabella. Well, she wasn't going to get to him first. Not this time. Kendra was about to step out, when she stopped and nearly gaped.

Incredulously, the two men had returned to

fencing. Even with blood trickling onto the ground, Adrian was not giving up…and this was just practice.

Again, she wondered what—or who—he really was.

****

After the noonday meal was finished the following day, Kendra slipped off to the stables once more. Her aunt frowned on her visiting the area at all, but she'd pleaded that Argenterie, her mare, would feel abandoned if she did not see her. Luckily, her uncle had supported her, saying a horse that bonded with its owner would also protect her. Beatrice had looked askance at both of them, but she'd finally given an indignant sniff in resignation.

Her aunt probably wouldn't be resigned to what Kendra had planned, though. Or her uncle either. When they'd arrived, she'd been told to stay inside the walls of the castle and not venture out, but she would go mad if she had to stay confined much longer. Since she'd come to Berwick Castle, she'd already had her fill with the antics of the court, the courtiers paying lip homage to anyone whose title outranked them, while the lords did the same to the king. The women, including the queen—*especially* the queen—flirted outrageously with the knights and noblemen alike and, in particular, with one special envoy from Scotland.

Hypocrisy hung so heavy in the atmosphere it was difficult to draw in a fresh breath. She missed the open spaces of the Welsh moors where ghostly apparitions drifted over bogs and the lonely cry of gulls filled the air over the pounding of the sea.

Today, she was going to *ride*.

"I would like my mare saddled, please," she said to

one of the stable lads who'd grown used to her visiting her horse.

His eyes widened. "I doona have permission to do that."

"Of course you do. You have my permission. She is my horse."

The boy stubbornly shook his head. "'Tis a rule no ladies are allowed outside the castle on account of…" He stopped.

"On account of what?" Kendra asked.

He shrugged. "Just on account."

Kendra was fast losing patience. "Surely, with the king's army wintering in Berwick, it is safe for a short ride outside the city gates."

He shook his head again. "I'd have my hide tanned, I would, if I let ye ride out alone."

Kendra sighed. She supposed she shouldn't blame the lad for not wanting to disobey orders. But she had to get away from the stifling constraints of the castle. "So, then. Let me speak to the stable master and ask him to allow you to be my escort."

The boy gaped at her. "Ye want…me…to go with ye?"

She sighed again. It probably wasn't the most proper of accompaniment—most likely, it wasn't proper at all at an English court—but she didn't have a knight in shining armor loitering about to take care of that discrepancy. "I'm sure you'll make a perfectly fine escort."

The boy's eyes turned owlish. For a moment, she thought he was trying to assimilate the whole idea, and then she heard a deep, masculine voice behind her.

"I will escort the lady," Adrian said.

Kendra felt her own eyes go round, but she quickly schooled her expression before she turned around. "Monsieur de Soules."

He bowed. "Lady Kendra."

"I thought you practiced fencing in the afternoons." As soon as the words were out, she felt her face warm. Lord, now he'd think she had been watching him! Not that she hadn't, but...

A corner of his mouth quirked up. "Occasionally not."

"Oh." She hoped she didn't sound as flustered as she felt. "I... I..."

"I will take that as an 'aye,' which means 'yes,' does it not?" Adrian turned to the lad. "Saddle the lady's horse."

The boy gulped and hesitated. "I am nae supposed to—"

"I will take full responsibility for the *order*." He emphasized the last word, and the stable boy paled. "And you are to be commended for your sense of duty."

At that, the young man's face flushed red and a smile replaced the earlier wobbling of his mouth. "Thank ye, sir. I'll have the mare ready in a thrice, sir."

He certainly had a sense of command. And the ability to charm and captivate, as well. She'd do well to remember that. Kendra had a feeling that no amount of cajoling or coaxing she might have done would have persuaded the stable lad to saddle her horse. She frowned. "I can—"

"The countryside outside Berwick teems with unrest." Adrian lifted a brow. "Would you rather have an untried lad lagging along with you, or me? At least, I can handle a sword."

That had to be the biggest understatement she'd ever heard. She doubted the legendary King Arthur could have wielded Excalibur any better. She looked up at Adrian, trying to determine if he was being humble— which she doubted—or mayhap a bit mocking. Then he bowed again, and for a brief second, she glimpsed armor on him once more. She blinked, and Adrian was only wearing tunic and braies, with a dark, woolen cloak.

"My lady? Do you wish to ride or not?"

How could he mix gallantry with so much authority? It was rather annoying that her own request for her horse had been denied, but she knew Adrian had a point. If she wanted to ride, this was the only way she was going to get to do it. Besides, it would give her time to spend with him. Not that he had indicated he was particularly interested in her company. She managed to stop another frown before it began.

"Are you sure I am not keeping you from something important?"

"*Non.* My horse needs exercise as much as yours does."

Kendra blinked at the blunt answer. The courtly response would have been "*Nothing is more important than you, my lady.*" But then, she didn't want insipid men paying her court, did she? *Not* that Adrian was. Paying her court, that is. She looked down to hide the confusion she felt around him. What in the world was wrong with her?

Another thought occurred as her mare was led out along with his mount. Mayhap he had another reason for going outside the city walls for a ride. He'd said there was unrest. She knew Scots harbored hatred for the first Edward and were nearly as hostile toward his son. Adrian was here to broker peace. If that failed—and it didn't seem Edward was willing to return to London—was Adrian riding out to scope the countryside for able-bodied men still left after the first Edward's massacre?

And was she functioning as a distraction of sorts?

****

Adrian had noticed immediately that Kendra was dressed differently this afternoon than when she usually went to the stables. Instead of one of her regular gowns, this one looked like it had a divided skirt, which meant she was intending to ride.

He watched for a few minutes to see who her escort would be. When no one materialized, he realized she was planning to go outside the gates alone. Was she planning to deliver a message to someone? And, if she was, did it come from her or from her uncle? Adrian doubted that Pembroke would send her on such a mission. Could she possibly have found out his own Templar connection?

Since Remy hadn't returned yet with instructions from the Bruce on how to proceed, Adrian deemed it best to keep a close eye on her.

They set out at a brisk pace, both horses trotting of their own accord. Kendra kept glancing at him as they followed the road along the river. Was she anxious?

"Do you have something on your mind, Lady Kendra?"

Her eyes held his gaze. And, if he weren't concerned about whom she might be planning to meet—and thwarting that plan if it existed—he'd take time to appreciate how the changing green of her eyes made him think of dark forests and lush meadows.

"I was wondering, how well do you know the lay of the land around Berwick?"

The directness of her question surprised him. Did she have some reason for asking? Her beautiful eyes were guileless, as was her expression.

"Why do you want to know?"

She blinked. "I…hmm, was just wondering."

Why? Obviously, his direct approach to the directness of her question wasn't working. He gave her his most charming smile. "Surely, you aren't thinking about exploring the countryside by yourself."

Instead of reacting like most women did, she simply stared at him. "What if I were?"

"It's really not safe."

"I'd be perfectly safe if I could dress like I do in Wales when I ride."

He lifted one eyebrow. "How can what you wear make a difference? Any villain along the road would see you are a noblewoman riding along."

"*Non!*" She shrugged a shoulder. "I dress like a man, with braies and tunic and boots, and stick my hair under a cap."

The idea of her wearing braies—the *image* of her derriere and long legs encased in such—made his blood rush to his groin. For a moment, he couldn't speak. "Are you saying the women in Wales dress like men?"

She gave him an annoyed look. "Of course not. The Welsh are civilized…at least, the ones on the southwest coast. It's just more *practical* to ride in braies than it is a dress when I'm riding across open moors without a human in sight." She looked around. "Besides, I don't see any highwaymen lurking about."

He drew his brows together in confusion. The image of Kendra in tight-fitting clothes had not left him, so he lagged behind in her abrupt change in subject. Then he realized she was talking about safety.

"One hardly ever *sees* highwaymen before it's too late. Besides, I'm sure your uncle would forbid such adventuring." Adrian watched her reaction closely.

Kendra grimaced. "If he didn't, my Aunt Beatrice certainly would."

So Pembroke hadn't sent her out. That didn't mean that she hadn't planned to make contact with someone, though. "You were willing to risk your aunt's indignation to ride out alone?"

"I was going to get the stable lad to come with me."

As if a boy hardly old enough to find his first whisker was going to be protection. Adrian narrowed his eyes slightly. But a young whelp would be easy to lose if Kendra had an assignation. All she'd have to do is deliver him to a public house and purchase an ale.

An assignation…maybe he'd been thinking about her motives completely wrong. Maybe she'd intended to meet a man for personal reasons. He'd learned from Pembroke that Lady Kendra was two-and-twenty. Certainly old enough to have a lover.

The thought did not sit well with him.

They rode for a few more miles before turning back. The course of their conversation had turned from his interrogating *her* to her, somehow, interrogating *him*. She peppered him with so many questions of how long he'd been in Scotland and how close he had been to his uncle that he was more than relieved to see the castle walls come into sight.

They were approaching the gates when he remembered, too late, exactly why ladies were not supposed to venture outside the grounds. But mayhap Kendra wouldn't notice. People tended not to look up.

No such luck. The hope had barely passed through his brain when Kendra reined in her horse with a gasp and pointed.

"Why is there a woman in a cage hanging from the wall?"

Chapter Four

"Who is that poor woman?" Kendra demanded as soon as they'd taken their horses back to the stable. "And what has she done to be so publicly humiliated?"

Adrian looked around the bailey, where too many people were about. "Mayhap we should go inside."

She stopped, hands on her hips. "I'm not going anywhere until I get an answer."

He was fast learning that Kendra was unlike any woman he'd ever encountered. "Do you want to stand out here and attract attention? If you do, it won't be long before your aunt finds out you've been riding."

She glared at him, and he bit back a laugh. He had a feeling Kendra did *not* like to be bested. But they were already drawing curious glances. "Mayhap you should change clothes and then ask your uncle about the cage."

Her green eyes sparked. "I told you I'm not going anywhere without an answer. And I don't need to talk to my uncle when I know *you* know why that unfortunate woman is imprisoned up there." She glanced at several men who had begun to linger and dropped her voice to a near whisper. "There's a walled garden behind the castle. We can go there."

The huskiness of her tone and the suggestiveness of such privacy immediately brought ideas to his head—and groin—of what could be done behind a trellis or a rosebush. He took a deep breath. From the stubborn set of her chin, he was sure she wasn't entertaining the same thoughts as he was. "Lead the way."

She turned on her heel and marched as straight-shouldered as any soldier toward a small gate that led to the back of the castle. In spite of himself, he lingered a few steps behind to appreciate the lithe grace of her determined pace.

The garden wasn't quite as private as he thought. A couple was strolling near the central fountain, and on the far end, a trio of older ladies, dressed warmly in cloaks and muffs, were taking in the fresh autumn air.

They'd barely gotten seated on a stone bench near the gate when Kendra folded her arms and lifted both brows. "Well?"

His eyes did a quick search to ensure no one was within hearing distance. "The lady is Isobel MacDuff, the Countess of Buchan."

Kendra's eyes widened. "A *countess*? Why?"

"It's a long story, but basically when Robert Bruce declared himself king of Scotland, she went against her husband's wishes and crowned Robert herself at Scone."

A most unladylike sound emerged from Kendra's throat. "Because she disobeyed her husband, she gets hung in a cage?"

"There's a bit more to it than that. When Robert killed John Comyn of Badenoch at Grey Friars, his kinsman, the Earl of Buchon, decided to switch sides and support the English."

"Lord have mercy!"

"The Lord isn't always merciful." Adrian

shrugged. "Then again, mayhap He is. The lady is alive."

"If you call being suspended in a cage living."

Adrian felt a muscle clench in his jaw. Reports from France had come in over the years of the imprisonment and torture of his fellow Templars who hadn't made it out of France. But it was hardly a comparison and certainly not one he could share. "If the Hammer had lived, she'd be dead."

Her eyes grew enormous. "Edward died three years ago. The countess has been up there all that time?"

His mouth tightened. "The current king may not have the same thirst for shedding Scottish blood that his father did, but he doesn't want to appear weak either. That's why the countess stays exposed to the people. As a reminder the English are still here."

"But... Robert Bruce has been acknowledged Scotland's king, at least by the French. Can't he request her release?"

Adrian wondered again how close her ties were with her French relatives. It was true that France and England were usually at loggerheads, which, in turn, made Scotland an ally, but Philippe still had out an edict for Templars. "It is one of the points I am hoping to get Edward to agree to. Bruce's own sister was secured in a cage as well, before being sent to a nunnery just last year, so I'm not sure how willing Edward is to negotiate about a second release."

"But...that's horrid. I will talk to my uncle. Maybe he can do something." She jumped up, not waiting for an answer. "I'm going to see him right now."

Adrian didn't try to stop her, although he doubted it would do any good. Pembroke would not want to get on the bad side of Edward. The king had a quick temper and was equally quick to punish, even if he wasn't as bloodthirsty as his father. And, if there was any chance at all that Pembroke and his Welsh army would side with Scotland if peace could not be found, he definitely wouldn't take a chance on angering Edward now.

Adrian rose with a sigh. There were no easy answers to the Countess of Buchan's dilemma.

****

Kendra didn't bother to change from her riding habit as she went in search of her uncle. He was going to know she'd been outside the castle walls when she asked him about the poor countess. Besides, now that she had seen what she wasn't supposed to see, there was no reason not to go riding. She just hoped he wasn't in the company of Edward since she knew, even angry as she was, that one simply didn't demand answers from a king.

Luckily, her uncle was with her aunt in the solar. Mayhap not totally lucky, given her aunt's disapproving perusal of what she was wearing. Well, *that* lecture was just going to have to wait. Kendra turned her attention to her uncle.

"How can the king do something so inhumane as to imprison a countess in a cage?"

"What were you doing outside the walls?" he countered.

"I went for a ride. Argenterie needed the exercise—"

"There are grooms here that can exercise your horse," her aunt said.

"I was about to go stark, raving mad trapped inside the castle," Kendra replied. "Besides, I don't like anyone else handling her."

Beatrice turned to her husband. "You should never have let her bring that animal. How are we ever going to find a suitable husband for her when she refuses to act like a lady?"

"The Countess of Buchan is a *lady*." Kendra couldn't keep the sharp edge off her tone. "And see where that got her!"

"She certainly did not act like one," her aunt retorted.

"Just because she did what she felt was right?" Her temper was still high. "Why is it that women do not have the right to an opinion?"

"Where do you get such ideas?" Beatrice closed her eyes as though praying for patience. "I suppose it is your upbringing. French women are too bold."

"You forget, Aunt, that my mother was Welsh. She always said the Celts valued their women's opinions and respected them. That once the country was ruled by matriarchy."

"Those pagan ways are past." Her aunt sniffed. "Wales is part of England now."

And her aunt had embraced Englishness in every way. Kendra flashed a look at her uncle, who had not said a word. "And England is Christian. Should not the countess be shown mercy?"

"Mercy was shown," Pembroke replied. "The lady could have been hanged for treason."

That was basically what Adrian had said. "And they call the Scots barbarians?"

Her uncle raised a brow. "Be careful what you say."

Kendra knew she should curb her tongue, but she

was still incensed. "Robert the Bruce has been acknowledged as the king of Scotland by most of the Continent—"

"That is not something we should be discussing," her uncle broke in. "And it would behoove you to watch your words. The very walls have ears."

She stopped abruptly. Even though she didn't like it, her uncle was right. Most of these old castles not only had hidden passageways, but also hidey-holes and crawl spaces between the walls where a person could lurk and listen to conversations. And intrigue at a royal court was a constant thing.

Beatrice gave her a hard stare. "I dare say you do not want to join the Countess of Buchan in her cage, do you?"

In spite of herself, Kendra shuddered. She couldn't imagine anything as horrible as being confined to a cage barely large enough to turn around in, day and night, with only minimal protection from the rain and cold. To say nothing about being exposed to taunts and jeers and rotten fruit being thrown. No woman should be subjected to any of that, regardless of what she'd done. However, to her aunt, she simply nodded. "Of course I wouldn't. I will watch my words."

"See that you do," her aunt replied.

"Especially in the coming days," her uncle said. "Edward's cousin, Thomas, the Earl of Lancaster, is coming for an extended visit. Things at court are about to become roiled. Words interpreted incorrectly could prove dangerous."

She wasn't sure what *things* he meant, but from his somber tone, she knew it wasn't going to be pleasant. "I will be careful."

"And no more discussing the Countess of Buchan's predicament," Beatrice added.

"As you wish, Aunt." Kendra kept her facial expression impassive. She would hold her tongue, but that didn't mean she wasn't going to pay the poor woman a visit.

****

Well past midnight, when Kendra hoped most of the castle was asleep, she slipped out of her bedchamber and to the servants' stairs at the end of the hallway. She wished she had her braies, but at least the dark blue dress she wore would help her blend into the night.

On reaching the ground level, she listened for any sound from the front of the castle. The Great Hall was silent, but she didn't want to take the chance of running into someone who might be drunk. Turning, she made her way out the back door, past the separated kitchens where a soft glow from banked fires lit the path. She moved quickly into the shadows of the keep until she could reach the curtain wall and the stone stairs leading to the battlements.

Stubbing a toe on an uneven step, she silently muttered a curse. Satin slippers weren't intended for sharp rocks, but she hadn't wanted to take a chance on wearing boots that might be heard by the guards.

Even though her gown was serviceable wool, she shivered when she reached the top and a gust of cold wind caught her. How could the countess abide being held in an open cage exposed to wind and cold? Kendra's hands fisted in anger at the thought of such cruelty. At least, the weather kept the guards in the barbican overlooking the gate and not anywhere near where the cage hung.

As she approached the spot, she heard the murmur of a masculine voice, too low to make out any words. Was a man visiting the countess? She'd been told only two female servants were allowed to attend her. Curious now, Kendra edged closer, squeezing into an embrasure and peeking around a merlon. As she did, she saw the shadow of a man sift through another embrasure several yards away. How in the world could a grown man fit through such a narrow space? She backed away and turned to see who it was, but the walkway was empty.

A chill slid down her spine that had nothing to do with the temperature. Who—or what—had she seen?

"Hello? Is someone there?"

That voice was definitely human. And female. Kendra moved closer and wedged in between the stone defenses and peered down. A single oil lamp illuminated a young woman near to her own age who looked up through the open latticework of the cage's roof.

"Who are ye?"

For a moment Kendra was so outraged she couldn't speak. The cage was not only exposed to the cold, but to rain and snow as well! What kind of brute would make a woman suffer such a thing? "My name is Kendra, and the Earl of Pembroke is my uncle."

Isobel's eyes widened. "Does he know ye are here?"

"No."

"Ye should go." The countess pulled her plaid arisaidh closer around her. "If ye are caught, ye'll be punished."

"Nothing my uncle could do would be this cruel."

"'Tis nae your uncle I fash about." The countess gave her a small smile. "'Tis Edward. He doesna like his orders countered."

Twice within the last two minutes, Kendra was speechless. The Countess of Buchan had been living in this human hell for nearly four *years,* yet Isobel was concerned about *her.* "Somehow, I am going to get you out of here."

Isobel shook her head. "There is naught that ye can do."

"There *must* be something. Maybe if I begged my uncle, he would—"

"Do nothing," another masculine voice said.

Startled, Kendra backed out of her space so fast she lost her balance. For a moment, she teetered on the edge of the battlement, and then one strong arm caught her waist, pushing her against the wall and pinning her. The scent of fresh soap and leather assailed her.

Adrian.

She looked up to see him gazing down at her, his unusual golden eyes sharp as a wolf's in the moonlight. He looked…hungry. Her pulse began to race, and suddenly she was aware of his body heat as he pressed against her.

"What in Hades are you doing up here? Don't you know it's dangerous?"

Her chin lifted. "I was careful."

"You nearly fell to your death just now." His voice sounded like a growl.

She bristled. "You scared me. You should have announced yourself."

He made a noise low in his throat that she couldn't

identify. "The guards would not have announced themselves. Do you have any idea what kind of entertainment you might have provided them?"

"They wouldn't dare lay a hand on me."

"*Non*? The only women who venture up here, besides the two assigned to Isobel, are camp followers."

"But I am not…" She became aware of something hardening against her lower belly. Odd parts of her began to tingle. Adrian's eyes narrowed, and he stepped abruptly away from her.

"Men are men, *mademoiselle*."

Feeling strangely bereft at his sudden move and flustered by her own reaction to what she'd just felt, she decided to change the subject. "And what are you doing out here on the ramparts at this hour?"

For a moment, he didn't answer. Then he held up the arm he hadn't used to catch her. He was holding a heavy sack.

Her curiosity returned. "What is in there?"

"Warm bricks." He moved sideways against the embrasure to allow his arm to extend down with them, and then he straightened. "For the countess."

"He's been bringing them every night since he arrived. I put them back on top of the cage in the morning for him to pick up." Isobel's voice floated up to them. "Thank ye again, kind knight."

"I do it gladly, my lady."

Kendra stared at him. He did this every night to keep the countess warm? What if he got caught? Surely he was putting himself at more risk than she was.

The man was truly infuriating. Just when she'd thought him cold and callous this afternoon when they'd ridden by the cage, now he turned out to be not only kind but caring.

She was so lost in thought as he guided her down the stairs that it wasn't until later she realized the countess had referred to him as a knight.

He had said he wasn't one. Why would she call him that?

Chapter Five

Adrian studied Remy seated across from him in the small library the next morning. He'd returned quicker than expected, which meant Robert had an urgent message.

"Has there been any change in plans?"

"Ultimately, no," Remy replied. "You're still to find out which direction Pembroke's loyalty runs. The Bruce is anticipating war, come spring."

A corner of Adrian's mouth quirked up. "There is the off chance that I could actually broker peace."

Remy grimaced. "Since Edward did not answer the letter Robert sent, asking for a truce, I'd say the chance of that happening is equal to Pope Clement granting pardons for Templars."

"Umm. No doubt an accurate description. How fare our brothers?"

"They prepare for war, keeping their skills honed."

Adrian nodded. "Edward will not be expecting an elite century of trained cavalry."

"That is why we've stayed hidden in the Highlands." Remy hesitated. "There is something else Robert wants you to do."

He nodded again. "I figured there was or you would not have nearly worn out your horse getting back. What is it?"

Remy looked uncomfortable. "He wants you to

ingratiate yourself with the niece. Any way you have to. Seduce her to get more information about her uncle."

Adrian's blood spiked at the same time he felt a chill run down his spine. The man in him would like nothing better than to get Kendra in his bed, lying naked beneath him while he pleasured her senseless. His Templar training told him it would be for the wrong reasons. He tried to compromise with his conscience.

"That lass may not be so easy to seduce."

Remy's brows lifted so high they nearly met his hairline. "Did I just hear you say you don't think you can?"

"Of course, I *can*." Adrian felt a moment of annoyance. "I'm saying Lady Kendra doesn't seem to be susceptible to the usual flattery."

His friend laughed. "I'm sure you can find a way to be persuasive."

Adrian wasn't so sure. That Kendra had gone to meet the Countess of Buchan last night should not have surprised him, yet he had nearly stumbled himself at seeing her on the battlements. Even though he'd only met her less than a fortnight ago, he should have known she would attempt something like that, based on her reaction when they'd ridden past the cage.

The little vixen was foolhardy, stubborn, strong-willed, and obstinate. And beautiful in an earthy, free-spirited, wood-nymph sort of way.

She was ultimately bound for trouble.

He'd meant what he said about men being men. If the guards had found her first... Lucifer's horns! He'd felt himself grow hard when he'd trapped her against the wall. For a brief moment, all he'd wanted to do was gather her delectable derriere—that had been jutting out earlier from the embrasure invitingly—in his hands and press her tightly to him while he took her mouth with his. And he was known for having nearly iron control over his emotions.

"I will think about it."

Remy sobered. "It was not a request."

Adrian studied his friend. "An order? The Bruce truly intends to fight, then."

"He's tired of hiding in the hills instead of taking his rightful place as king of Scotland. He's tired of skirmishes that result in small victories. He wants to retake a string of northern castles from coast to coast."

Adrian released his breath in a whoosh. "So we will be making a final stand."

"That's what Robert is preparing for." Remy gave a Gallic shrug. "Unless, of course, you can convince Edward he's a fool who should go home."

"I may actually have some help with that."

"Oh?" Remy looked intrigued. "How so?"

"The Earl of Lancaster is due to arrive at any moment. Even though they're cousins, he's been at odds with Edward for years."

"Over Piers?"

"In part." Adrian thought back to the bits and pieces of information he'd been able to gather this past week. "Edward's war has become expensive, and there are a number of nobles who would like to curtail the Royal fiscal policies."

"Telling a king what to do often causes heads to be separated from bodies," Remy remarked.

"True, but in this case, Lancaster happens to be the wealthiest man in England. He can raise an army practically equal to Edward's."

Remy's brows rose again. "Edward would be fighting two wars, then."

"Precisely. The question remains, though, which side Pembroke would favor. If he backs the king over Lancaster, which I would expect him to do, it means Robert loses the alliance." He paused. "If there is one."

"Well, you can use the niece to find out." Remy grinned once more. "It is not exactly a repulsive assignment."

Adrian nearly choked. Repulsive, no. Alluring, enticing, tempting, yes. Seducing Lady Kendra would be one of the most interesting, challenging, and enjoyable things he'd ever done. Except he'd be doing it for the wrong reasons.

The lady wasn't bound for trouble. She *was* trouble.

****

Kendra had actually put on one of her better gowns—a pale green watered silk that accented her eyes and closely molded her body—for this evening's dinner. Her aunt thought she'd done so in honor of the Earl of Lancaster having arrived, but she wore it for Adrian. The memory of him holding her on the battlement last night—especially what she had felt pushing against her belly before he stepped away—burned hot in her head, nearly searing her brain.

She watched him as he took a place several seats over from her. Since the table was round, it was easy to observe him without being obvious. Unfortunately, Queen Isabella had taken the seat next to him.

How different Countess Isobel was from Isabella. Apart from their contrast in coloring and dress, the countess seemed kind and brave, while the queen was haughty and flamboyant. The one who was imprisoned in a cage had more dignity than the one who lived in a castle.

Kendra turned her attention to the newcomer. The earl was seated next to Piers Gaveston, and that contrast could not have been more clear either. Piers had a slight frame, his hair carefully clipped short, his velvet cote-hardie and snowy linen shirt immaculate. Lancaster was tall, signs that he enjoyed both food and ale evident in the beginnings of jowls and a paunch. He hadn't bothered dressing for dinner but still wore his travelling cloak thrown back over one shoulder, his tunic, braies, and boots dusty from the journey.

The differences didn't stop with physical appearance, either. The earl practically sneered at Piers every time the man spoke.

"How are the king's Cornish lands doing?" Lancaster asked.

"The earldom is Piers', not Ours," Edward nearly snapped.

His cousin shrugged. "I thought the title was returned to the Crown when Gaveston was banned from England two years ago."

Edward glared at him. "As you can see, he has returned."

"Only because the threat of ex-communication was lifted, I dare say."

Gaveston adjusted his sleeves. "There was no reason for that threat to be made in the first place."

"No?" Lancaster's gaze slid to Isabella and then back. "Philippe was most concerned over his daughter's welfare in England if you remained."

Adrian shrugged a shoulder. "The French king

agreed to marry his daughter to an English one. *L'affaire est néglée, non?*"

Although Adrian's voice was level, the intensity in his golden eyes made Kendra think of an eagle who'd just spotted his prey. He glanced at Isabella.

"And it seems the queen is quite content with her circumstances."

Kendra frowned. What did he mean by that? If the woman hadn't been wearing a crown, she'd be little more than a hoyden. But then, in the little she had observed, Edward did not seem to mind his wife's flirting with other men. She glanced sideways at Adrian. Did he enjoy the queen's attention? She couldn't tell.

He had barely spared a glance at herself when he came in, and he hadn't spoken directly to her either. Had last night's episode left no impact on him?

Lancaster turned to Adrian. "And what brings you to this table? French knights are considered suspect in England these days."

"I do not claim to be a knight." Adrian's gaze didn't falter. "I am part Scots through my uncle John de Soules and am here to broker peace on behalf of Robert the Bruce."

Lancaster studied him and then turned to Edward. "A war that has taken too much from the English coffers. Maybe you should agree to acknowledge the Scottish king since you cannot seem to overthrow him."

Edward narrowed his eyes. "You forget your place."

Lancaster smirked. "I assure you I do not, *cousin*. The barons are not happy with what this war has cost us. There is talk of changing the law to rule by council instead."

The king's face turned nearly purple. "You come close to speaking treason of Us!"

"Do I?" Lancaster shifted his eyes to Piers and back to the king. "The nobles want a king who will lead them to victory. Mayhap I could be of assistance."

Adrian intervened. "If the English nobility wants to stop wasting money, then mayhap you could *assist* in brokering peace, my lord."

Queen Isabella suddenly tapped her spoon against her goblet, halting all conversation. "I grow quite weary of this nonstop talk of war. I am sure you gentlemen..." She gave Adrian a sideways glance through her lashes and then smiled at Lancaster. "...do not want to bore the ladies present?"

"I believe the queen is quite right." Kendra's uncle spoke for the first time. "My own dear wife is near bored unto tears, I'm afraid."

Kendra looked at her aunt, who dutifully dabbed at an eye with a lace handkerchief. She bit the inside of her lip to keep from laughing. She had never once since she'd arrived in Wales seen her aunt shed a tear. Especially not from boredom. But then she looked at her uncle with renewed respect. He had quite adeptly shut down a conversation that might just have led to open warfare.

"Quite so. I do beg forgiveness of the beautiful ladies present." Lancaster fixed his gaze on Kendra. "And this is your lovely niece, I presume?"

"Yes," her aunt said quickly. "Lady Kendra is actually *my* niece by blood and granddaughter to the late Constable of France."

Kendra shot her aunt a look. Why was that

important? She hated having a pedigree like a prized mare. She had been apprised of the wealth the earl had accumulated and how powerful he was. Her aunt had lectured her quite thoroughly before coming down to dinner. The earl was also a descendent of the Plantagenets of Anjou, and somehow her aunt must think this whole French-English connection important. As far as she was concerned, it seemed one never knew which side to be on. They were at odds more than they were allies. At any given moment, loyalties might change. It was enough to—

"So what do you think?" the earl asked.

"What?" Lord, she'd been woolgathering so badly she hadn't caught a word of the conversation. Why was Adrian glaring at Lancaster while the queen was looking at *her* with narrowed eyes.

Lancaster looked amused. "I just threw the gauntlet down—figuratively speaking—and I have challenged Monsieur de Soules to a fencing match tomorrow. I've been told he is quite good."

"He is." The words came out before she thought, and she felt warmth creep up her neck. "I mean, he and his men practice in the bailey..." She stopped. Good Lord. Would Adrian think she'd been watching? She had, of course, but to blurt the information out... Heat flooded her face.

"He is very strong, isn't he?" The queen stroked Adrian's forearm with her hand and then turned to Lancaster. "I will be glad to take over the awarding of the prize since Lady Kendra seems a bit confused."

Edward fixed her with a look. "You have your place in the stands, and you will act accordingly. The gentlemen have agreed that Lady Kendra will award the prize."

"Prize?" she asked.

Adrian turned his golden gaze to her while Lancaster spoke. "The prize, my dear, is a kiss from you."

****

The dinner had been a near disaster. If it hadn't been so late when Adrian finally left the private dining room, he'd have summoned Remy or Pierre from their slumber and taken to sparring in the bailey. Adrian clenched his fists, wishing he could hit something. Preferably Lancaster.

Lancaster had also come dangerously close to Adrian's true identity. Although he knew Edward didn't think England owed allegiance to Rome and so far had not searched for Templars, if he suspected one lurked in his court, he might feel obligated to have him arrested as a show of strength for Lancaster. And, if the man were going to keep goading Edward, insinuating he was weak where his father had been brutal, peace would never be brokered with the Bruce. The whole thing was a tenuous situation at the best.

And now, he had tomorrow's competition. He had no doubt he could win, considering the extensive training he'd undergone for years, but would he make more of an enemy of Lancaster if he did? The man was already suspicious. But if he let himself lose, Kendra would be forced to kiss the earl.

Adrian halted abruptly. It wasn't that he yearned for a kiss from a lady. Queen Isabella had made her willingness to give him that—and more—very clear. He sighed, then turned abruptly toward a side door that led outside to the barracks. He'd wake up Remy *and* Pierre and work off some of this bottled tension.

Like some besotted, green lad, he wanted a kiss from Kendra.

One that had no ruse behind it.

****

Queen Isabella stepped quickly back into the shadows of the hallway when Adrian stopped walking. Sitting so close to him at dinner had stirred the banked heat she'd felt for him ever since he'd arrived. She usually had only to crook her little finger and the man in question came willingly to her bed. That Adrian de Soules had not only piqued her interest more. She had been willing to play cat-and-mouse for a little while longer until that idiot Lancaster had proposed a challenge tomorrow and made the outspoken ward of Pembroke the trophy. She had seen the way the chit looked at Adrian when she thought she wasn't being observed. The little bitch wanted him, although Isabella was pretty sure she didn't know a thing about seducing a man.

But courtesan skills could trump that kind of naivety easily. Isabella fully intended to let Adrian know what he'd be missing if he didn't become her lover. That was why she'd decided to follow him to his bedchamber tonight.

Unfortunately, it didn't look like he was going there. Isabella turned around, pressing her lips together. Another time, then. She would wait.

Chapter Six

Kendra didn't think she'd slept a wink, so she was surprised when her maid Elsie pulled open the heavy drapes and sunshine streamed through the window.

"Sakes! What time is it?" she asked, sitting up.

"'Tis near mid-morn, my lady."

"Mid..." Lord, she never slept that late! Kendra swung her legs over the edge of the bed, then winced as her bare feet touched the cold floor. Argenterie would be wondering where her treat was. She reached for the serviceable brown muslin kirtle she'd worn the day before.

"Oh, no, my lady! Ye cannae wear that!" Elsie opened the wardrobe and rummaged through the few gowns there, withdrawing a bright yellow satin. "This is better."

"That's a banquet dress. Why would I wear it in the morning?"

The maid gave her a look that clearly said, without words, that she must be daft.

"Ye have nae forgotten the swordplay this day between Lord Lancaster and Monsieur de Soules? 'Tis all the folks in the castle have been talking about." Elsie tilted her head. "And ye are to play a part, I heard."

She could hardly have forgotten the challenge. The idea of awarding a kiss was what kept her awake all night. She'd never kissed a man before. What kind of a kiss was expected? She'd never *been* kissed, either, unless she counted the wet, sloppy attempt of a French count's son when she was four-and-ten. She'd bloodied his nose.

As she'd tossed and turned throughout the night, she'd gone from feeling her whole body warm at the thought of kissing Adrian—would he kiss her back?—to having her blood chill at the thought that Lancaster might win the match.

Her uncle had told her the earl had fought for Edward I as soon as he came of age and had remained beside him for ten years. The current king's father hadn't gotten the moniker of "The Hammer" for nothing. If the earl had fought with the first Edward for that length of time, he was no doubt excellent with a sword.

Better than Adrian?

Kendra closed her eyes, thinking about watching Adrian practice in the bailey. Although he'd kept his shirt on, the sleeves had been rolled up, revealing the strength in his forearms. As he'd grown damp with sweat, the material had clung to him and she'd seen the muscles in his back ripple with every maneuver. She already knew that he moved with stealth-like grace, since she'd danced with him.

Was he stronger than Lord Lancaster? The earl was heavily muscled, even if he had extra weight. And he seemed close in age to Adrian. She had no idea what kind of actual fighting experience Adrian had. Would he win? The thought of kissing Lancaster—even a mere peck—was slightly repulsive. And, if the custom was for the winner to kiss her back… She wasn't sure what the punishment might be for bloodying an earl's nose.

Maybe she should have insisted the queen be the prize-giver after all. The thought had barely formed when she pushed it aside. Isabella was already way too flirtatious. Although, if Lord Lancaster won...

She clutched her head with both hands.

"Is something amiss?" Elsie looked worried. "Are ye nae well?"

That would depend on who won the match. Kendra rubbed her temples. Mayhap she could plead a headache? It wouldn't be a lie, with the pounding that was starting. Then she dropped her hands and lifted her head. She wasn't going to hand the queen a golden opportunity to kiss Adrian. *No. No. No.*

"I will be fine," she replied as she took the yellow kirtle from Elsie.

Adrian had to win. He just had to.

****

"You have got to let the earl win," Remy told Adrian as they walked toward the bailey before the match. "We cannot let him suspect our true strength."

Adrian clenched his jaw. He'd not gotten much sleep last night thinking about the dilemma. The Templars were the Bruce's hidden weapon, the force he did not want anyone to know he had. Could Adrian, as a Frenchman who claimed not to be a knight, possibly win and not arouse suspicion? "I hate losing."

"Well, consider we might be needing Lancaster as an ally, albeit an unknown one," Pierre added. "It could behoove Robert's effort if Edward's forces were split."

Adrian set his jaw. "But it would also make Pembroke choose between Lancaster and Edward, and an alliance with Robert would be out of the question."

"We do not know which way the wind blows with

Pembroke," Pierre pointed out.

Remy gave him an arched look. "Of course you have a way of finding out."

"You don't need to remind me, brother."

Hellfire and damnation. He didn't want to think of that dilemma either. The Bruce expected him to seduce Kendra to extract information from her. *It wasn't a request*, Remy had said. And Adrian would have no qualms in doing just that, were Kendra one of the regular ladies of the court who used cunning and guile to get what they wanted. Deceit and intrigue were part of the nature of those who followed in the king's wake and hovered around him, hoping to advance their stations.

But Kendra wasn't one of those women. Unlike the manipulative queen, Kendra was outspoken and honest to a fault. She had been outraged—and no doubt still was—at the treatment of the Countess of Buchan. She took her horse an apple every morning, and pilfering that rare fruit was practically tantamount to a crime. And she even said thank you to the serving wenches at dinner.

She was a woman who deserved to be courted by a man with honorable intentions, not someone who basically led a double life. And if she found out he was a Templar…

He should let the earl win.

He spotted her immediately as he stepped into the bailey. Wooden benches had been placed around the periphery. She was perched on one, looking as wary as a pigeon about to take flight, although mayhap "canary" was a better choice of words since her gown was the color of buttercups in a field. Her aunt and uncle were seated on one side of her, while Edward and Gaveston were on the other. Isabella had chosen another bench, making sure she was surrounded by courtiers and her ladies-in-waiting, although it was obvious to Adrian that Kendra was the one who held center stage. Not that she looked happy about it.

"*Elle est delectable, n'est-ce pas?*" Remy whispered.

"*Oui.*" He clipped his answer, not willing to discuss just how delightfully pleasing Kendra looked. The color of her kirtle brought out the burnished gold in her reddish hair and made her skin look like smooth ivory.

She gave him a wide-eyed look that seemed almost desperate before she cast her gaze down. What kind of a message was she sending?

His attention was diverted as Lancaster strode into the bailey, followed by a squire who carried his sword in its sheath. The young man ceremoniously bowed to the king and then to Lancaster, who drew the sword out with a deft *swish,* snapped his arm at an angle, and held the sword upright in front of him.

Adrian managed to keep himself from grimacing at the theatrics as he pulled his own sword, unbuckling the belt and handing it to Remy. He acknowledged Edward before he walked to his place opposite Lancaster.

The earl made a show of a fancy figure eight before assuming his fencing position. "Are you ready to prove your mettle?"

Adrian didn't answer the question. "*En garde.*"

They engaged with a clash of swords that made the servants, piled in behind the seated nobles, whoop with glee. Adrian caught a glimpse of Kendra frowning, and then he turned his attention to the match.

He hadn't expected an easy round, but Lancaster was surprisingly light on his feet despite the extra weight. And he was an experienced warrior, not some court dandy who played with rapiers. As they continued to thrust and parry, Adrian took notice of which moves the earl used most. More than likely, they were also the ones other English soldiers would employ.

However, after more than a quarter hour of sparring, with both of them jumping and leaping, neither drawing first blood, he could tell the earl was tiring. His footwork was not as fast, his blows a bit sluggish. If Adrian were going to lose the match, he needed to do it now before it became apparent to those who watched.

He glanced at Kendra. She sat still as a marble statue, her face chalky white, hands clenched tightly in her lap. Her eyes widened as she met his quick look and in that moment, he sensed her anguish.

She was frightened to death of bestowing a kiss. Lucifer's horns! Had she never kissed a man before?

The revelation was so astonishing he barely managed to sidestep a sharp thrust from Lancaster. Spinning, he turned on his heel and struck, slicing through the earl's sleeve. A small spurt of red followed.

The crowd went wild as Adrian grounded his sword. Lancaster narrowed his eyes, ignoring his wound, and then grounded his blade as well.

"I wonder where you trained, *Monsieur* de Soules?" he asked. "You fight like a soldier."

"Just lots of practice." Adrian avoided looking at Remy and Pierre as he made his way toward the bench where Kendra now stood. If she were scared nearly witless at the prospect of awarding a kiss, he wasn't about to let Lancaster take advantage of her.

He bowed deeply in front of her. "My lady. I know I have won the privilege of receiving a kiss from you as my just reward, but might I instead have the honor of kissing your hand?"

She looked flustered and confused. "Of course."

He took her hand, brushing his lips across her knuckles, ignoring the urge to turn her hand over and nuzzle her palm. Straightening, he gave a quick nod and then walked quickly away before he changed his mind.

By all the saints! How could he bring himself to seduce a woman who'd never been kissed, just to get information? A woman's first kiss should be special... Then a strange sensation washed over him, thinking he might be the first to show her such simple pleasure.

Mayhap it was a starting point.

****

Kendra stared after Adrian in confusion. Her fingers tingled from his grasp, and even though he'd barely brushed against her hand, it felt cool to the air after the warmth of his lips. She'd breathed such a sigh of relief when he'd won the match. Why was he walking away?

Edward gave her a strange look as he and Piers left the bailey. She turned to her aunt, but Beatrice and her uncle had already risen to follow the king. "Quite extraordinary," was all her aunt said.

Slowly Kendra became aware of the tittering conversation of the ladies behind her.

"Monsieur de Soules did not claim his reward," one said.

"He barely kissed her hand," a second one added.

A third one giggled. "He probably didn't *want* a kiss from her."

Someone else joined in. "She's so *plain*, Lancaster probably wouldn't have claimed the prize either."

"Maybe he lost on purpose to avoid it," the giggler said.

Although Kendra did not turn around or acknowledge she'd heard them, she felt shame creep through her. She'd been so engrossed in her own worries, about having to kiss Lancaster, that it hadn't occurred to her that Adrian might not want to accept a kiss from her. He'd had a grim look on his face at dinner last night when the earl proposed the match. She hadn't considered it might be because *she* was the prize.

"Well, well." Queen Isabella approached her. "You certainly botched that. It would have been better if I had presented the favor after all."

Kendra lifted her chin, hoping her face didn't look as fiery red as it felt. "Monsieur de Soules was simply being gallant."

The queen waved a dismissive hand. "Gallantry is not nearly so much fun as enjoying a man's hot tongue in one's mouth."

Kendra felt her eyes widen in shock. Merciful heavens! What would *that* feel like? *How* would it feel? And… She inhaled sharply. Was that what had been expected of her?

"But you would have kept the kiss chaste, wouldn't you?" Isabella laughed as she turned away. "Such a wasted opportunity."

Kendra's face heated again as the queen left. She *had* been thinking a peck on the cheek was what constituted the prize. It hadn't even entered her mind that a man might want *more*. Or the boisterous, raunchy crowd as well. She glanced around. Nearly everyone had scattered, although the tittering ladies lingered nearby, giving her side looks.

She raised her chin and, with as much dignity as she could muster, she moved in the other direction. She might have disappointed everyone this afternoon, but she never intended to be their entertainment. They'd have to find that elsewhere.

But the biggest disappointment, and one she'd never admit to anyone, was that Adrian had turned away. He hadn't wanted her kiss. She would do well to remember that.

Chapter Seven

The door to the Great Hall burst open and all who sat at the High Table ceased conversation as a woman on a white hart rode in. The hood of the scarlet cloak she wore hid her features, but her voice was anguished when she spoke.

"Please help me find my brachet hound which was stolen from me!"

A knight rose from the table and came forward. "I am at your service, my lady."

The sound of Elsie entering the bedchamber roused Kendra from the dream. In her half-sleep mode, she thought she'd seen the knight's shadow leaving the room.

She blinked herself awake. Ghosts probably abounded in Berwick Castle, considering its bloody history and how many times it had changed hands between the English and the Scots. And she'd seen a similar shadow the night she'd visited the countess. But what was the portent?

Then again, mayhap the dream was only her mind reliving yesterday's disaster with a better ending. The knight had looked like Adrian, although she didn't recognize either the hall or the people at the table.

She frowned at the maid. Dawn's light had barely broken. "What are you doing here so early?"

"I did not mean to waken ye, my lady." She set

down the pitcher she'd been holding. "I brought hot water for your ablutions, but ye doona have to get up just yet. It will stay warm."

"I'm awake, so I might as well get on with the day." Kendra pushed the covers back and sat up. "Do you know if there are ghosts about?"

The maid's eyes widened, and she looked around as if one might pop up somewhere. "Nae that I've seen, but..." She surveyed the room again. "...'tis better nae to speak of them, lest ye attract one."

Kendra started to reply, then thought better of it. The spirits she'd encountered on the Welsh moors had never caused her harm, but servants were often a superstitious sort, and no good would come of rumors flying that she was touched in the head. Especially not after yesterday's embarrassing scene in the bailey. So she simply nodded.

The maid finished attending to her quickly— probably not wanting to confront a shade if one had been accidently summoned—which left Kendra with almost an hour before the night's fast would be broken.

She went down the back stairs and walked outside. Voices and sounds of pans banging came from the kitchens, and she slipped inside the door to pilfer an apple. Thank goodness, the courtyard was still empty. Kendra looked up at the battlements. She'd heard a voice that night, but only seen a shadow. Would Isobel tell her who it was? Why not ask?

Her mind made up, she quickly climbed the tower steps, then waited for the guard to disappear into the barbican before inching along the wall to where the countess' cage hung.

In the still gray light, she made out no shadows, but

Isobel looked up as she settled into an embrasure.

"What are ye doing here?"

"I…" How to lead into the conversation? "I…brought you an apple." Kendra handed it down. She'd get another one for her horse later.

"Thank ye!" Isobel bit into it with a crunch and closed her eyes to savor the taste. "Monsieur de Soules tries to bring me fruit when he can, too."

Adrian was not exactly the person Kendra wanted to talk about. Her pride still smarted from his rebuff, however politely it had been done. The countess was probably the only person in the castle who had not heard of what happened. "He is very kind."

"Aye."

"Have you known him long?"

"Nae. Not long." Isobel gave her a guarded look. "Do ye fancy him?"

Kendra felt herself blush. Hopefully, the bars of the cage kept the countess from seeing her too clearly. It didn't matter if she fancied Adrian. He didn't fancy her. "He is…quite courtly."

Isobel smiled. "So ye are interested, then."

"I didn't say that!"

"Ye dinna have to. I had eyes—and ears as well— that night the two of ye were here."

The memory of how close he'd held her made her blood heat. Better not think about that. He was just ensuring she didn't fall to her death. Better to get to why she was here.

"That night… I thought I heard someone talking to you. A man."

"It must have been the wind. It sounds almost human sometimes."

The voice had been too low for Kendra to make out words, but she doubted it was the wind. "I know this sounds strange, but I thought I saw a shadow of a man disappear."

Isobel gave her another guarded look. "How could a man disappear from here?"

"I…don't know." Kendra had the feeling that the countess was hiding something, but what—or who—it could be, in an open cage, was a mystery. But a prisoner was probably the safest person to confide in. "I… I've encountered…ah…fetches before."

"Ye have the Sight?"

"No. I just sense invisible beings sometimes. Like a presence." Kendra hesitated. "Do you think me mad?"

Isobel smiled again. "I'm Scots. Most of our castles are riddled with ghosties."

Kendra breathed a sigh of relief. "I thought I saw another shadow this morning." She told the countess of her dream. "I have no idea who the people were or why someone would ride a deer into the room. And a white one, at that." She started to laugh at how silly it sounded when she told it out loud, but to her surprise, Isobel had sobered.

"I had a white brachet hound once," she said.

****

Adrian stepped back into the shadows of the keep and watched as Kendra climbed down the tower steps. She must have been up visiting Isobel again. He'd been on his way up to collect the cold bricks when he noticed movement along the wall.

Obviously his cautionary warning to Kendra last time about the danger she placed herself in went unheeded. He suspected most of any unasked-for advice did the same. Stubborn little vixen.

But there was also another danger to these visits. The countess had been imprisoned for four years without benefit of a friend to confide in. Kendra had many of the same strengths and character traits as Isobel. It wouldn't take long for them to become friends.

And the Countess of Buchan knew who he was. She was one of the few who knew the Earl of Orkney had provided refuge for the fleeing Templars three years ago and that they were now the Bruce's secret weapon.

If that information got into the wrong hands... If Kendra learned of it and told her uncle, it might give Edward the edge he needed to actually win this ongoing war with Scotland.

But how was he going to stop the visits when she took no heed to what he said?

****

Not quite ready to face the gossips of the court— she didn't need to hear any more remarks about how plain she was—Kendra decided to forego breaking her fast in the Great Hall. Instead, she went to the kitchens and took another apple for Argenterie since she'd give hers to Isobel, and selected some cheese and a warm bannock for herself. Thanking the cook, who'd grudgingly become accustomed to her entering his domain, she made for the stables. Her mare would be better company than humans.

Inside the warm stall, she gave the horse her treat, then made sure she had fresh hay before plopping down in a corner to eat the bread and cheese. Kendra had just finished brushing the crumbs from her skirt when she heard voices.

Adrian's and Lancaster's.

Not wanting to be seen by either of them, she ran a hand over the mare's flank to still her and flattened herself against the stall's wall. For an appalling moment, she wondered if they were actually going to discuss *her*, but then she realized they weren't even talking about the match.

"Since you are Robert the Bruce's envoy, I assume you know where he is?" Lancaster asked.

Adrian's response was measured. "No one knows where *King* Robert is."

"It must be difficult for a *king* not to have a place from which to conduct business." Lancaster paused. "If my cousin were to actually consider some kind of truce, how would you get in contact?"

Another measured response. "A message can be sent."

The earl chuckled. "I don't suppose you'd be willing to tell me where?"

"Do I strike you as a stupid man?"

Lancaster's voice changed. "No. You do not. And, judging from your skill in yesterday's match, you strike me as much more than simply an envoy filling in for your deceased uncle."

"Mayhap it was just a lucky blow. As I said, I practice a lot."

"In the sense that I was fool enough to let it happen, yes, but no man has ever lasted for a quarter hour against me," Lancaster answered. "I will remind you I saw combat alongside The Hammer himself, and you do not fight like a Scots."

"Why should I? I was raised in France," Adrian

replied.

There was a brief silence before the earl spoke again. "There are rumors about a Scottish alliance with France. Are you loyal to Philippe, then?"

Adrian gave a short laugh. "Why all the questions, Lancaster? Did your cousin ask you to ferret information from me?"

The earl snorted. "Edward isn't bright enough to think of that."

"Is it wise to say something that could be taken as a treasonous statement?"

"Mayhap not in front of an Englishman, but I suspect such a statement is safe with you," Lancaster said.

"You trust me?"

"I don't trust you at all." The earl's voice turned grim. "Nor do I think you are who you say you are, but time will tell."

Kendra heard him leave, the sound of his boots fading away. Lord have mercy! She might have her own suspicions that Adrian was hiding something, but if someone as powerful as the Earl of Lancaster did, Adrian could be in real danger. Should she say something to her uncle?

Argenterie chose that moment to poke her head over the half-door of the stall and nicker. Kendra held her breath. Maybe Adrian would go about his business and ignore the mare. Then she heard his footsteps approach and tried to flatten herself further against the wall.

"*Bon jour, ma douce jument.*" His hand stroked the mare's muzzle. "Your mistress should be here soon..." His voice trailed off as he spotted Kendra. "*Mon erreur.*

I see she is already here."

****

Queen Isabella stepped behind the curtain of the second-story window as she observed Adrian and Kendra leave the barn together. Her eyes narrowed. She'd wondered where he was when he didn't appear in the Great Hall this morning. He and the little trollop must have arranged an assignation. What did she have to offer that Isabella didn't?

Whatever it was, the bitch needed to be stopped. Even though Isabella thought men were basically stupid creatures, Adrian de Soules was a very *attractive* one. And he was French as she was. She liked attractive, muscular men in her bed. Especially French men. Unfortunately, they were difficult to find in this god-forsaken outpost. Why the English kept fighting the Scots over Berwick Castle was just another example of their stupidity.

But more to the point, what needed to be done about Kendra de Clermont? Poison was always easy, but given that she was not only the Earl of Pembroke's ward but also the granddaughter of the late Constable of France, a hornet's nest would be stirred on both sides of the Channel should she mysteriously die.

Better to get her married off. Beatrice had lamented more than once that she feared no Englishman would offer for the girl, given her brash, outspoken behavior. But perhaps Isabella could help with that. She smiled as she walked back to her bedchamber. She knew the perfect man to take care of the situation.

Gerard de Nogaret.

He was a cousin of her father's councilor, Guillaume, and had been instrumental in bringing the

Templars to heel. Her father Philippe had written that many of the tortures for making the Templars talk had been devised by Gerard.

He'd be the perfect person to take Kendra de Clermont in hand. Isabella's father would see the advantage of an alliance to the Earl of Pembroke as well. And Gerard would be taking the hussy to France, well away from here. Away from Adrian.

Isabella entered her chambers and went straight to her *escritoire*. She'd write the letter immediately, inviting the man for an extended visit.

Chapter Eight

"So you think Lady Kendra will tell her uncle what she overheard?" Remy asked Adrian the next morning as they approached the archery field just outside the walls, for practice.

"I am not certain," he replied. When he'd found her hiding in her mare's stall, his first instinct had been that she'd not wanted him to find her. "The earl was fishing for information, but I gave him naught."

"But he still drew conclusions," Pierre said. "Could the girl have done the same?"

"I don't know." Oddly, she had not asked any questions as he walked her back to the castle. Had he given her any cause to become suspicious?

"She has both English and French connections," Pierre went on. "Either could be dangerous for Bruce and to the Brotherhood."

"Especially since we do not know where Pembroke's alliances truly lie."

"Or Lancaster's, for that matter," Remy said. "We know he thinks little of Edward. If he found out who we are—what we are—would he inform Philippe in order to gain French backing to overthrow the king and claim the crown?"

Adrian furrowed his brows. Was Lancaster ambitious enough to try such a coup? He didn't doubt the man would use every resource available, if that were so.

Logic told him Kendra had already been in the stall when he entered. Had she known Lancaster was going to come to the stables? Had she meant to meet the earl? The thought of how insistent she'd been to get outside the walls the day of their ride had lingered with him. Was she supposed to have delivered a message to the earl that was thwarted because he'd accompanied her? Mayhap to let Lancaster know how things lay before he arrived? And now, was she to deliver a message from the earl to someone who waited to carry it to France?

Adrian hated to think Kendra was involved in any kind of espionage. It was dangerous work, as the Templars well knew, but he doubted that would stop the headstrong woman.

Remy halted abruptly. Adrian had been so lost in thought he'd almost bumped into him. Such woolgathering was dangerous as well. "What is it?"

"Look." Remy pointed toward the field.

Adrian followed his gesture. Kendra stood between Lancaster and Gaveston, a lady's bow in one hand and a quiver of arrows in the other. As they approached the trio, he heard her sputter.

"Why can't a woman practice on this field?"

"Your presence is a distraction, my lady," the earl said. "How can my men concentrate on hitting the target with you in their midst?"

"Are your men not disciplined?" Gaveston asked. "Are they so easily distracted?"

Lancaster assessed him. "Mayhap the lady is not a distraction for *you,* but soldiers are a different matter."

Gaveston held his gaze, ignoring the taunt. "Perhaps you fear she might best your soldiers?"

"Fear?" The earl laughed. "My men fear nothing."

Gaveston gave him a cool smile. "Then allow her to shoot."

"She is a *lady*."

Adrian stepped closer. Perhaps Lancaster simply meant what he said, but he might be trying to hide the fact that Kendra had skills that most women didn't. Skills that might be useful for a spy.

"I would be interested in seeing Lady Kendra *attempt* to hit the target myself." He bit back a grin when she glared at him. He'd emphasized the word to goad her into giving the shot her best so he could assess for himself. He bowed. "Ladies first, of course."

Lancaster gave him a withering look, which he ignored. He was much more interested in the stance that she took. She turned her side to the target, nocked the arrow, and started to cant the bow, but stopped. Instead, she eyed the target, one finger over the arrow, keeping it in place, while she lifted her other elbow, drawing the bowstring back to her ear and loosing the arrow in a straight point of aim.

She smirked at him when it hit dead center of the bull's-eye.

Somehow, he wasn't surprised. When he'd seen her begin to lift the bow skyward to cant and then change her mind, he suspected she was well practiced. When had she learned? And, more importantly, why?

"*Touché, mademoiselle*," he said. "I believe you have proved your point."

"And mayhap you think you can best me?" She chose another arrow from her quiver.

He hid a smile. "I'll accept that challenge, my lady."

"*Très bien*," she replied. "Then I believe it is your turn."

Adrian nocked his own bow, tempted to cant it just for show, but Lancaster was already too suspicious of him. He drew, aiming a bit left, so his arrow would land next to hers instead of displacing it.

She arched a brow and promptly put her second arrow on the other side of his.

He let himself grin at that. If Kendra had any instructions to draw information from him, she had an odd way of proving it. Most women would use seduction to achieve their ends, just as he'd been ordered to do. But then, Kendra de Clermont was not most women. Challenging him at archery could be a distraction that she was clever enough to try while she sought information.

****

"What in the world were you thinking?" Beatrice stared at Kendra, then shook her head. "Do not bother to answer. You obviously were not thinking at all." She turned her eyes upward to the ceiling of the solar they were sitting in. "How in the world am I ever going to find you a husband when they are probably afraid you might place an arrow in their heart while they're sleeping?"

"It would be a dagger, at that close range."

"Do not use a smart mouth with me, niece," her aunt snapped. "You are well past marriage age, and our visit here at Berwick is a golden opportunity to rectify that situation."

Kendra sighed. She should have known she'd be in huge trouble for her display this morning, but she missed practicing her defense skills. If an English nobleman were put off because a female knew how to do something besides sew and embroider, so be it. *She* wasn't looking for a husband at Berwick.

"It is possible that I may never marry."

"That is exactly my worry," Beatrice said. "But we may be able to salvage your reputation if you start acting like a lady."

Obviously, her aunt hadn't gotten the point. "I miss the freedom I had in Wales."

"Freedom to roam around like a ruffian! Riding a horse astride, leaving your hair undone, using a weapon... Who taught you that?"

There wasn't any way she was going to give her aunt the names of the soldiers she'd pestered into teaching her. Beatrice would probably go directly to her uncle and insist they be punished. "I did a lot of observing. Then I practiced with a page's bow." Those weren't lies, just not the entire truth.

Her aunt gave her a shrewd look. "Well, your *practicing* stops now. No noble's son will want a wife who tries to best him."

She probably could *best* most of them. Not that she was interested. Although, to be honest with herself, she did want to prove something to Adrian. If he didn't find her attractive enough to accept a kiss for winning the fencing match, then she'd wanted to show him she was as able as he was to land an arrow in the bull's-eye. And, she *had*. Her lips twitched.

"Are you finding this conversation amusing?"

She forced a bland expression. "Of course not, Aunt."

"Good. Then I expect you to conduct yourself as befitting the Earl of Pembroke's niece. You need to hold polite conversation with every man in speaking distance tonight."

"Polite conversation that is meaningless drivel?"

Her aunt frowned. "It will be a start to proving you can behave like a lady. And what you call meaningless drivel gets interpreted as being agreeable."

Agreeable. Adrian had hardly spoken a word to her as he'd escorted her from the barn yesterday. Instead, he'd given her sharp looks as though he thought she'd intentionally hidden in the stall to eavesdrop. She'd only hidden because she wasn't ready to face him after the rebuff at the fencing match. Not that she would explain that to him.

"Do I have your word?"

"On what?"

Her aunt sighed. "On *trying* to be agreeable. Polite. Pleasant."

Kendra held back her own sigh. The easiest way to end this un-agreeable conversation was to *agree* with it. "I will try."

At least, when her aunt was present.

****

The midday meal had just been served in the small dining room when a messenger rushed in, followed by a disheveled Hubert.

"I tried to stop him, Your Majesty." The castellan straightened his jacket. "But the brute nearly knocked me over."

Edward looked mildly annoyed, but Lancaster spoke before he could. "The message must be important."

"It is, my lord," the messenger replied. "Robert Bruce has commenced raiding again!"

The king slammed his goblet down. "Where?"

"Linlithgow, Your Highness. The castle has been taken."

"That close?" Edward looked at Pembroke. "We were in residence there just last month."

Pembroke asked a few more questions, then dismissed the man. He turned to the king. "The Bruce grows bold, knowing you are hardly more than two days' ride away.

"Perhaps because my cousin does not invoke fear like his father did." Lancaster gave the king a loathing look. "If I were to command the army—"

"We are still your king!" Edward's face mottled. "Do not rely too much on Our goodwill because we are blood."

"And the English should stick together," Gaveston added.

"You should talk," Lancaster nearly sneered. "*Frenchman.*"

At the word, as though all present collectively remembered Adrian was both French and at court on the Bruce's behalf, all eyes suddenly turned to him.

"What do you know of this?" Lancaster demanded.

"Nothing," Adrian answered. "I am only an envoy."

"An envoy mayhap intended to distract us by speaking of a truce?" Lancaster raised a skeptical brow. "While your Scottish rebel continues to plunder?"

The conversation from the barn came back to Kendra. The earl first questioning Adrian of the Bruce's whereabouts, then alluding to the fact that Adrian wasn't who he pretended to be. Was that true? Was he a spy instead of a peacemaker?

Adrian gave him a Gallic shrug. "The only intention of King Robert that I am aware of is that he seeks a truce with England."

"He has a strange way to go about it," Edward said.

"With all due respect, Your Majesty, perhaps this latest raid happened because he grows impatient. I have had nothing to report regarding progress." Adrian's voice remained steady.

The king studied him. "For your sake, We hope you speak the truth."

Kendra felt a frisson of fear slide down her spine. While Edward didn't have the taste for battle and blood that his father did, he was not as weak as the Earl of Lancaster thought. The continual goading the earl had done since his arrival didn't help matters either. It only invoked Edward's anger. Anger that could be misdirected.

God help Adrian if he were found to be a spy.

Chapter Nine

"She's not here," Remy said the next morning as he and Adrian joined Pierre at the archery field.

"Not surprising," Pierre replied. 'News of yesterday's feat travelled like rushes-on-fire throughout the castle. I imagine her aunt has forbidden another appearance."

His comrade was probably right, but Adrian had looked forward to another bout. Of actually testing her skills, challenging her. Kendra intrigued him. She had looked so vulnerable—frightened, even—at the fencing match, all because she was supposed to bestow a kiss. Which made him wonder if she'd ever kissed a man. And that thought, in turn, had made him want to be the first to do so. She had a wide, full mouth, with plump lips that were soft and ripe for such. It had taken every bit of his iron resolve to act the gallant knight and take her hand instead.

But the Kendra who'd shown up for archery practice yesterday was defiant, outspoken, stubborn, *and* highly skilled with the bow. He also wanted to know how she'd acquired that.

"Did Pembroke make any comments?"

Remy shook his head. "The earl seemed as surprised as everyone else."

That was intriguing news too. Had she learned in France? He thought about what information he'd been able to gather. She was two-and-twenty and became Pembroke's ward several years ago. She was also the granddaughter of the former Constable of France, who had been King Philippe's first in command. She had been of betrothal age before she came to England, yet no match had been made. The possibility existed that she had trained from a young age, much as pages and squires did, to become a spy.

The French court had used women before. Philippe was still looking for the exiled Brotherhood. And, Adrian reminded himself grimly, Kendra hated the Templars. After yesterday's news that Robert had commenced raiding, he needed to keep a closer eye on her.

"I think I will go in search of Lady Kendra."

Pierre grinned. "I thought you might."

"From what you said about Lancaster's insinuations, we need to know where Pembroke's loyalty lies," Remy added. "You should use your attraction to her."

He didn't need reminding what Bruce was expecting him to do. "Lady Kendra is not a loose lady of the court."

His friends exchanged glances. Pierre's grin vanished. Remy narrowed his eyes.

"Have a care, *mon ami*. We are here on a mission for the Bruce. Do not lose sight of that."

"I'm aware why we are here." Adrian turned and strode away. Lucifer's horns! He was hardly wearing his heart on his sleeve. Finding a woman intriguing didn't mean he was besotted. Ever since Angelique, he had stayed in control of his emotions.

He found Kendra in the ladies' solar, embroidering.

The act seemed so foreign that for a moment he stood in the open doorway, watching. She held the loop close to the window's light, then muttered under her breath as she pulled several stitches loose and redid them.

Kendra tossed the material down. "*Merde! Bon sang!*"

"Such language."

Startled, she looked up. "What are you doing here?"

"I wondered what you'd found to do that was more challenging than archery practice." He grinned as he entered the room. "I had no idea you were interested in doing altar cloths."

"I'm not." Kendra frowned. "I'm being punished."

He sobered as he took the seat across the small table from her. "For what?"

Her frown deepened. "You know for what."

His own brow furrowed. "For showing up for archery practice yesterday?"

"For not acting like a *lady*." She nearly spit the words.

"You *are* a lady."

"Not according to my aunt." Kendra picked up the embroidering loop again. "*This* is what ladies are supposed to do."

Adrian was tempted to smile at her disgust, but he sensed it would probably just make her more angry. "Well, I'm sure the Lord will appreciate your effort."

She gave him a sour look. "The Lord won't see it, since no priest would allow this mess anywhere near an altar."

She probably had a point. His mouth twitched in

spite of himself.

"You're trying not to laugh, aren't you?" She jabbed the needle into the cloth. "Go ahead. I don't blame you. I can't sew a straight—ouch!" Kendra jerked her hand away, a prickle of bright red blood on her fingertip. She stuck it into her mouth.

Any inclination Adrian had to laugh disappeared at the sight of her sucking on her finger. His own blood rushed straight to his loins as an image of her sucking him struck with the force of a lightning bolt. As he stared, she removed her finger and licked the tip once more. *Mon Dieu.* Had she any idea of how sensual that action was?

Another droplet appeared. Before she could repeat her actions, he leaned over the table. "Allow me."

He took her hand, kissing the finger softly before slowly closing his own mouth over it. She gave a surprised jerk, but he held her wrist firm, allowing his tongue to swirl around the appendage, savoring the salty taste of her skin as well as the slight callus on the pad…

A callus that probably came from archery practice. Lots of it. That reminder brought his lustful thoughts back to reality, and he released her hand. Her breathing was shallow, her eyes dark as a forest as she stared at him. He took his own deep breath just as her maid appeared in the doorway.

She gazed at them with open curiosity, then darted a look behind her. "Lady Pembroke is on her way upstairs."

Adrian rose, grateful for the maid's warning. "I will leave you to your…embroidery, Lady Kendra." Then he winked, watching a pink blush spread across her cheeks before he turned and walked out the door.

The seduction had begun. He just wasn't sure whose it was.

****

Kendra tried not to stare at Adrian that evening at dinner. She *tried* not to look at him at all, but that was impossible, given the round table and that he always sat a few seats away, where she had a clear view. At least, she wasn't seated next to him. She wasn't sure if she could breathe, let alone eat, that near him.

He had *licked* her finger. Slowly. Deliberately. Had swirled his *tongue* around it. A tongue soft as velvet, yet capable of powerful strokes. Strokes that sent powerful impulses coursing through her body and a strange quiver in that private area between her thighs. Thank God Elsie had arrived when she did or Kendra might have dissolved into mush. Even now, hours later, her finger still tingled, the sensation shooting through her once again.

Why had he done that?

"Your Highness," her aunt said to the queen, "I was wondering if my niece might join your ladies with their embroidery for the rest of the week?"

Isabella looked amused. "She is quite welcome to spend all day in my private solar with my ladies."

"Excellent!" Beatrice said. "Perhaps one of your ladies could teach her to do more careful stitching, as well."

Kendra bit back a groan. She had hoped being stuck with that miserable task for one day would have sufficed as punishment. Obviously, her aunt was taking no chances she might do something else that was not ladylike.

"Of course," Isabella answered. "I understand your niece made quite a spectacle of herself yesterday."

"I must apologize for that. I'm afraid she has been allowed too much freedom to do as she pleased at our home in Wales." Her aunt slanted a look at Kendra. "We had a chat earlier. There will be no more unladylike behavior, including riding her horse."

What? Kendra's temper rose. It was bad enough they were discussing her like she wasn't present. Now she was going to be restricted to the castle? "Argenterie needs to be exercised!"

"One of the stable hands can do that."

"But—"

"If I may interrupt?" Adrian proceeded without waiting for a response. "I never let anyone else ride my own destrier. A finely bred animal such as Lady Kendra's Andalusian fares better with only one rider."

Kendra shot him a grateful look while the queen narrowed her eyes.

"I agree." Pembroke looked at his wife. "I know you have no interest in equines, but Andalusians are sensitive and quite loyal to their owner."

"Really, my lord. You make that animal sound like a knight in service to the king," she answered.

Edward glanced at Lancaster before turning to Beatrice. "Actually, my lady, We wish all Our knights—and *lords*—were that loyal without Our demanding it."

Lancaster eyed him coolly, and Pembroke spoke before the earl could retort.

"I see no reason why Kendra should not continue to exercise her horse."

For a moment, Beatrice looked nonplussed. Then

she lifted her chin slightly. "Your ward actually rode away from the castle several days ago. Given that half-barbarian Scots roam the countryside, it was dangerous. Do you condone that?"

"If I might interrupt again?" Adrian smiled at Beatrice. "I escorted Lady Kendra on that ride and made sure we stayed on the main road."

"You cannot be responsible for her every time she decides on a whim to run off."

Kendra strove to hold onto her temper. "I didn't run off—"

"You went without a by-your-leave," her aunt said. "You obviously did not think about danger."

Edward held up his hand. "Mayhap a compromise could be reached. If Lady Kendra wants to exercise her mare—and We agree that it is a fine animal—then she will need to have an escort each time she rides out."

"A champion, so to speak," Gaveston said. "Like knights of old."

Edward smiled at him. "Exactly. Knights used to swear allegiance to a lady."

Gaveston smiled back. "Like Lancelot did with Guinevere."

"I was not present at the Round Table," Adrian said, "and I do not claim to be an English knight, but I offer my services as Lady Kendra's...er, champion. Since I have to exercise my destrier as well, I will escort the lady whenever she leaves the castle."

Kendra's jaw dropped, and she closed her mouth quickly. Her aunt gave him a speculative look, but her uncle slowly nodded. "That might be the best solution."

"Then that is settled." Edward turned his attention to his food. "This looks delicious."

The queen sat perfectly still, her eyes hard as she stared at Kendra. The noise of the conversation, which had resumed, drowned out the snap of the wooden spoon that broke in her hand.

****

Adrian found Kendra the next morning in the stables, brushing her mare. "Are you planning to go for a ride?"

She started at the sound of his voice and then shook her head. "I am not allowed."

He lifted a brow. "I thought we had the issue settled last night at dinner."

Kendra gave him a little smile as she resumed brushing. "You do not know my aunt well. She is not willing to surrender until her terms have been met."

His mouth quirked. "You make it sound like a war."

"To my aunt, it is. She has very definitive ideas on how I should act."

"Ah. Like the flighty, frivolous ladies of court."

She grimaced. "Pretty much."

"Why? Surely, your aunt realizes what an insincere and ambitious lot they are."

"My aunt is ambitious, too," Kendra replied. "She wants me to make a match with an English noble that will enhance my uncle's holdings."

Marriages for alliances were common enough, but the thought of Kendra being married off so the earl could accumulate more wealth and power made him angry. From the English aristocrats he'd encountered, every one of them would try to break her spirit, to make her amenable and biddable, just like her aunt wanted. His wood nymph was too unique for that. And the sudden image in his mind of her coupling with another man—of some imbecile *taking* her—instantly made his blood boil.

"And what do you want, Lady Kendra?"

She looked surprised at the question. "Does it matter?"

"It should." He paused. "Do you not wish for a home of your own and *enfants*?"

A fleeting expression of wistfulness crossed her face and then was gone. "I have not thought of children."

Because she was a French spy? He hesitated. "That is unusual. May I ask why?"

She continued to brush her mare without looking up. Was she not answering because his question was totally out of line? Or was she trying to come up with some excuse to cover possible espionage? "I should not have asked such a personal question. Please accept my apologies."

Giving her mare a final pat on her neck, she put the brush down and turned to him. "Can I trust you with a secret?"

Mon Dieu. Was she going to tell him she was searching for Templars on Philippe's behalf? He wasn't sure he wanted to know. They would be sworn enemies.

He swallowed. "Of course. You have my oath."

"Spoken like one of King Arthur's knights." She smiled a little.

He smiled back. "I did say I was your champion, my lady."

"So you did." She looked around, then lowered her voice almost to a whisper. "The reason I cannot marry is because I see and hear things."

"See and hear things?"

Kendra nodded. "People, actually. People…" She took a deep breath. "People who are no longer alive."

Adrian blinked. Of all the possibilities he had half-expected her to say, seeing or hearing ghosts was certainly not on the list. "I'm not sure I understand."

"Most people don't." She explained about her experiences on the Welsh moors and the most recent ones on the battlements by Isobel's cage. "If I married a man who acquired my dowry and was only interested in advancing himself, he'd have me declared mad or…worse, accuse me of witchcraft."

Adrian winced. She was right. Although most of the Inquisitions headed by the Catholic Church involved heresy—or the false accusation of such—there were pagan rites still practiced that the Church also wanted to eradicate. Any phenomenon that could not be logically explained to an inquisitor was suspect.

"Do you recognize these…spirits?"

She shook her head. "Not usually. The one who visited the countess seemed protective."

"But he didn't acknowledge you?"

"No. But he wasn't there for me. He was there for Isobel." Kendra tilted her head. "You believe me then?"

He'd thought of her as an otherworldly wood nymph, but perhaps there was a reason. "Why not?" He grinned. "I grew up in Brittany, near the forest of Broceliande and the lake where the faerie queen supposedly resides."

"The Lady of the Lake from the Arthurian legends," Kendra said.

"Well, I've never seen her, but folklore about the fae abounds." He shrugged. "And there have been mysterious occurrences of people entering the forest and never coming out."

"I remember hearing those stories when I was a child," Kendra said, "but I always thought they were told to scare me from wandering into our own woods."

He grinned again. "Did it work?"

Her mouth twitched before she broke into a grin too. "*Non*. It only made me more curious."

Adrian laughed aloud. He had no doubt Kendra had had an inquisitive streak at an early age. "So you went and explored anyway?"

"*Oui*. I've always felt more at ease with animals than people."

He could imagine her taming the wild creatures of the forest. It just added to his image of her as a wood nymph. "Had you actually gone to Broceliande, you might have been lucky enough to encounter the Lady."

"I would have liked that," Kendra replied, her tone serious.

A corner of his mouth lifted. "I suspect the Lady would too."

She looked up at him. "You're teasing me."

"Only a little."

"Ummm. It is rather ironic that Lord Gaveston mentioned Lancelot last night, since Brittany is where his legend began." She studied Adrian, then got a mischievous look in her eye. "Mayhap you knew him?"

Adrian assumed a wounded expression, admiring her quick wit. "Do I look like I'm several centuries old?"

She paused as if to consider, and he had an overwhelming urge to prove to her how young and virile he was by crushing her saucy lips with a deep, hard kiss. Her own eyes darkened as she seemed to sense his intent, and he wondered if perhaps she really did have a touch of fae.

And then the moment was shattered by the clattering of horses' hooves entering the bailey. Kendra stepped back, and Adrian went to the doorway to see the French banner of Guillaume de Nogaret being furled as knights ran out to assist the party.

He narrowed his eyes. What was the Templar nemesis doing here?

Chapter Ten

Queen Isabella dabbed a bit of frankincense oil behind her ears, pulled a few curls loose from her plaits to frame her face, checked the kohl around her eyes, and smoothed the silk folds of her gown before descending the stairs. *Finally*, Gerard, the cousin of Guillaume de Nogaret, had arrived. And not one minute too soon.

Adrian had followed Kendra out to the stables again this morning, like a dog after a bitch in heat. Did he really tumble her in the hay like a common wench? Isabella was fond of feather mattresses herself and certainly not anything as stiff as straw that might scratch her skin. The maid she paid to keep an eye on the little hussy's door at night had reported no comings or goings. Still, that didn't mean Adrian wasn't enjoying the girl's favors.

Not for much longer, though. The missive she'd received from de Nogaret just a few days ago had assured her he was more than willing for a marriage alliance with the Earl of Pembroke's niece. That Gerard had arrived practically on the heels of the letter just showed how eager he was.

Soon, very soon, she would have Adrian all to herself. She might have to punish him, though, since he'd vexed her quite enough by not responding to her flirtations. But once he'd experienced her various skills, he'd soon forget Kendra de Clarmont.

Isabella smiled. It was time to have a talk with Beatrice.

****

Kendra sensed the tension in Adrian as soon as she saw the French banner being furled in the bailey. The transformation from the relaxed teasing that had quickly been turning into something much more personal was gone. His shoulders were rigid, his jaw set, his gaze intense. "It looks like King Edward has some French visitors."

"*Oui. C'est la bannière de Guillaume de Nogaret.*"

Kendra widened her eyes. "Why would King Philippe's councilor come here?"

"A good question." Adrian glanced at her. "Has your uncle said anything about a visit?"

"No. Why would he?"

He shrugged, but it looked forced to her. Why?

"I would think if King Edward were expecting an emissary from France, he might have mentioned it," he said.

"Mayhap he did, but my uncle does not confide in me."

Adrian studied her for a moment. "But he might mention it to his wife. Has your aunt said anything?"

Kendra shook her head. "My aunt would hardly tell me anything that might make me...*curious.*"

A corner of his mouth lifted. "I guess she would not, at that. And I suspect whatever Edward's machinations are, he is clever enough not to divulge them, in spite of what Lancaster thinks."

"And I think the earl is too full of himself, even if he is the richest man in England."

"Money equates to power." Adrian looked thoughtful. "I wonder if mayhap Lancaster invited the French councilor to pay a visit. It would be like him to do something like that to annoy Edward."

"They certainly do not like each other." Kendra smiled. "I sometimes think men are more conniving than women."

"That's an interesting theory. I must..." Adrian's voice drifted off as the man at the front of the entourage threw back his fur-lined hood to reveal his face. "That's not Guillaume."

Kendra peered around Adrian. "Then who is it?"

He narrowed his eyes. "It is his cousin, Gerard."

"Do you know him?"

"We've never met." A muscle twitched in Adrian's jaw. "I wonder why he is here."

"I guess we will find out soon enough," Kendra replied.

****

Unfortunately, her words turned out to be prophetic a few hours later. Kendra was grateful she was sitting on the small settee in her aunt's receiving chamber when she heard the disastrous news. Her legs would surely have given way if she had been standing. She was still finding speech difficult.

"You...want...me...to marry Gerard de Nogaret?"

"Yes!" her aunt beamed. "It is the perfect solution."

The perfect solution for getting her out of her aunt's sight. Kendra swallowed hard, trying to gather her wits. "I realize that I have not been an ideal ward, Aunt, but I didn't realize you were so desperate to get rid of me."

Beatrice gave her a quizzical look. "Wherever did you get that idea? But no matter. You know very well marriages among the nobility are arranged for various reasons."

"But I am not an English aristocrat."

"Actually, you are better. You are a *French* aristocrat. You forget that my father—your grandfather—was the Grand Chamberlain and Constable of France! And, if I need to remind you, Gerard is cousin to King Philippe's most trusted councilor."

The French king might trust him, but Kendra didn't. Although she'd been told he was only thirty, his face was all hard lines, his mouth tight, his eyes hard. When he'd looked her over—now she knew why—as she'd emerged from the stables that morning, he'd reminded her of a predator stalking prey.

"Does Uncle Aymer know of this?"

"Of course he does! I told him of the betrothal right after I spoke with Queen Isabella."

Kendra was beginning to smell a royal rat. "This was the queen's suggestion?"

Beatrice waved a dismissive hand. "It does not matter whose suggestion it was. The queen said King Edward was most pleased that the Earl of Pembroke's niece would be wed to Lord de Norgaret since it puts the French squarely on the English side if fighting continues with Scotland."

"So I am just a pawn in the chess game of war."

"As I said before, marriages are arranged for many reasons. In this case, King Edward fears that rebel Robert Bruce might be trying to solicit France's help."

"But King Philippe already acknowledged Robert

Bruce as Scotland's king," Kendra protested.

"That is precisely why Edward favors this marriage," her aunt replied. "Your uncle is a powerful earl, and as his nephew-by-marriage, Gerard would be honor bound to convince his cousin, the *councilor* to Philippe, to side with England." Beatrice patted her hand. "Isabella was quite right. This marriage is the perfect solution to put an end to this nonsense."

"But Robert Bruce wants a truce. If Edward doesn't want the war to continue, why doesn't he just sign it?"

"Pride, for one thing." Her aunt grew thoughtful. "From what your uncle told me, signing a truce would look like surrender on Edward's part, particularly since his father was a force to be reckoned with."

"Edward the First was a brutal monster."

"Cease that kind of talk at once! The very walls have ears." Beatrice looked around the empty room as if expecting someone to emerge from somewhere. "It is not a woman's place to discuss war *or* a king's decisions."

Kendra frowned. "If I can't talk about war or royal decisions, why do I have to be a pawn to them?"

"There is no sense in continuing this topic." Beatrice paused and then relented a little. "In a way, you do have power, even though men will never acknowledge it."

"How so?"

"By marrying Gerard de Nogaret, you could be the very vehicle to actually bring peace to England. Think of how many lives could be saved if this fighting finally stops. You have a responsibility which you should feel honored to carry out." She smiled benignly. "You will work things out with your marriage. We all do."

****

Adrian took his seat in the private dining room that evening, hardly noticing that Queen Isabella had moved her chair ever closer. He was trying not to glare at de Nogaret.

Not Guillaume, but his cousin. Adrian had told Kendra the truth when he said he'd never met the man. But he had certainly heard of him. Word had drifted from the Continent that Gerard had been instrumental in getting the captive Templars to confess to heresy in order to have a quick death rather than die by slow torture.

His first thought had been that de Nogaret had learned of the Templars taking refuge in Scotland. But that thought had been eclipsed by the announcement just before dinner that a betrothal had been arranged between the French lord and Kendra.

The idea struck him like his destrier's shod hoof in his belly.

"I propose a toast!" Isabella smiled brightly as she lifted her wine goblet high. "To the happy couple on their upcoming marriage!"

Adrian turned his gaze to Kendra, seated beside de Nogaret. She wouldn't meet his eye, instead studying her trencher as though some fascinating bit of food had been put in it.

"*Oui!*" Gerard lifted his cup as well. "There is much to be gained by this union."

"Hear! Hear!" Lancaster said. "My cousin has finally made a wise decision."

Edward glowered at him, although he raised his goblet to drink. Adrian dropped a utensil to the floor, leaning down to pick it up as the others followed suit. He wasn't about to toast the marriage. The only other person who didn't drink was Kendra.

Gerard sharpened his gaze. "Do you not care for wine, Lady Kendra?"

She lifted her chin. "I am not feeling well."

"Please forgive her manners, my lord," Beatrice said. "The wonderful news has overwhelmed her."

"Understandable," Gaveston added, "since the marriage announcement was a surprise to all of us."

Adrian glanced at the king. This betrothal wasn't Edward's doing, then, if Gaveston knew nothing about it. His glance shifted to Pembroke. Was the earl behind the machinations? If Pembroke sought an alliance with the French, did that mean he meant to put his considerable might behind Edward? Or Robert? Edward I had appointed him Lord Lieutenant of Scotland, but after the slaughters at Berwick and Dunbar, some nobles had lost their taste for more blood. And Pembroke's lands were in Wales, a country fiercely proud of its origins, just as Scotland was.

Gerard chortled. "King Philippe has always said his daughter could keep a secret."

Adrian stiffened. This was Queen Isabella's doing? Pieces of this odd puzzle suddenly fell into place. In the several weeks since he'd been at court, the queen had flirted outrageously and offered barely disguised invitations to copulate on several occasions. He had done his utmost to ignore any insinuations, while remaining polite as her rank demanded.

"I will admit the idea was mine," the queen purred as she placed a hand on Adrian's sleeve and smiled at Kendra. "It has been obvious to this court that our dear earl's niece prefers Frenchmen to English knights."

The queen's smile looked more feral than sincere. Kendra paled, and Adrian bit back a curse as he maneuvered his arm from Isabella's touch. Unfortunately, the queen had used Kendra's lack of interest in husband-hunting as a weapon to her own advantage.

She must have seen Kendra as both competition and an obstacle to be cleared from her path to his bed. And, like her father, she wouldn't let anything—or anyone—stand in the way.

But after his conversation with Kendra in the stables this morning, Adrian knew why she feared getting married. What his kinsmen in Brittany might see as the Gift would not be seen as such by English lords interested in tractable wives, and certainly not in mainland France, where the Pope's influence was nearly as strong as the king's.

His blood turned cold as he glanced at de Nogaret. A man notorious for nefariously burning Templars at the stake for heresies they didn't commit would have no tolerance for a wife who—besides not being biddable— also saw and heard *spectres.* The Church considered anyone with what it considered unnatural skills as a witch and a pawn of the Devil. Philippe would see it as a threat, as well.

Mon Dieu! If de Nogaret ever found out...Kendra would be tied to the stake as well.

****

Restless, unable to sleep over the events of the day, Kendra finally tossed the covers aside, donned her woolen wrapper, and padded silently to the door of her bedchamber.

She had no idea what time it was, but the noise from the Great Hall had ceased some hours ago, so it might be near dawn. Thankfully, she heard no servants yet stirring as she made her way out the back door of the keep and toward the battlements. She had to talk to someone about her impending doom, and the countess might enjoy the company.

All was silent as she approached the cage, but she had the sense that another presence lingered nearby. Stopping, she scrutinized the walkway. The soldiers on guard were near the barbican as usual, and there wasn't any place along the wall that a human could hide. Although, of course, the presence she felt wouldn't *be* human any longer.

Then, suddenly, she saw the shadow along an embrasure. The shape was that of a large man, dressed in what seemed to be leather and metal armor that belonged to an earlier time. Hoping to find out who he was, she called softly. "Wait!"

The form paused, the coifed head turning toward her. Hoping the figure would become more clear, Kendra strained to see and then gaped as it vanished over the side of the wall. Peering down, she saw nothing.

She pondered as she approached the cage. This was the second time she'd seen the spirit. Last time, the countess had denied its presence. Did she not know? Was it possible the shade was that of a man who'd inhabited Berwick Castle at an earlier time and was trying to protect the countess?

Not surprisingly, Isobel was awake when Kendra slipped into the nook above the cage, her oil lamp providing a dim glow. Had she been conversing with the spirit?

"Why are ye here at this hour?"

"I could not sleep," Kendra replied. "I needed to talk to someone."

"Does it have to do with the French contingent that arrived this morning?"

"*Oui*. How did you know?"

The countess shrugged. "The only benefit from living in a cage suspended above the walls is that I see everyone who comes in and leaves."

Did that include the shadow man? But then, spirits didn't need to use conventional means of moving about. "The man is cousin to King Philippe's councilor. Queen Isabella arranged a betrothal for me."

"Ah," Isobel said. "Ye earned her wrath because of Adrian, I suspect."

"But we have not done anything!"

"'Tis the fact that Adrian has nae done anything with the queen that has her peeved."

Kendra's heart fluttered to hear it, then she frowned. Did Adrian share such confidences with Isobel? "How do you know?"

"Because if he had, she would nae want ye gone." The countess smiled. "And Adrian did declare himself your champion, nae?"

She felt herself blush. "He told you that?"

"Aye." She eyed Kendra. "Ye should trust him. He will keep ye from this marriage, if ye ask."

Her heart lurched again. Could he? "How? My aunt and uncle have approved the match, and the king wishes an alliance." As much as she was attracted to Adrian—and she had trusted him with her secret—what could he do? "Adrian is only an envoy."

"He is…" The countess paused, then began again. "Ye just need to trust him. He will protect ye, much like he does me."

Adrian did protect Isobel. He brought her warm bricks at night and plaids for warmth and probably more palatable food than the normal gruel she got. "But he hasn't been able to secure your release."

"Nor have I asked him to," Isobel replied. "Do nae misunderstand. I hate this cage, but securing Scotland's freedom is more important than my captivity."

Kendra suddenly felt her problem was minor compared to what the countess had endured. "You are so brave."

"Nae brave. The Earls of Fife have always crowned Scotland's kings. Since my brother is held hostage by England, it was my duty to do so."

"And you defied your husband, too."

"I have nae regrets about that." Isobel was quiet for a moment. "My marriage was an arranged one which I did nae want."

Kendra stared at her. "Like mine is?"

"Aye. But I accepted it because my father wished an alliance with the Comyns when he thought John Balliol would remain king."

"It is always about power and status, isn't it?" Kendra tried not to sound bitter. "What a woman wants matters not to men."

"To most men, no," Isobel agreed, "but 'tis nae always the case. Love matches are made."

Kendra felt herself blush. "Adrian de Soules does not love me."

"Mayhap nae yet, but he reminds me of a man I ken who would do anything for the lady he loved," the countess answered, "including defying his king."

"What happened to him?"

"He was exiled, but his lady went with him, so I doona think he cared."

"This lady was a friend of yours?"

"I dinna have the pleasure of meeting her since she was an ancestor of mine from Perth, but the story of the love match she made—in defiance of the king—was always one of my favorites." Isobel tilted her head up. "Lord de Soules declared himself your champion when he dinna have to. He has honor."

Kendra turned thoughtful. "If Adrian were even willing to defy Edward—out of a sense of duty or honor or something—he would void any chance of a truce with King Robert."

"Mayhap. Mayhap not. Edward is more wily than some of his retainers give him credit for, but the Bruce will nae back down. One way or another, Scotland will win her freedom." The countess arched a brow. "Meanwhile, ye stand to lose yours. What will ye do?"

Kendra wished she knew the answer.

Chapter Eleven

At the sound of footsteps outside the stables, Adrian turned from saddling his horse, hoping that Kendra had decided to join him for his morning ride. They had much to discuss. Unfortunately, it was Gerard who darkened the doorway.

Adrian led his destrier out. "If you want to check on your horses, they are in the stalls at the far end."

"Actually, I thought to ride out with you." Gerard snapped his fingers at a stable boy. "See to it that my horse is saddled at once. And make haste."

The lad ran off, white-faced, to do his bidding. Adrian kept his expression impassive. He always took care of his own mount. He wasn't looking forward to more of de Nogaret's company, either. Last night's dinner had been unpleasant enough. "You are interested in seeing the countryside?"

"Not particularly. I am interested, though, in why my betrothed intended to ride out with you."

So Kendra had planned to come. He didn't like that de Nogaret was already controlling her movements. "She has a mare that needs regular exercise. King Edward appointed me her…bodyguard."

"Which she will no longer need, now that I am here."

Adrian forced a nonchalant smile. "The reason the king gave me the task is that I am envoy to Robert

Bruce. The peasants and villagers still resent English knights, so Lady Kendra is safer riding with me."

"Then she should be safe from these villains with me as well, since I am no English knight."

He held on to his rising temper. "As a Frenchman, you are hardly familiar with the country."

"You are French yourself…" His sentence was cut short as his horse was led out. He mounted and didn't speak again until they cleared the gate. "What is a Frenchman doing in service to a rebel king?"

"Robert Bruce holds nearly every castle north of the River Tay, which hardly makes him a rebel any longer."

"Except in the eyes of an English king," Gerard replied. "And you have not answered my question. How did a Frenchman become a Scottish envoy?"

"I am part Scots, as my uncle was." He kept his voice even. The last thing he needed was to cause this cousin to Philippe's councilor to become suspicious.

"Yet your accent remains strong," Gerard said. "How long have you been in Scotland?"

He was going to have to be very careful. Had de Nogaret been asked to look for exiled Templars? It seemed likely. "My uncle's health started failing several years ago. Since he had been Robert Bruce's envoy, he wanted me to continue his work."

Gerard's eyes looked cold as gray granite. "Two kings claim the throne. The field seems a bit crowded."

"I suppose it could be seen that way."

"I wonder…" Gerard sounded speculative. "Why Robert Bruce has become so successful in recent years? He was left with only a ragtag group of men after his defeat at Methven and the massacre in Argyll. It takes money to back an army."

The hair at his nape began to prickle. "Many Scots rallied behind him."

"I am not talking about farmers with pitchforks. The number of men Robert Bruce now commands need sustenance." He slanted Adrian another look. "Guillaume thinks the treasure the Templars absconded with arrived in Scotland along with the heretics themselves who are funding Bruce's operation. What do you think?"

Adrian's blood chilled. He was going to have to be very, very cautious. If de Nogaret even had an inkling that the treasure lay buried beneath Henri St. Clair's castle at Roslin—or that the Templars were Bruce's secret weapon—neither France nor the Church would stop at anything short of total annihilation.

"I think those rumors died years ago, since no Templars have been seen."

"One would hardly expect them to ride about with their emblazoned red crosses." Gerard flicked a fly from his hand. "That does not mean they are not here."

"I suppose it is a possibility," Adrian kept his tone as neutral as he could.

"Indeed."

Adrian looked straight ahead. If there were any bright spot to this conversation, it was that perhaps Queen Isabella's invitation and suggested betrothal to Kendra had been simply a convenient reason for de Nogaret to come here. Mayhap the man didn't intend to go through with it? Adrian's hope was short lived as de Nogaret spoke again.

"*Quel coup ce serait...*" Gerard smiled widely, although the humor didn't reach his eyes. "...if I brought home Pembroke's niece as a wife along with the Templar treasure. *Un grand triomphe, non?*"

It would be a total *coup*. He was going to have to send Remy to warn Bruce. Adrian managed to shrug. "As you say."

"One more thing," de Nogaret said as they turned their horses to head back. "While I am here, my intended bride will have no more need of your services. Stay away from her."

He spurred his horse viciously, causing it to scream as it broke into a gallop.

Adrian didn't follow him, instead clenching a fist as he watched the mistreatment of the animal. Men like that treated their wives the same way. There wasn't any way he was going to let that happen to Kendra.

Stay away from her? Not only had he Robert's order to do the exact opposite, now he had his own reasons to protect her. He would have to be careful, but the gauntlet had been thrown.

****

Kendra threw down the altar cloth she was supposed to be embroidering, causing her aunt to look up from her own work in consternation.

"Having a temper tantrum like a child does not become you."

Kendra clamped her mouth shut. Her aunt had no idea just how much she wanted to stamp her feet and throw every movable object in the solar. And maybe some non-throwable objects as well. Right now, her anger made her feel strong enough to pick up the small table and toss it across the room. And mayhap the chair her aunt was sitting in. *With* her aunt still seated.

"I *despise* Gerard de Nogaret!"

Her aunt arched one brow. "You hardly know him."

She knew all she needed to know. He had been pompous and arrogant at dinner, but this morning, he had forbidden her to go out riding. *Forbidden* her. As though he already were her lord and master. When she'd tried to walk past him, he'd grabbed her arm, none too gently, and nearly dragged her back to the keep, where he'd marched her to her room with *orders* to stay there. She'd only waited for the sound of his boots to disappear before she sought out her uncle. Unfortunately, he and the king had gone hunting, and by the time she got to the stable, Adrian's horse was gone.

"I do not want to marry him."

Beatrice laid down her embroidery. "What a woman *wants* is rarely relevant. Lord de Nogaret holds much power in France. You will have servants to meet your every demand and coin to spend on whatever you wish to have. You should be grateful."

What she wished to have was her freedom. Gerard de Nogaret had already denied her an opportunity to ride her own horse here in England before they were married. She could only imagine how restricted her movements would be once they were in France. And if he should ever find out about her ability to see spirits... Kendra shivered as a shudder ran all the way down her spine.

"You know I do not care about that." Kendra tried to keep from sounding desperate. "All I want to do is go home to Wales."

"And do what? Ride astride your horse like a man? Spend your time on the boggy moors or climbing the hills?"

"Yes! That is exactly what I want to do."

Beatrice's mouth tightened. "Your uncle has been too lax with you. From the time you came to us, he should have heeded my warning that you learn the skills a gentlewoman needs to have. Instead, he let you run wild as a heathen."

"I don't want to be a gentlewoman—"

"Obviously. How fortunate we are that Lord de Nogaret is willing to overlook your inadequacies." Her aunt picked up her embroidery. "Now go and make yourself presentable for dinner."

Kendra had a feeling he wouldn't overlook them for long, but she didn't say it. As she left, she thought of the conversation she'd had with the countess last night. She agreed that Adrian could be trusted. She wouldn't have divulged her secret otherwise. Her earlier suspicions that he was more than simply the envoy he said he was remained, but she instinctively felt she had nothing to fear from him.

He'd agreed to be her champion, but that was in the context of escorting her outside the city walls when she wanted to ride. Helping her escape a marriage she did not want was an entirely different matter. Adrian was trying to secure a truce between Scotland and England. And Edward had approved the marriage.

Isobel herself had said Scotland's freedom was more important than hers...and she had endured living in a cage for nearly four years! If Kendra asked Adrian for help, he would have to defy the English king. That would mean no truce would be signed.

She couldn't ask Adrian for help and be responsible for Scotland losing a chance for independence, however slim it might be. Fighting would continue. More lives would be lost.

She would have to find another way to avoid marrying Gerard de Nogaret. She had to.

****

"We would be remiss as hosts if we did not have an extravagant event to welcome Lord de Nogaret to England," Queen Isabella said as she managed to seat herself beside Adrian at the evening meal, although she looked at her husband. "Do you not agree?"

"Yuletide is approaching in little more than a fortnight," Edward said. "We could surely have a huge feast then."

"Yule? That will be celebrated by the peasants and servants as well. We must do something special." The queen smiled at Kendra. "Something to celebrate the betrothal also."

Kendra felt sick. She might as well have been talking to the castle walls this afternoon instead of her aunt. Her uncle had been stuck behind closed doors with the king and Lancaster after they'd returned from hunting. Rumors flew that Robert Bruce had his eye on Edinburgh next. Her uncle—and certainly the king—would not want to be bothered with her pleas not to marry. Such a thing would be insignificant to them if the rumors were true and Robert was marching east. Then again, other rumors suggested he was turning back to Dunbarton.

"I think His Majesty's suggestion for a Yuletide festival is quite all that is needed."

Gerard leveled his gaze on her as she spoke. "I do not require my bride to *think*."

Kendra felt her face heat in anger. She had no

intention of being some mindless chit who sat silently throughout a conversation. She wanted to tell the condescending lord just that, but both her aunt and uncle were giving her stern looks. She became aware that Adrian was watching her also, his expression sympathetic.

She looked down as her face flamed again, this time in embarrassment for being reticent. Did he think her weak for not responding? Surely, he didn't think she was in agreement with this betrothal? She stole a glance through her lashes. He was still watching her. She closed her eyes, then slowly opened them.

More than anything, Kendra wanted to believe what the countess had said. That Adrian would keep her from this marriage if she asked it. That he would protect her. But the messenger that arrived this afternoon had only solidified her intention of not involving him. Regardless of which direction, if Robert Bruce were on the move, Adrian was already in a dangerous position.

"Might I suggest a competition to test my French warriors' skills with yours, Your Majesty?" Gerard asked. "Nothing as elaborate as a tournament, of course."

"That is an excellent idea!" Queen Isabella exclaimed. "It has been frightfully boring here at Berwick this autumn."

"My knights could use some real competition as well," Lancaster said. "We could find out if my cousin's men could best either of us."

Edward frowned. "We remind you that *your* knights are still Ours to command."

"I meant, of course, that I was their liege lord. You

will have a chance to see how well-trained they are." Lancaster smiled. "And how well they obey me."

"Is that a threat to His Majesty?" Gaveston demanded. "It sounds like one."

"Not at all," the earl replied blandly. "Only that my men are well prepared for battle."

"We do not have to limit the competition to just our knights." Gerard looked at Adrian. "I would invite Robert Bruce's envoy and his men to compete as well."

Adrian gave him a steady look. "There are but three of us, and we are not here to do battle."

"But of course you would be invited to participate," Queen Isabella said. "We have all seen you practice with your soldiers." She laid a hand on his arm. "You are quite skilled."

Kendra bit her lip. Nearly every night at dinner, the queen managed to touch him. She often made suggestive remarks as well, although she usually did so when the king was engaged in conversation with Gaveston. Had the countess been right about that too? Was the queen growing more bold now that she thought she'd effectively eliminated Kendra from their own personal, private rivalry?

"I would be very interested in testing those skills," Gerard said, his granite eyes penetrating. "Especially since you are representing the Scottish king."

"As his envoy." Adrian held his gaze, unwavering. "In place of my late uncle. And the offer of a truce still holds."

"If Robert Bruce is advancing, the king would appear weak if he accepted a truce now," Lancaster interrupted.

Edward glared at him. "We have not yet decided

what to do."

Lancaster shrugged. "It would appear cowardly to sign."

Dear Lord. This conversation was turning from bad to dangerous. The earl's goading of his cousin might make the king dig in his heels and refuse any kind of treaty, which put Adrian in a very precarious position. Kendra had no illusions that Robert Bruce would ever forfeit the Scottish crown, and his army had been steadily growing, strengthening, and claiming one victory after another. The people followed him and, if Adrian sought to advocate for Robert Bruce, the man must have some honor. It would behoove King Edward to agree to parley, but Lancaster seemed bent on keeping the waters stirred.

"Do We have to remind you, *again*, that you walk a fine line, cousin?" Edward snapped.

"I simply state the obvious." Lancaster glanced at Adrian, then turned back to the king. "Berwick will be overrun by Scots."

Gerard glanced from one of the men to the other. "Mayhap we could open the competition to include any Scots in the vicinity?" He gave a Gallic shrug when the earl and the king both stared at him. "You could see what strengths these vassals really have."

Edward looked thoughtful. "It is always wise to size up the enemy."

"The Scots do not need to be your enemy," Adrian said.

"That still remains to be seen," the king answered, "but We like the idea of opening the competition to anyone interested in participating. We can see what the possible recruits of Robert Bruce are capable of."

"For once, cousin, I agree with you," Lancaster said.

"Then it is settled," Queen Isabella said. "We shall prepare for a great event—and a great celebration for Lord de Nogaret's upcoming marriage—that no one will forget."

That no one will forget. An idea began to form in Kendra's mind based on something her aunt had said. It seemed preposterous at first, but as the table conversation turned to the mundane and she wasn't included, the thought kept growing. If it worked, she would not have to ask for Adrian's help at all. Gerard de Nogaret would not want to marry her.

She stifled a smile. If the queen truly wanted an event that no one would forget, Kendra thought she might just be able to deliver one.

Chapter Twelve

"We must warn Robert that de Nogaret is in England," Adrian told Remy and Pierre the next morning as they rode their horses outside the castle gates. "And that he is asking questions about the Templars."

"Do you think Philippe could have been sent a missive that the Bruce has a group of mounted knights with him and gotten suspicious?" Remy asked.

"Doubtful," Adrian answered. "Only fifteen or twenty of our brothers ride at any given time. That's not enough to alert anyone to the presence of nearly one hundred of us."

Pierre nodded. "Many Border soldiers have sworn allegiance to Robert after he's taken their castles. Some of them are knights as well, so it would not be unusual to see a group of them with our king."

Remy raised a brow. "You are sure de Nogaret was invited to Berwick? That he did not ask to come?"

"The queen admitted she'd extended the invitation." Adrian grimaced. "She said Edward wishes for an alliance through marriage,"

"Since when did England and France ever agree on anything?" Remy snorted. "More than likely, the queen just wants Lady Kendra gone."

"Still," Pierre said, "if Pembroke's niece marries the French councilor's cousin, that pretty much solidifies which side France will defend."

"And don't forget Pembroke," Adrian added. "In all of my conversations with the earl, I have not sensed that he is willing to support Scotland's independence."

"Even though he hasn't approved Edward the First's bloody massacres nor favored the current king's spending?"

Adrian shrugged. "I think he fears Lancaster attempting a *coup*. He has the armies, and if Pembroke pulls his support from Edward, England will fall."

"Mayhap our work here is done then," Remy said. "I doubt Edward will sign a truce, with Robert on the move."

Pierre nodded again. "Especially if Lancaster keeps niggling at him for cowardice."

"You could give the king a deadline to sign the truce, with the offer that Bruce will cease raiding," Remy suggested.

"Robert already sent him a letter prior to my arrival saying almost as much. So far, he's ignored it." Adrian shook his head. "Ultimatums rarely ever work."

"That would give us a reason to leave court, though," Pierre said, "and be out of de Nogaret's line of fire."

Adrian eyed him. "Are you not forgetting Lady Kendra?"

"I think we already have our answer regarding Pembroke," he replied. "Besides, she will not be of use to us if she's marrying a French lord and leaving."

Remy grinned. "Of course, if you want to follow Robert's order and seduce the lady—"

"Shut your mouth!" Adrian turned on him. "She does not wish this marriage."

Remy regarded him for a moment. "So *that* is how it is between you."

"There isn't anything between us." Adrian was aware that his face grew warm. By the saints! He hadn't blushed since he was a green lad. "I declared myself her champion. That vow means something to me."

"Has the lady told you she does not wish to marry?" Pierre asked.

"I have not had the chance to talk with her alone," Adrian answered, "but I can tell from how she looks and acts at dinner."

Remy looked skeptical. "She could just be behaving like a real lady would do—"

"Kendra *is* a real lady!" Adrian felt his temper rising. "Both of you have heard the rumors that de Nogaret helped torture our brothers in France. I've watched the man mistreat his horse. He will expect Kendra to act as docile as an animal, which she won't do. De Nogaret would break her spirit." He took a deep breath. "Besides, Countess Isobel told me they had a conversation and Kendra told her as much."

"What do you plan to do, then?" Pierre asked.

"I am not sure yet." Adrian felt a muscle in his jaw twitch. "But when you speak with the Bruce about de Nogaret's suspicions, ask him if he would grant sanctuary to her."

Both men gaped at him. Finally Remy spoke. "That will incite full blown-out war with England for sure!"

"Not necessarily." Adrian smiled grimly. "The trick is not to let them know where she's gone."

****

Three days had passed since the dinner where the competition was mentioned. The next morning, Kendra had pleaded that she was not feeling well, which was not a lie. She felt sick to her stomach every time she thought of marrying Gerard de Nogaret, and it hadn't been difficult to retch in front of her aunt nor had it been hard to look feverish...a warm brick placed against each cheek in turn had done its job. Beatrice had backed away, suggesting she stay in her chambers until she felt better.

The competition was to be held today. Her aunt had come this morning to tell her she needed to attend but, when Kendra repeated her sick act, had quickly decided otherwise. That suited Kendra just fine. No one would be checking on her until it was too late.

She crossed the room to the wardrobe and took a bundle from the bottom of it. Even though she'd doubted she'd be able to wear them, she'd hidden the braies and shirt she wore in Wales amongst the gowns she'd packed. She'd just had no idea of how handy they would be for today. Kendra dressed swiftly, then secured her hair under the hood of the short cape that completed her outfit.

By the time she'd retrieved the bow and quiver she'd hidden in her mare's stall, the fencing competition was well underway. She was pleasantly surprised that Gerard had been eliminated in an earlier round, but as she watched Adrian block and parry against the Earl of Lancaster without taking advantage of several opportunities to advance, she realized he was not trying to win. A few minutes later, the earl's sword made contact with Adrian's shoulder and the match was done. Adrian didn't seem upset over the loss at all. Why?

She shifted her attention to the French lord

standing not that far away. His eyes narrowed as he scrutinized Adrian. His look was so intense, Kendra didn't think he'd taken any notice of the archers waiting their turn, but she still adjusted her hood to keep her features from showing. The time for recognition was not yet.

"Archers! Draw your numbers!" the bailiff in charge of the competition announced.

Kendra moved forward with the others, thankful this was an open competition that required no names be called out. She reached into the bowl the bailiff held to take a slip of paper.

"Laddie, yer hand looks too soft to pull a bowstring."

She froze. Had anyone nearby heard? She didn't dare look in the direction of Gerard. Then a man standing beside her laughed.

"Ye are a mite small to be competing. How old are ye, lad?"

Dear Lord. She hadn't anticipated having to speak. At least not until after she'd shot. She pitched her voice as low as she could. "Old enough."

A second man chuckled. "His voice has nae even changed yet."

"Ye might want to wait a year or two to try your hand," the first man said.

Kendra shook her head vehemently.

Another voice spoke. One that she recognized immediately.

"Is there an age limit?" Adrian asked the bailiff.

She didn't dare look up as she waited for the answer. If Adrian recognized her, he'd more than likely stop her from competing. She *had* to compete. Her aunt had said no man would marry a woman he was afraid might put an arrow in his heart while he was sleeping. She had to prove to Gerard de Nogaret that she was capable of doing just that.

"There is no age limit," the bailiff replied.

"And the competition is open, *non*?"

"It is, *Monsieur*."

"*Bon*."

There was a moment's silence before one of the men who'd laughed replied, "We were only jesting."

Kendra heard Adrian's footsteps retreat and breathed a sigh of relief. If she could just get through the competition... She glanced at her number. Twenty. She was next to last. She moved to the back of the line, careful not to draw any more attention to herself.

A number of the archers were fair shots. Gerard managed to put four arrows in the center of the target. She watched covertly as Adrian took his stance and was surprised, once again, that each of his six arrows fell outside the bull's-eye. He was deliberately choosing to lose at archery too. Why?

By the time it was her turn, Kendra had tallied up her competitors' scores. Only one had managed to place five arrows inside the eye. Another had tied with Gerard for second place.

Adjusting her position, she focused on the target. This was her chance to prove she was not the wife that a French lord would want. Taking a deep breath, she released five arrows straight-on in rapid succession, each one hitting inside the center. The crowd gasped, then silence fell as she canted her bow for her last shot. The arrow arched, seeming to suspend itself in midair before tracking downward to knock all the other arrows off the target with its impact.

The crowd roared its approval. Kendra bowed from the waist as a man would, then straightened and threw back her hood, letting her hair tumble down. Smiling, she turned to look at Gerard.

His face was white with fury, his eyes like slate as he stared back.

****

The banquet that evening was held in the Great Hall. Half of it had been cleared for dancing later, but the other half had trestle tables crowded together so all those who had competed that day could be included. Kendra sat at the first table with her aunt since, other than the queen, only men were seated on the dais.

Lancaster gave her a scrutinizing look while Gaveston regarded her curiously. Her uncle and the king were engaged in conversation. Adrian smiled at Kendra while Gerard continued the cold, penetrating stare he'd used earlier.

"Are you happy that you have offended your betrothed?" Beatrice asked.

She was *very* happy, but that wasn't the answer her aunt wanted to hear. Gerard had yet to speak a word to her. He'd left the field abruptly, not waiting for prizes to be awarded. And Beatrice had confined her to her chamber the rest of the day to ponder on her grievous misbehavior. Kendra bit back a smile. There had been no *mis*behavior on her part. "Lord de Nogaret should not be offended. He did quite well."

"You know very well that is not what I mean," her aunt replied. "You humiliated him. How many times do I have to tell you that men do not like for a woman to best them?"

Adrian hadn't cared the day she'd challenged him at practice. He'd *grinned*. But that wasn't the answer her aunt wanted either. "Do you not think Lord de Nogaret should know what he's getting?"

Her aunt looked at her as though she'd suddenly sprouted snakes in her hair like Medusa. "I should hope *not*. You may have already done unrepairable damage."

She certainly hoped she had. "If his lordship is truly offended, then mayhap I am not the best choice of a bride."

"That hardly matters. The king has decided he wants this alliance with France."

Kendra raised her chin. "I am sure there are many daughters of English nobles who would suit."

"None that have your connection." Beatrice arched a brow. "Do you not realize how powerful your uncle truly is?"

"Why does that matter? I'm *your* niece, not his daughter."

Her aunt looked appalled. "You are his legal ward! An alliance with France through marriage would bring good relations to England."

"I doubt I am important enough for that."

"But your uncle's title is." Her aunt regarded her. "Why do you suppose my husband is so involved in conversation with the king at this moment?"

Kendra looked back at the dais. Was her uncle really discussing her fate with the king? Almost as though she'd sent a silent message, they both glanced in her direction. She looked quickly away.

The conversation was brought to a halt by the sound of pipe and flute as the minstrels tuned their instruments. Serving wenches hurried to clear the remaining trenchers from tables and refill wine goblets. Kendra was about to take a sip of hers when Gerard approached, his expression stony. She set her goblet down, trying to quell what felt like a bevy of quail taking flight in her stomach.

"I believe the honor of the first dance is mine," he said.

He wanted to dance? Dear Lord. From the hard look in his eyes she thought he was going to publicly disparage her. She'd rather bear such umbrage than to have to dance with the man. "I—"

"That is gracious of you, my lord," Beatrice said, planting a subtle elbow in Kendra's side. "My niece was just telling me how foolish her actions were today."

She had done no such thing. But protesting was not going to get her anywhere, especially since Gerard had taken hold of her wrist rather painfully and nearly dragged her up.

"Of course," she said.

His grip on her wrist didn't loosen, and she wondered if she'd have a bruise as he led her into the round. By the time the dance ended, she was sure of it since each time they met his hand had felt like a vise.

As they left the floor, she rubbed both wrists gingerly. He glanced down and smiled, although his eyes remained hard. "Let that be a lesson."

Kendra stared at him. He'd bruised her wrists on purpose? "A lesson?"

He leaned closer. "A lesson, my lovely betrothed. No woman makes me look like a fool."

"I did not mean to make you look like a fool."

He grabbed one of her wrists again, bending the thumb back just enough to make her wince. "And I do not like a woman who talks back to me either."

Kendra jerked her hand back. "Then mayhap, *my lord,* you should marry someone else!"

He smiled again, but it looked more like a sneer. "And give up my chance to an earldom?"

"You won't inherit an earldom if you marry me. That is not the way English law works."

"*Peut-être pas.*" He shrugged. "Perhaps not. But you are Pembroke's legal ward. He has no heir. Once you bear me a son, I will have King Philippe apply pressure on Edward to have the child declared the heir...which means I will control the earldom until he reaches his majority."

Kendra felt as though her horse had kicked her in her stomach. She hadn't thought about that. Nearly two decades of a Frenchman in control of an English earldom could very well have the opposite effect from what everyone thought. Judging from Gerard de Nogaret's expression, she was pretty sure his intention was not altruistic. And she definitely did not want to think about *how* begetting that son would happen.

But one thing was clear. Gerard de Nogaret had no intention of ending the betrothal.

****

From his self-assigned post against a wall safely out of sight of Queen Isabella, Adrian watched as de Nogaret led Kendra back to her aunt and then walked toward where the queen was seated. A moment later, Kendra rose and went the other way, to the rear serving entrance to the hall. Adrian looked around, then casually started across the room.

He'd been wanting to talk to her all day, but she'd been sent to her chambers shortly after the prizes had been awarded this morning. He'd recognized her almost instantly. The sight of her in braies that revealed shapely legs and a nicely rounded derriere had caused an instantaneous reaction, and he wondered why no one else realized the "lad" was a woman. A part of him wanted to carry her off before she was recognized and reprimanded for her behavior. Another part of him admired her spunk, which was why he'd come to her defense. He'd had a hard time not laughing at the expression on de Nogaret's face when he realized the person who'd placed each of those arrows perfectly was Kendra. She'd put the man in his place without a single word.

Adrian glanced around the room once more before he stepped through the servant's entrance that led to the kitchens. He suspected she was on her way to visit Isobel in her cage.

The bailey was dark, save for several oil lamps attached to posts, but a nearly full moon shed enough light that Adrian could make out Kendra's form as she emerged from the tower to the battlement. He probably should just wait for her here so she could have her private conversation, but snow had begun to fall, and the walkway along the crenellations would be slippery. She'd nearly fallen once before.

Quickly, he made his way up the stairs, then hesitated as he heard Kendra's voice, flattening himself in the shadows of the tower wall.

"I don't know what to do, Isobel. I can't marry Gerard de Nogaret."

The countess' voice drifted upward. "Your plot dinna work?"

"No," Kendra replied. "I thought if I proved I was

as skilled with a bow as any man, he would not want me. He is furious, but he refuses to cancel the betrothal."

Adrian cursed silently.

"Would ye dare try to best him at something else?" Isobel asked.

"It wouldn't make any difference," Kendra answered. "He wants this marriage to have a son, one to be declared heir to my uncle's estates so he can rule them."

Adrian cursed again. He knew the man had no honorable intentions. Kendra deserved better than a man who would only use her.

"If only I could have remained in France with my father," she went on. "I could have lived my life unnoticed."

"But ye said your father was dead."

"He is. He owed too much money to bear the burden." Kendra's voice was bitter now. "I blame the Templars for lending him the money."

Adrian inhaled sharply. *Mon Dieu.* He'd almost forgotten.

There was a moment of silence. Then the countess spoke. "Do ye hate all Templars then?"

Adrian held his breath, waiting for an answer.

Another silent moment. "I've never met one, but as a group, I do. I blame them for lending my father too much money. The money lender knew he had a gaming problem."

"That is one man who mayhap made a bad decision," Isobel replied. "The Templars lent the French king money, too, and look how he repaid them."

"You sound as though you are defending them."

Adrian tensed. Would the countess betray him, albeit unwittingly?

"I am only saying ye should nae judge what ye doona ken." There was a pause. "There are many who doona understand why I did what I did, including my husband."

"Oh, Isobel! I am sorry!" Kendra sounded close to tears. "How selfish of me to be concerned over my petty problems when you have lived in this cage for years."

"Doona fash. Edward will nae let me die or starve. I am still a valuable hostage to him," the countess said. "And your concern is nae a petty one. Ye must get away."

"But where can I go? My aunt and uncle are my only relatives in England."

"There are places in the Highlands where ye would nae be found," Isobel answered.

"But how would I get there? I don't know the country."

There was another pause, longer this time. "Lord de Soules knows the country. Ye should ask him."

"But I can't involve him when he is trying to broker peace with King Edward!"

"I have been told Robert Bruce is on the move. Edward will sign no truce now." The countess hesitated. "Lord de Soules will probably be leaving soon. Go to him before it is too late."

"Do you really think he will take the risk of helping me?"

"Ye willna ken until ye ask."

Adrian heard the hint of laughter in Isobel's voice and then a shuffle on the battlement. He stole down the steps before Kendra would find him standing there eavesdropping.

By the time she descended the steps, he was casually walking across the bailey. She stopped when she saw him.

"Lady Kendra. I saw you leave the hall," he said as he approached her. "Is something amiss?"

"I…" She paused. "I needed some fresh air."

He wanted to encourage her to talk without revealing what he'd heard. "You did not look well. I thought to check on you."

"You followed me out?" She looked quickly around. "Did anyone see you?"

Did she think Gerard had followed her as well? "I'm sure a number of people did, but I didn't hasten after you." He moved closer. "Is something wrong?"

She hesitated again, then grimaced. "Besides my being forced to marry a man I don't even like?"

"You shouldn't be forced to marry him."

"I wish you could convince my uncle and aunt about that."

Adrian took her hands in his. "There are…" He stopped abruptly when she winced. Frowning, he looked down at her wrists which, even in the moonlight, bore the beginnings of dark bruises. "*Mon Dieu*. Did that bastard do this?"

She tried to pull her hands free, but he held fast. "Tell me."

Kendra nodded as a tear trickled down her cheek. "He told me I made him look like a fool."

"He *is* a fool." Adrian used his thumb to wipe the tear away, then let his fingers slide along her cheek to cup her chin. Her eyes widened as she looked up at him. The next thing he knew, he'd bent and covered her mouth with his.

The sensation sent a jolt like lightning through his body. Her lips were velvet soft and pliant under his. He circled her waist, drawing her close, as he swept his tongue across their crease, pleased at how readily she parted them for him. She tasted slightly of salty tears and wine and something much more intoxicating. He deepened the kiss as she wrapped her arms around his neck to meet his challenge.

A sudden noise from the kitchens not far away broke into his rapidly fogging mind, bringing him back to reality. He reluctantly broke the kiss and stepped back.

"If I am to assist you to get away, we probably should not be seen together."

Her eyes went wide again. "You will help me?"

And in that moment, he knew he no longer had a choice. She might hate the Templars and even him, if she found out he belonged to the brotherhood, but it was a chance he would have to take. Leaving her to a fate with a brutal husband was not something he could do.

"I will find a way."

****

From a window in the darkened kitchen, Queen Isabella observed them break apart and go their separate ways. She hadn't been able to find Adrian earlier, had only seen him leave shortly after the little bitch had gone out. It had taken her a good twenty minutes to disengage from conversation with Gerard, given how angry he was that the stupid girl had bested him. She'd spent precious moments reminding him how he could bring her to heel, once they were wedded.

Meanwhile, the tart had arranged a tryst with Adrian. That he was besotted was clear. She could sense desire and lust in a man, based on her own many encounters with paramours.

The bitch needed to be gone. Sooner, rather than later. Isabella narrowed her eyes. The marriage would have to be moved up.

Chapter Thirteen

"Good morning, my lady!" Elsie said as she drew back the curtains to allow the sunshine to stream into Kendra's bedchamber. "What excitement we'll be having today!"

She blinked, her mind not quite awake. What did the maid mean by excitement? Surely she couldn't know about the kiss Kendra had shared with Adrian! Odd parts of her body tingled as she remembered how hard and firm, yet gentle, his lips were as he claimed hers, and how smooth and warm his tongue. She'd never even considered what a man's tongue inside her mouth might feel like, let alone having her breasts pressed against the hard ridges of his chest. It was a good thing he'd held her tight since she'd been lightheaded enough to faint. She had *never* swooned in her life, but it had been a glorious, dizzying moment she definitely wanted to repeat. But Elsie didn't know that.

"What excitement?"

"Everyone in the castle will be going out to find the right log for Yule!" her maid answered.

Yule. She'd almost forgotten the season. Even though the Catholic Church banned its practice, in Wales many still celebrated the pagan rites. With much pageantry and a great show, the Holly King, who had taken the crown at midsummer, would fight and lose the battle to the Oak King, symbolizing the rebirth that spring would bring. She doubted that ritual would take place in Berwick.

"What do they do here?"

"There will be lots of arguing and boasting amongst the men throughout the day as each will claim he's found the best tree, but once the decision is made, there will be a grand festival this eve when it is lit to burn for twelve nights until the Christ's Mass."

"You said everyone in the castle goes out. Do the women just follow the men around?"

Elsie grinned. "Nae, my lady. We are in charge of gathering mistletoe."

Mistletoe. Although the Welsh still held to the ancient Druidic tradition that the plant had mystical qualities, the French had enthusiastically embraced the Nordic tradition of kissing under it. As much as she would have welcomed another kiss from Adrian, she was going to have to avoid any hangings of it since Gerard de Nogaret had most recently come from the French court. The idea of a kiss from him made her stomach roil. She managed somehow to smile.

"I am glad the servants are given leave to partake in all the activities."

"Aye." Elsie gave her a speculative look. "But are ye nae excited? Your betrothed will surely make a show of kissing ye!"

Dear Lord, how would she tolerate it? Nausea rose as reality slammed into her. She would have to tolerate a lot more than kissing if she were forced to marry the man. Kendra pulled down the sleeves of her night rail to cover the bruises on her wrists. She couldn't go through with it. She couldn't.

But Adrian had said he would help her escape. Would he? She was sure he had meant it last night, but that was after they'd kissed. If his mind functioned at all like hers, he could have spoken in the heat of the moment. She would have agreed to *anything* he'd asked after that kiss.

But this morning was another day. In spite of what the countess had said about Edward not signing a truce if Robert Bruce was on the move, Kendra could hardly expect Adrian to forsake trying to get one. And, if he helped her get away, that chance would be gone.

She was still contemplating that dilemma at the end of the day. She'd seen Adrian earlier that morning as he and his two men prepared to join the castle party, but he had barely glanced in her direction. Nor had he spoken to her that afternoon when everyone had returned and mulled wine was served in the Great Hall. He'd said they shouldn't be seen together if he were to help her get away. Was that why he acted so distant? Or did he regret what he'd offered to do?

And now, after the feast in the hall had been served and the trestle tables pushed away, he was on the far side of the room.

Her attention was diverted by horns trumpeting the arrival of the log. Nobles and servants alike gathered on either side of the large entrance, forming an aisle. Four squires, dressed in red tunics and green leggings, somberly carried the log on their shoulders as they marched through the crowd to the large hearth near the dais.

King Edward rose, accepting a pitch torch from his castellan, and moved forward to light the tinder beneath the log. The fire caught immediately, and the crowd to roar in approval, for the quick lighting was a portent of prosperity for the coming year. Kendra turned to leave, hoping to get to her chamber unnoticed, and bumped into Gerard. She tried not to recoil at the contact.

"Where are you going?" he asked.

"I...thought to retire, my lord."

An eyebrow rose. "Like you did last night?"

A chill ran down her spine. Dear Lord! Did he know about the kiss? A moment later, he gripped her wrists and rubbed them hard. She winced in pain, but managed not to cry out. "You are hurting me."

His brow went higher. "You have no idea what kind of pain I can inflict. Do not disappear from me again."

She willed her body not to tremble. She would not show fear. She. Would. Not. She forced her chin up. "Do you wish to cause a scene at King Edward's feast?"

His eyes narrowed, but he released her. Then he smiled coldly. "I believe the queen wishes to make an announcement for which you need to be present."

Kendra glanced around. Queen Isabella had come to stand alongside Edward and was watching them. She smiled when she caught Kendra's eye, but the smile looked sinister. The fine hair at her nape began to rise.

The herald trumpeted again, causing the large crowd to fall silent.

"We have one more cause to celebrate Yule this evening." The queen lifted her goblet. "Since Lord de Nogaret is needed back at the French court, King Edward and I will be hosting his wedding to Lady Kendra de Clermont right after we celebrate the Christ's Mass."

The crowd roared again, but all Kendra heard was a loud buzzing in her ears. In less than a fortnight, she was to be married. There wasn't any way Adrian could arrange her escape that quickly. She was trapped.

The buzzing grew louder, turning into what sounded like rolling thunder, before a gray haze descended and she felt herself falling.

****

If he'd needed any proof Kendra's situation was dire, Queen Isabella's announcement convinced Adrian something had to be done and quickly. He'd been observing the exchange between Kendra and de Nogaret and saw the bastard grip her wrists, and her wince. It had taken every ounce of will power not to march across the room and plant a fist in his face. The man had already turned his back on her to accept congratulations when she started to swoon. Luckily, a man servant had been passing by and caught her.

He watched as the servant carried her out, Pembroke and her aunt following in his wake. Adrian started to step forward, but Remy put a restraining hand on his shoulder.

"It is not your place to go to her."

Adrian jerked away. "She may have been hurt in the fall."

"Showing an interest in her is the worst thing you can do," Pierre warned.

His men were right. If he were to succeed in getting Kendra away, he didn't need to make de Nogaret any more suspicious than he already was.

"We won't have time for either of you to ride to the Bruce and get his permission for sanctuary."

Remy raised a brow. "You truly trust her enough to

take her to Robert's camp? If she saw the number of men he has, she could send word—"

"Kendra is no spy." As soon as the words were out, Adrian realized how truly he believed them. Gone was any concern that she might be gathering information for her uncle. After she'd trusted him about her ability to see *spectres*, he realized she preferred to be as far away from the English court as she could get. "I trust her."

"What if she identifies us as Templars?" Pierre asked. "You know she blames us for her father's debts."

He frowned. "We've been in Scotland for three years. It's not as if we wear our surcoats anymore."

"But more than a hundred men in Robert's army that have French accents still?" Remy looked skeptical. "The lady is smart enough to add two and two together."

Adrian set his jaw. "There are many Frenchmen who've chosen exile after losing their lands to Philippe."

"But what if she finds out?" Remy persisted.

"If it comes to that, I will deal with it." Adrian looked from one man to the other. "Do you really want to leave her to her fate with de Nogaret? We have all heard the cruelty he imposed on our brethren. And they are *men*. What chance would a woman have defending herself against the bastard?" He gave both of his comrades a piercing look. "And we are still knights."

Remy and Pierre glanced at each, their expressions turning sheepish.

"You should not have to remind us that we have a duty," Remy said.

"Or that we are still honorable," Pierre added.

"What do you want us to do?"

"I am not sure yet," Adrian answered. "I need a few days to come up with a plan that will get Kendra to safety."

Remy sighed. "I suppose this means any hope for an actual truce with Edward is gone."

Adrian gave him a sharp look as an idea began to form. "Perhaps a truce is the very thing we need to use."

"*What*?" Pierre gave him a quizzical look. "As the Scots say, 'Have ye gone daft?' You know Edward will not sign—"

"Probably not," Adrian agreed, "but he can't very well openly refuse a final offer with de Nogaret here unless he wants to risk looking like an arrogant fool."

Remy drew his brows together. "But the Bruce has made no such offer."

Adrian smiled grimly. "Not yet."

****

Kendra sputtered as the pungent odor of something that smelled awful filled her nose. Her eyes sprang open, and she realized she was lying on the bed in her chamber.

"I do hope you are feeling better." Her aunt removed the cloth she had been holding to Kendra's face. "Although it is easy to see why you were overwhelmed with such a lovely surprise."

Slowly, the recollection of fainting—and the reason why—came back. Kendra blinked at her aunt. "I was not—"

"Of course you were," Beatrice cut in. "For the queen to offer to include your wedding in the Yule festivities was so considerate."

The queen's *consideration* had nothing to do with it. As Kendra's mind cleared, she knew Isabella just wanted to get rid of her as quickly as possible.

"You are feeling better, are you not?"

She started at the sound of her uncle's voice. She hadn't realized he was standing in the doorway. Then she saw Gerard behind him, and her blood chilled.

"Lord de Nogaret should not be in my bedchamber."

"What does it matter?" he asked, stepping completely inside and moving toward the bed. "I am your betrothed. Soon enough, we will be sharing quarters."

She shivered, and it had nothing to do with her blood feeling frozen. "I do not want to marry you."

Beatrice looked stricken. "Forgive her, my lord. She is obviously still feeling the effects of her swoon."

"I am not." Kendra pushed herself into a sitting position against the headboard and pulled back her sleeves to show her bruises. "He did this to me."

Her uncle frowned, but Gerard spoke before he could. "I had no idea that I had inflicted such distress. I remember your moving away just as I reached for you." He smiled at Kendra. "I had no idea your flesh was so delicate. I will have to remember that in the future."

Beatrice beamed. "There now. You see? It was simply an accident that won't happen again."

Kendra stared numbly at her aunt. She was right that an *accident* wouldn't happen again. Gerard's statement had been a warning, not an apology. She turned to her uncle, determined to make one more effort.

"Please. This has nothing to do with Lord de

Nogaret. I do not wish to marry anyone, only to live a simple life in Wales."

He looked troubled, but Gerard cut in once again. "It seems your niece may have sustained an injury to her head."

Beatrice nodded. "That would explain her speaking utter nonsense. Please forgive her, my lord."

"Of course." Gerard smiled again. "I am looking forward to making her my bride."

"Mayhap we should let Kendra get some rest," Pembroke suggested.

"An excellent idea," Beatrice replied. "She just needs time to gather her wits about her."

Kendra closed her eyes, trying to keep from shaking, as she listened to their footsteps recede. Obviously she was the only person who had caught Gerard's innuendos. He'd already told her she had no idea how much pain he could inflict. But if her aunt and uncle accepted his story about her bruises, why would they believe anything else she said?

She desperately needed to talk to someone. She couldn't very well seek Adrian out, but maybe the countess could offer a suggestion on what to do.

Kendra sat up, glad the room wasn't spinning. Carefully, she made her way to the door and opened it a crack. Then she quickly closed it. A guard had been posted in the hall. Had that been Gerard's doing? Did he suspect she planned to run away?

She crept back to bed, slipping between the covers without bothering to undress. Could Adrian possibly help her escape in time to avoid the wedding? She had no idea how he would do so, but she had to ask him. With a guard stationed at her door, it was highly unlikely she'd not be watched from this moment on.

Kendra buried her face in her pillow. She was not going to cry. She was going to come up with a plan. Somehow she had to convince Gerard she didn't need a guard, that she hadn't meant what she said. That she'd only been distraught. That meant being pleasant to him, no matter how much she detested the man.

Could she do it?

Chapter Fourteen

Her hands were bound. People laughed and jeered as a guard jerked the rope she was tethered to, causing her to stumble as she crossed the bailey. The iron flogging pole already had wood heaped around it, faggots placed on top for easy lighting. At the sight of the executioner waiting with a pitch torch, she dug in her heels, trying to resist her inevitable fate, but they'd taken her boots, and her bare feet had little traction. The crowd pressed closer as she was shoved atop the pile and the guard began to wind the rope around to bind her in place. In another minute, the dried kindling would be lit, the heat instantly traveling up the metal as the wood caught. She closed her eyes, remembering what the auld healer has whispered to her. If she inhaled deeply, the smoke would kill her before the flames did.

A whizzing sound past her ear made her eyes pop open. The man who had started to tie her lay at her feet, an arrow through his chest. Before anyone could react, a horse's hooves thundered through the crowd, scattering people like chaff in the wind. A knight in ancient leather armor bore down, slashing his sword to the right and left to clear a path to her. At the last possible moment, the big destrier skidded to a stop and reared, using its front hooves as it had been taught. The knight bent down, encircled her waist, and scooped her into the saddle in front of him before he dug his heels into the horse's flanks and they galloped away.

Kendra sat up with a jerk, her heart pounding as she stared into the dark shadows of her bedchamber. There was only silence. The dream had been so real. Had it been a vision? As a child, before the ghosts had started to appear, she'd had several such lucid dreams.

Still shaking, she groped for the candle beside her bed and lit it. The soft glow lent a reality to her surroundings. The wardrobe by the door. The chest of drawers with ewer and basin to one side. The small table and chair by the shuttered window. Everything was normal. She held her breath, though, half-expecting an apparition to make an appearance, but none did.

Had the woman in the dream been *her*? She'd almost felt as though she were someone else. Had the dream been a portent? Was she actually going to meet such a fate if Gerard de Nogaret discovered her unusual ability?

Or could this be the way the Countess of Buchan met her end? She'd heard her uncle say John Comyn wanted an heir and he could not remarry while his wife still lived. Edward I had decided Isobel would make a better example of what happened to traitors if he kept her alive in a cage, but would his son be persuadable? Especially since there could be a truce now?

Kendra lay back on the pillow and stared at the ceiling. Who had the knight been? Several days' growth of beard obscured his jaw and the nose guard on the helm hid most of his face, but she'd glimpsed dark eyes. He'd seemed vaguely familiar, but she knew she'd never met him. Had she seen him, though? The hair at her nape began to rise.

He reminded her of the shadow man she'd glimpsed on the ramparts when she'd visited Isobel. If only she could go up there and visit the countess and tell her of the dream. But the guard was still at her door.

She rolled over and punched her pillow. Tomorrow she would persuade Gerard she had changed her mind, even though she would have to lie, deceive, and mislead to do it. Tomorrow she would find a way to talk to Adrian. Tomorrow she would get a message to Isobel too. She needed to know who the shadow man was and why he visited her.

Was he the same man as the knight who'd rescued the woman in the dream? And *who* was he?

****

As it turned out, Kendra received a reprieve of sorts when she went down to break her fast the next morning. First, the guard left and no one replaced him, so maybe it had only been done as a threat of what could happen if she kept resisting. More importantly, though, Edward had taken a party hunting, and Gerard had gone with them. Adrian had not.

She found him in the stables, tending his horse. Approaching the stall, she saw he was wrapping the destrier's leg. "Has he gone lame?"

"No, but it has to look like he did." He smiled at her. "It was the only way I could beg an excuse not to go hunting."

Kendra gave him a hopeful look. "Does that mean you've come up with a plan?"

His smile faded. "Not yet."

"The Christ's Mass is only ten days away!"

He inclined his head. "I am aware of that, my lady."

"I'm sorry." Kendra hadn't meant to sound so abrupt, but she hadn't slept after the dream, and she was desperate. "I had the most horrible vision last night."

"Vision? You mean apparitions?"

"No." Looking around to be sure she wouldn't be overheard, she told him of the dream. "I don't know if it pertains to me or the countess."

Adrian looked thoughtful. "Do you have the Sight too?"

"No. At least, I don't think I do. I can't foresee the future."

"But have you had visions like this before?"

"A few, when I was a child, before I could see ghosts." Kendra hesitated. "But they were usually about things that had happened long ago."

"How long ago?"

She shrugged. "It would depend. Once I thought I visited Charlemagne's court, and another time I saw a battle in Scotland between people who were painted blue and invaders with long, blond plaits hanging from beneath helmets."

"What happened to you in those visions?"

"Nothing. I was more like an observer than *in* the vision."

Adrain gave her an intent look. "But last night, you thought you were the person being burned at the stake?"

"I…I'm not sure. It felt so *real*."

"And you said you didn't recognize the knight who rode to your rescue?"

Kendra shook her head. "I had the strongest feeling he was the ghost—I think the shadow man who visits the countess is a ghost—but I couldn't be certain."

"Have you asked Isobel about this?"

She shook her head again. "The first time it happened, she suggested it was the wind, but she also said just about anyone who is Scots believes in ghosts, so it wasn't a definitive answer. And, last night, there was a guard at my door."

Adrian was surprised. "A guard? Why?"

"I suppose either my aunt or Lord de Nogaret wanted to teach me a lesson. That if I don't behave, that is the consequence." Kendra sighed. "I suppose I need to comply."

"*What*?" He gave her an incredulous look.

"I don't mean *really* comply. I will just say I've had time to think things over and decided this was the best arrangement." She grimaced. "And then try to act like it is. That way, no one will get suspicious about my escaping."

"That is not a bad idea." Adrian studied her. "Mayhap you do need a guard."

Kendra nearly gaped at him. "How will I escape if I have a guard following me around?"

Adrian smiled at her. "The guard will be me."

She blinked. "*Es-tu fou?*"

"*Non.* I have not lost my mind." Adrian folded his arms across his chest. "The more I think about it, the more brilliant it sounds."

"*Je ne comprends pas.* Explain."

"It is quite simple. It would not be proper for de Nogaret to guard you himself if he is your betrothed—"

"Don't call him that!"

"*Excusez-moi.*" Adrian inclined his head to her in apology. "As I was about to say, having a common soldier following the Earl of Pembroke's niece around would not do either."

"That is true. I can—and *will*—act highly offended." Kendra tilted her head to one side and looked up at Adrian. "But Lord de Nogaret doesn't seem to like you."

"I know." Adrian smiled. "That makes it all the better."

"Then why do you think he will agree to let you be my guard?"

"He won't have to." The smile widened into a grin. "Edward himself made me your champion."

"But that was before all of this happened."

"True, but Edward does not like having his orders countermanded. *Especially* not by a Frenchman." Adrian sobered. "And one that *he* didn't invite here."

Kendra stared at him, her mind spinning in dizzying circles as hope sprang up. "Do you think it will really work? I'm not—" She stopped as two soldiers entered the barn and turned her attention to the horse.

Adrian gave the animal a casual pat on his neck. "It will work," he said before he stepped back. "It will work."

****

It *was* going to work. Adrian kept his expression carefully impassive as he took his seat in the king's private dining room that night. He hoped Kendra was able to do the same. He didn't look in her direction lest he catch her eye.

They had been waiting in the king's receiving room when Edward's hunting party returned that afternoon. Kendra had managed a magnificent performance in appearing contrite. Her uncle had looked relieved, but De Nogaret only lifted both brows and demanded to know why Adrian was present. That was when Kendra truly out-did herself, saying that he had used his diplomatic skills as an envoy to persuade her to see what a wonderful opportunity this was. De Nogaret remained skeptical and said he wanted a guard accompanying her at all times, to which she had demurely—demurely!—replied that King Edward had appointed Adrian her champion and, of course, she would not want to go against the king's edict. De Nogaret tried to protest, but Edward interrupted him, declaring Adrian Kendra's champion once more.

A brilliant *coup de grace.* Adrian bit back a grin.

The grin disappeared when the conversation shifted to talk of Robert Bruce's recent raids.

"Perhaps the way to put down the Scottish rebellion is to arrest every noble supporting the Scottish rebellion," Gerard offered to the group.

"That would mean surprise attacks throughout the winter." Lancaster glanced at the king. "Something currently you are not prepared to do."

Edward looked annoyed. "We would be foolish to attack Scots—and particularly Highlanders—on their home terrain when the snow closes the mountain passes and footing is treacherous everywhere."

"So you want to wait for a warm, summer day to fight?" Lancaster needled.

"Mayhap a *hot* day, such as one the temperature of Hades, would better suit you." Gaveston looked down his nose at the earl. "It would be a preemptive visit to your final resting place."

"Is that your attempt at humor?" Lancaster asked. "If so, I am sure you will be joining me there."

"*Mes chers seigneurs.*" Gerard held up a hand. "I did not intend to start an argument. I merely meant that perhaps following France's example might work. Rest assured, my cousin Guillaume will not stop searching until he has rounded up every Templar still living."

Adrian tensed. Was de Nogaret in England for dual purposes?

"I am glad to hear your cousin still pursues them after three years," Kendra said.

Gerard slid his glance to Adrian before looking at Kendra. "Why would this concern you?"

"They were responsible for my father's death," she replied.

"Kendra, I am sure no one wants to listen to your family troubles," Beatrice intervened quickly. "All that is in the past."

"I agree," her uncle said. "We need to be concerned with the present."

Kendra tightened her mouth. "Still, I'm glad the Templars are out of power."

Adrian felt like he'd swallowed a hot coal.

"So you see the wisdom of agreeing with me," de Nogaret answered. "Unfortunately, though, some of them managed to escape, along with King Philippe's treasure. We don't where it is."

"Maybe Robert Bruce has it." Lancaster gave Edward a pointed look. "The Scottish forces seem to be well funded."

Edward glared at him. "We would know if there were Templars roaming about."

Lancaster studied him. "Would you?"

Adrian forced himself to keep his shoulders relaxed and his fists unclenched. He didn't know if the earl was only goading the king again or if he actually suspected the exiled Templars were in Scotland.

"I am sure King Philippe would have sent word to our king if he had extracted information to that effect," Pembroke said.

Edward nodded. "We have not received any such missive."

"That's because their leader, Jean de Moray, has been of no help." De Nogaret laughed, but the sound was chilling. "And believe me, we've tortured him extensively."

Adrian tried not to wince. He was all too aware of the atrocious methods the French king and his puppet Pope used to force confessions.

De Nogaret turned to Kendra. "Since you dislike the Templars, perhaps you will enjoy hearing about the pain I inflicted?"

Kendra's eyes widened. She was, no doubt, remembering the bruises on her wrists that had still not disappeared. Adrian summoned every ounce of willpower he had in order not to leap across the table and pummel the arrogant Frenchman to a pulp, both for his brethren and for Kendra.

"That will not be necessary, my lord," she said.

De Nogaret gave her a penetrating look. "As you wish."

To Adrian, that sounded more like a warning than an acquiescence and, judging from how chalky Kendra's face had turned, he was pretty sure she had gotten the implication too.

His resolve to see her to safety hardened. The plan he was putting together would work in getting her away, but if she discovered who Bruce's secret army really was, there was a risk she would send word to her uncle. Adrian was glad Remy and Pierre did not attend these dinners. They would balk at taking anyone who hated the Templars to Bruce's camp. If she betrayed them, not only would the Templars be arrested and returned to France, but Bruce might also lose the war.

But what other choice did they have? To stand by and do nothing while Kendra was forced to marry a man who had already abused her and threatened more of the same was not an option. If there was one principle still left in the Templar code, it was honor.

And that meant getting Kendra to Bruce's camp was a chance Adrian needed to take.

Chapter Fifteen

The arrival of an invitation for Edward and his entourage to a Yuletide festival at Bamburgh Castle, a day's ride south, set the ladies of the nobility abuzz. Queen Isabella immediately gathered her ladies-in-waiting to plan a new wardrobe for herself.

"Good heavens," Kendra said to Adrian as she was the last female to leave the Great Hall after the midday lunch. "We are leaving in four days and only staying a total of three while there. Why does the queen need a new wardrobe when neither Governor Forster or his wife has seen any of the many gowns, kirtles, and surcoats she already owns?"

Adrian gave her an amused look. "A question most men would ask."

She frowned. "Are you comparing me to a man?"

"Hardly." *Mon Dieu.* If only she knew how often he thought of her as a woman. One which, in spite of telling himself he was doing the honorable thing by helping her to escape, was still a woman he very much wanted to claim as his own. "I only meant that most ladies would use any excuse for a new gown."

Kendra gave an unladylike snort. "It's almost more of an insult if you are comparing me to the queen's ladies."

He smiled. "Trust me when I say that is the last thing I would do." She was nothing like those simpering fools. Neither was she the skilled courtesan that Angelique had been nor was she sultry and flirtatious like the queen. Quite the opposite. Strong-willed, opinionated, and free-spirited, Kendra possessed as much inner strength as the countess. Her aunt had been right about one thing. Kendra did not act like any of the ladies at the court, but somehow, her individual traits only made her more attractive to him. And utterly *female*.

Kendra looked somewhat mollified. "Well, I pity the poor seamstresses who will be going without sleep and working their fingers raw trying to get the new gowns ready. And for naught."

"I agree." He looked around the emptying hall. "But it seems even the men are moving at fever pitch to get ready."

"I wonder why the invitation came on such short notice," she said. "I'm sure Sir Reginald knew King Edward had decided to winter at Berwick."

"Perhaps he heard that the banner of de Nogaret had been seen riding north," Adrian replied. "It would behoove him to know who lands on English shores." He had other thoughts, though, as to why the invitation had been issued.

Sir Reginald Forster, while serving as governor for the Crown, had Scottish roots and also secretly sympathized with Scotland's desire for independence. On more than one occasion, he had "allowed" messengers to slip by his guards and patrol. Adrian wondered if such a message was the reason for this hastily called visit.

"Is Bamburgh Castle much bigger than Berwick?" Kendra asked.

"Much bigger." Adrian quirked up a corner of his mouth. "Are you thinking you might find a secret tunnel through which to escape?"

Kendra's eyes widened. "There are some there?"

Adrian regretted his attempt at jest. "I am sure there are, but don't think to act on that. If you didn't get lost underground, you'd surely be caught when you emerged. The castle has been well fortified for centuries."

"Centuries?"

"*Oui*. Since it sits high on a cliff overlooking the North Sea, there has been some sort of fortress there since the time of the Picts, if not before them. The Saxons made it their capital when Ida invaded."

"That was nearly nine hundred years ago!" Kendra exclaimed.

Adrian nodded. "Actually, there is a bit of legend before that happened."

"What kind of legend?"

"You must promise not to laugh. You'll probably find the story strange and mayhap even unbelievable."

Kendra lifted one brow. "You are talking to someone who sees ghosts, remember?"

"Ah. In that case…" Adrian grinned at her. "You remember me telling you that I grew up in Broceliande?"

"What does Brittany have to do with Northumberland?"

"Patience, my lady. You also recall the day we spoke of your ghosts that I mentioned the *Notre Dame du Lac*?"

"*Oui*. The Lady of the Lake who may or may not exist. Go on."

"And you have heard she raised a son whom she sent to King Arthur's court to be a knight?"

"Of course." Kendra smiled. "Every French girl has read of Lancelot."

"Some say he was the perfect knight." Adrian paused. "Others, the worst of traitors."

"That is rather the way it is with Robert the Bruce, is it not?"

"It is." Adrian was only a little surprised she'd made that connection. It just proved Kendra had a keen intellect.

"But what does Lancelot have to do with our visit to Bamburgh?" she asked.

He smiled again. "Because Bamburgh Castle was once known as Joyous Garde, Lancelot's home."

Kendra drew her brows together in confusion. "What? I thought Arthur's wars were fought in southern England. Why would he send Lancelot this far north?"

"Depends on which side of the story you're on," Adrian replied. "Some say Arthur wanted to build a defense against the Northmen, and he gave the castle to Lancelot as a reward for commanding the fortress. Others say the king wanted to get his first knight as far from his wife as he could."

Kendra grimaced. "I always thought Guinevere was much maligned."

Adrian nodded, trying to hide a smile. "I imagine you would."

"Women always get blamed for things beyond their control..." Kendra stopped and peered at him. "Are you laughing at me?"

"Not at all." He managed to assume a serious expression. "I suspect Queen Guinevere was probably as strong-willed as you are."

"Do you mean stubborn?"

"That is a compliment, believe it or not." His lips twitched at her indignation. "In any case, we'll be visiting a castle that holds many secrets. Mayhap you'll even see a ghost or two."

She lifted her chin. "And I hope you are right beside me to meet one."

"So we can all have a nice chat?"

Her eyes sparked green fire. "You are making fun of me again."

"Not at all," he said, but he didn't hide his grin this time. Kendra had no idea how beautiful she was when her ire was up. He would have to remember that.

****

Any plans Kendra may have harbored about escaping while at Bamburgh Castle quickly vanished as the king's party approached it several days later. Unlike Berwick, nestled against the high banks of the River Tweed and having steps that led down to it, Bamburgh sat isolated atop a volcanic whinstone outcrop that rose one hundred fifty feet above the sea. Craggy cliffs dropped straight down from the thick walls with miles of empty beaches as far as the eye could see. No forest surrounded it, and the only road approaching the gates was steep and narrow, without cover.

It wasn't surprising that this place had been a stronghold for over a thousand years. It was impregnable. Which also meant it would be impossible to escape unseen.

"I do hope the governor's wife has hot baths waiting for us," Queen Isabella complained as her coach halted to wait for the portcullis to be raised. "It's been a horribly cold day."

Kendra glanced down from her mare and didn't answer. Not that the queen was speaking to her in the first place. Light snow had fallen when they started out, but the clouds had cleared, leaving the day sunny, with a light wind from the North Sea following them. To Kendra, the air was more crisp than cold. Even if the weather had been wet and miserable, she didn't see how the queen could be chilled since she was wrapped in numerous furs and had five of her ladies-in-waiting crowded into the coach for warmth as well.

"I only hope Sir Reginald has good French cognac instead of the nasty whisky the Scots like," Gerard said from beside Kendra.

On her other side, she could practically feel Adrian bristle. Even in Wales, the Scottish malts were highly sought after, and the few times she'd managed to sneak a few sips, she'd thought the flavor smoky and smooth.

"The nasty whisky you speak of is aged anywhere from eight to twenty years," he said, "compared to two years for brandy."

Gerard sniffed. "The *eau de vie* of cognac is from the finest white grapes, not from anything so common as barley."

"A man can live on barley," Adrian replied, "but it is doubtful grapes will sustain him."

"You truly are *bourgeoisie* then, to prefer a grain-based drink."

Adrian gave a Gallic shrug that was as nonchalant as any Frenchman she'd seen at court, and Kendra almost smiled at the gesture. She doubted Gerard could top it.

But which liquor was better wasn't the real issue.

Gerard had been hurling barbs at Adrian throughout the long, long day, and Adrian had managed to deflect most of them, although she sensed he would like nothing better than to come to blows with the offensive Lord de Nogaret.

She blamed herself for what they'd had to endure since the start of the journey. If she hadn't insisted on riding her own horse—albeit in a lady's heavily skirted riding habit—the men would not have positioned themselves on either side of her. Gerard had claimed his position as her betrothed and Adrian had taken his as her declared champion.

But her mare had needed the exercise. It had been hard to hold her to a springy trot for most of the morning. Aside from hating the closed-in feeling of a coach, Kendra had not wanted to listen to her aunt lecture her for hours on behaving properly while at Bamburgh and, worse, talking about her upcoming nuptials. She doubted she could have borne that discussion for long without blurting out something that might give away what she was planning to do.

That was a chance she didn't want to take. Better to tolerate the tension riding between two men who didn't like each than to risk suspicion.

She just hoped she could pilfer some of Sir Reginald's liquor regardless of whether it was whisky or cognac. Men weren't the only ones who would be needing drink this evening.

****

As he entered Bamburgh Castle a few minutes later, Adrian couldn't remember a time—other than escaping aboard the ship to the Orkneys three years ago—when he'd been so glad of a reprieve.

His jaw actually ached from grinding his teeth throughout the day to keep from sparring with de Nogaret. His fists had clenched and unclenched so many times, he'd finally wrapped his reins around the saddle's pommel to keep from pulling at his poor horse's mouth. The stallion, sensing his tension from the grip of his thighs, had danced sideways most of the morning. Or perhaps that was because Kendra's mare seemed to do the same. The animals might have sensed their owners had the same attraction to each other.

Sir Reginald himself greeted the king as soon as they entered. "Welcome to Bamburgh, Your Majesty. May I show you to your rooms, as the journey has been long and you might care to rest for a short time?"

He gave Adrian a subtle glance as introductions were acknowledged and servants began to escort the rest of the entourage to their rooms. As an envoy instead of nobility, he would not be staying in the keep itself. De Nogaret sneered at him as he was led up the stairs of the castle along with Pembroke, Lancaster, and Gaveston.

The small chamber Adrian had been assigned near the wall of the inner ward contained a straw-stuffed mattress on leather straps that held it up from the dirt-packed floor, a rough-hewn table and chair, and a tin basin, with ewer, on a wooden shelf. It was quite the contrast to the luxury of the featherbed with its ornate canopy and velvet drapes at Berwick, but Adrian suspected Sir Reginald had wanted to make clear that he considered a *Scottish* envoy of no import. The room also offered privacy for talk.

Spies and traitors were known to lose their heads if they weren't careful.

Adrian wasn't surprised when the door opened a short time later and Sir Reginald stepped inside, quickly closing it behind him.

"I assume your guests are all occupied with bathing and being refreshed?"

"I sure as hell hope so." Reginald glanced around the room. "I'm sorry for the accommodations—"

"Don't be concerned. I've had far worse," Adrian said. "I'm guessing your invitation wasn't because you wanted to celebrate Yule with the king?"

"Hardly. I prefer as little exchange with Edward as possible, but the Baron of Roslin sent a message that Guillaume de Nogaret's cousin had set sail to England, and he wanted to know why."

That Henri St. Clair had spies along both the English and French coasts was no surprise. His ancestors had served with the Conqueror and still retained their Norman-French roots, albeit they had little respect for Philippe or his puppet pope. But the baron had given sanctuary to the Templars and guarded their sacred treasure, so he needed to know the movements of anyone closely connected to the French king.

Adrian felt the bile rise in his throat as he answered. "From what I can gather, Queen Isabella initiated a marriage proposal between the cousin, Gerard, and the Earl of Pembroke's niece, Lady Kendra de Clermont."

"Women—even queens—generally do not meddle in the affairs of men," Reginald said. "Why would Queen Isabella do that?"

He felt his face heat. "I have turned down the queen's advances. She thinks it has to do with Lady

Kendra."

Reginald gave him a shrewd look. "Would it not have been easier to tup Isabella like dozens of other have?"

"I did not want to be a conquest." He grimaced. "Nor did I want to run afoul of Edward. The woman is still married to him."

"Which means little to her. She is a Jezebel," Reginald replied. "Are you sure that getting rid of Lady Kendra is the only reason for the marriage proposal? Isabella is Philippe's daughter, remember."

"I don't need reminding."

A corner of Reginald's mouth turned up. "I suppose you don't, at that." He turned thoughtful. "Such an alliance with Pembroke would substantiate the information the Baron of Roslin was given."

"What is that?" Adrian asked.

"That France will not come to the aid of Scotland."

Adrian stared. "What? Even though Philippe acknowledged Robert's right to the crown?"

"We both know the French king is only interested in what best serves him. He knew Edward the First posed a danger to France, so he acknowledged Bruce. Edward the Second is weak in comparison." Reginald shrugged. "Since Isabella married him three years ago, Philippe probably thinks it more advantageous to side with the English now."

"Henri St. Clair knows this for certain?"

"Is anything certain these days? But the baron said he had it on good authority that it was true."

Good authority probably meant a spy within the French court itself. "Robert will have to be told."

"I will try and ferret more information from my

illustrious guests. Unless I discover something more, I will not speak to you again while you are here." Reginald turned to the door. "Godspeed."

****

Dinner at Bamburgh, unlike Berwick, was held for everyone in the Great Hall. Kendra looked around the large, rectangular room for the raised dais, but found none. Instead, at one end of the hall was a round table, much like the one in the private dining room at Berwick except much larger.

"We are to eat at the same level as the knights?" Queen Isabella asked in disdain as they were all seated.

Sir Reginald gave her a bland smile. "My apologies, Your Highness, if the seating displeases you. As governor, and not royal, I did not think to install a dais."

"Quite understandable," Edward said. "We respect a man who does not try to elevate himself beyond his station."

"We do have a similar table at Berwick," Gaveston added.

"That is different. It is private," the queen snapped at him. "Monarchs should always be seated above the rest of the people."

"I am sure your beauty will stand out regardless."

Gaveston spoke the words smoothly, his facial expression neutral, but Kendra detected a hint of sarcasm in his voice. She hid a smile. The fact that the earl and the queen barely tolerated each other was evident to nearly everyone, except possibly Edward. Or, perhaps, the king just didn't care. His marriage to France's Princess Royal had not been a love match, after all.

"Indeed it will." Lancaster let his glance slide over Edward and then back to the queen. "Your lovely countenance is obvious to nearly everyone."

Possibly sensing tension, Sir Reginald intervened. "While this table is set at floor level, it might interest you to know it was found two hundred years ago when the castle was rebuilt using stone."

The queen looked bored. "And why would that be of interest to me?"

Sir Reginald kept his smile affable. "The etched carvings in the table were mostly sanded away when it was refurbished, but it was thought to possibly date back to the sixth century, before the Vikings arrived."

The hair at Kendra's nape began to prickle, much as it did when she sensed an invisible presence. She'd never had that reaction to an inanimate object before. She placed her hand on the wood and felt a warm vibration. Removing her hand quickly, she kept her eyes down. She had felt *something*, but she had to hide her feeling of excitement from Gerard and, for that matter, from the rest of the group as well.

When she thought she had her feelings under control, she looked up to find Adrian watching her. She looked away, not daring to acknowledge him by smiling. It was something of a small miracle that he even sat at their table tonight. Gerard had been quite vocal—before the king arrived—that mere envoys should not be seated amongst nobles, and Sir Reginald had agreed, until Gaveston pointed out that Edward expected Adrian, as Lady Kendra's protector until she got married, to be at her side. Sir Reginald had looked surprised and Gerard had glowered, but the arrival of the king and queen—and Edward's quick assent to

Gaveston's suggestion—had put an end to the matter.

Kendra was really beginning to like Gaveston.

But the tingle at her nape remained, and her fingers itched to feel the wood again. She managed to keep her hands clenched in her lap. "Bamburgh has been the site of fortresses for centuries. Were other artifacts found from earlier times?"

"Oh, yes," Sir Reginald answered. "A carved fragment of a stone chair thought to be part of a throne, several Anglo-Saxon knives and swords—or parts of them anyway—along with bits of metal helmets with petrified bones, most likely from the Viking period, are in the gallery on the third floor." He paused. "And there is a portrait."

Kendra widened her eyes. "A portrait from Saxon or Viking times?"

"Well, I'm not sure it's that old," Sir Reginald answered with a smile, "although no one has really been able to say. The canvas is very brittle, and some of the oils have cracked, but it was preserved under glass when I got here."

"Who is it?"

"That is one of the reasons we can't tell how old it is." He hesitated again. "No one seems to know who the woman is."

Kendra felt the hair at her nape rise, practically standing on end.

****

Later that evening, when the dancing had been going on for over an hour, Kendra managed to slip out of the Great Hall unnoticed and return to the third-floor gallery. Sir Reginald had given them all a quick tour after dinner, then taken the men to the castle's scriptorium for brandy while the women dressed for the Yule ball that was the focal point of the visit. She had intended to turn right around and go back to study the portrait, but her aunt—not wanting to take any chances on her embarrassing them—had taken hold of her arm and insisted that she help Kendra dress and lecture her, once more, on proper behavior.

But now she stood in the narrow room, dimly lit by a few sconces burning at intervals along the wall. The picture, while faded and cracked, showed an attractive young woman with reddish curls and blue eyes. Kendra thought how much the Countess of Buchan resembled her. Tilting her head to look at the portrait from a different angle, she nearly fell against the wall when the lady seemed to smile at her. And then she heard her voice. The lips weren't moving, but the words were clear.

"Ask a boon of Edward for your wedding gift. Ask him to release my kinswoman from her cage and send her to a convent as I was sent."

Kendra took a deep breath. She'd heard ghosts before, but none had ever spoken directly to her. She had been more of an observer. "The Countess of Buchan?"

"Aye…" The voice trailed off.

The air shifted, making the flames flicker in the sconces as a semi-transparent form gradually emerged in the dim light. Kendra blinked. It was the shadow man from Berwick's battlements.

For the first time, she could see his features. He was incredibly handsome, with high cheekbones, a straight nose, full wide mouth, and chiseled jaw. Black hair brushed his shoulders, and his dark eyes smoldered as he gazed at the portrait.

"*I have kept your kinswoman safe, my love, and now I return to you.*" The apparition turned to Kendra and began to fade away. "*Welcome to my home, my lady.*"

"What in Hades was that?"

Kendra nearly jumped out of her skin at the sound of another voice, decidedly human. She turned to see Adrian standing only a few feet away.

"What was that?" he asked again.

"You actually saw him?"

"I suppose it was a *him*. It sounded like a man." Adrian frowned and looked around. "But it disappeared. Men can't do that."

"No, but spirits can."

Adrian gave her an incredulous look. "I saw a spirit?"

Kendra smiled. "Well, you did say that maybe you'd meet a ghost at Bamburgh."

"I was jesting… I think." He searched the room with his gaze.

"I suspect he came home."

Adrian turned his attention back to her. "Who?" Then comprehension dawned. "Are you saying that was Lancelot?"

"I suspect so." Kendra gestured to the portrait. "Especially if this is Guinevere."

Adrian looked more closely. "She looks like Isobel."

Kendra nodded. "The countess told me once that an ancestor of hers had defied her king to be with the man she loved."

"And Lancelot was exiled because of Guinevere."

"It would seem to fit." Kendra looked at the picture again. Although it had to be a trick of the lighting, she thought the woman's eyes were brighter and she looked happy. "I think they are finally united again."

Adrian made an unusual sound, something close to a soft growl. When she turned to him, he was watching her intensely. Did he think she was mad? But he had seen—and heard—the specter himself. "Do you think I am being overly romantic in thinking Lancelot and Guinevere are together again? That their passion remains?"

"If anyone would understand passion, it would be those two." Adrian reached for her hair, and began pulling pins out of it.

"What are you doing?"

"I want to see your hair loose, like in the portrait."

"I can't go back out there with my hair loose!"

"I'll give them back." He stuck the pins in his surcoat and arranged her curls across her shoulders. "Later."

The feel of his large, warm hands threading through her hair and sliding slowly over her shoulders made Kendra shiver while, at the same time, she felt incredibly warm. *Really* warm. She looked into his amber eyes and saw a flame flicker in them.

Adrian smiled and reached for Kendra, drew her close, and covered her mouth with his.

And, just before her eyes fluttered close, she could have sworn Guinevere smiled.

Chapter Sixteen

"I cannot begin to tell ye how grateful I am to ye," the Countess of Buchan said to Kendra as she stood on the castle steps waiting for the wagon that would take her the short distance to the Carmelite friary in the village. "I doubted I would ever set foot on soil again."

"I am just glad the king saw reason." As soon as they'd returned from Bamburgh the day before, Kendra had watched for a chance to approach the king to ask for a boon. The opportunity had presented itself almost miraculously at dinner last night when the king, obviously pleased with pledges of support from Sir Reginald and in a festive mood, had asked what sort of gift Kendra might like for her wedding. She had answered that she wished for only one thing...that since this was the Yule season, the king show mercy and benevolence by removing the countess from her cage.

Her aunt had given her an approving look while her uncle and Gaveston agreed that such an act would go a long way in lessening the Scots' hatred of the English. Adrian added that it might even soften some of Robert Bruce's demands, and he would immediately send one of his men to relay the message. But mayhap it was Lancaster who, in scoffing that Edward I would never do it, was the decision maker for the current king. He'd declared Isobel be moved the next day.

Isobel smiled at her. "Even so, if ye had not asked,

it would not have happened."

"I cannot take the credit for thinking of it, though," Kendra replied. She had told the countess of her encounter with the spirits of Lancelot and Guinevere. "I wonder if your ancestor's spirit managed to influence Sir Reginald to invite us to Bamburgh."

"Mayhap. There were those who accused her of witchery in enchanting both Arthur and Lancelot."

"Do many people know you are related to Guinevere?"

Isobel shook her head. "At the time, the queen was blamed for the breakdown of the Round Table and her name considered a pox, so the lineage became a secret passed down only through my mother's line, the de Clares."

"De Clare?" Kendra widened her eyes. "That name is similar to mine, de Claremont."

Isobel studied her. "Ye were able to see Lancelot and hear Guinevere speak to ye..." She smiled again. "It is possible that ye are a descendent of hers as well."

A little shiver slid down her spine, but it was warm, not cold. "That would make us relatives."

"Mayhap. I would be proud for ye to be my kinswoman."

"As would I." Kendra paused, thinking about her plan to escape. If there were no wedding, her boon might not hold. "Do you think the king might change his mind once I am gone?" She was tempted to tell Isobel about her intention, but the countess gave her an astute look that made Kendra think she probably already knew.

"Even if he does, once I enter the friary's doors, I have sanctuary. Edward would not be willing to challenge the Church. With the Pope ensconced at Avignon, he would risk war with France as well." Isobel patted Kendra's hand as the wagon arrived and a guard came forward to help her into it. "Do not be concerned for me. Ye must see after your own welfare."

Kendra nodded, fighting tears as she watched the countess being driven away. She prayed that Edward would not take revenge for her fleeing her intended marriage.

That is, if she were able to flee. The Christ's Mass was only three days away. After their shared kiss at Bamburgh, Adrian had promised she would be gone by then. She had to trust him, but her blood turned cold.

What if he couldn't do it? Dear Lord, what then?

****

"You are not ill, are you?" Beatrice asked Kendra at dinner that night when she pushed her plate away after just one bite.

"I...I am not hungry."

"I imagine wedding jitters are setting in." Queen Isabella smiled. "After all, we will soon be celebrating your wedding feast."

Adrian noticed how pale Kendra was and wished he could reassure her that he'd already put his plan for her escape into motion. This morning, he'd sent Pierre with a message to Bruce, as he'd told the king he would do. But Pierre would not be riding west just yet. He would be waiting just several miles down the road to escort Kendra.

But Adrian needed to separate her from de Nogaret's watchful eye first. He might have been able to get Kendra away sooner, except the man always insisted on accompanying them for the morning ride that Kendra took to exercise her mare.

De Nogaret chuckled. "Rest assured, Your Majesty, that I am having no such jitters."

Pembroke frowned. "Perhaps this is a subject best left alone."

Adrian heartily agreed. Kendra appeared close to losing whatever minute morsels of food she might have eaten. He turned to the king. "Will you be arranging a royal hunt for the marriage feast?"

Kendra threw him a startled look, and he only hoped the slight smile he gave her would assuage her worry that he was not approving anything. He couldn't tell because she looked quickly down.

"Of course," Edward said. "We will need plenty of fresh game."

"Since it is Yule, mayhap a contest would not be amiss?" Adrian asked. "Whoever kills the first boar gets a prize?"

"An excellent idea! A bit of competition amongst the knights will be good."

"And," Adrian continued, "mayhap the first hart taken will be the one to grace the wedding table."

Edward nodded. "We like that idea as well."

Adrian smiled. "I look forward to being the person who delivers that stag to the kitchens."

"I will be the one to do it!" de Norgaret said.

"Well, I suppose it comes down to who is out there earliest to hunt, then," Adrian replied. "I will ride out as soon as dawn breaks."

De Nogaret narrowed his eyes. "So will I."

"May the best man win." Adrian smiled again. "I will be honored to present such a gift to Lady Kendra."

"That honor belongs to me!" De Nogaret declared.

"Hmmm." Adrian grew thoughtful. "Perhaps you are right. I had not considered you might resent another man providing your bride with sustenance." He sighed. "Very well. I acquiesce."

"You can still compete for the boar," Gaveston said.

"I could." Adrian rubbed his jaw, considering. "I doubt, though, that I could keep from loosing an arrow if I spied a hart." He contemplated a moment more. "Mayhap it would be best if I simply withdrew from the hunt. After all, there are enough knights to provide the game."

"That is true," Edward said. "We are pleased that you act in such a courtly manner."

Adrian inclined his head. "My staying behind will also ensure that Lady Kendra has a safe escort for her morning ride."

Kendra flashed him a quick look as she reached for her goblet, although he noted she didn't drink.

De Nogaret glared at him. "Lady Kendra does not need to ride tomorrow."

She turned her gaze on him. "We agreed that I was allowed to exercise my mare daily."

"Only if I am present," de Nogaret answered.

"I have my champion to guard me."

"He will not be your champion much longer."

"That is true," Adrian cut in, "but with the wedding only two days away, tomorrow will be Lady Kendra's last chance to ride."

Her eyes widened slightly, and he hoped she understood that *last chance* meant being ready to leave for good.

Pembroke looked at de Nogaret. "I hope you

realize how much my niece loves to ride and you will not deny her the opportunity once you are wed."

From the tight set of the man's jaw, Adrian was quite sure he would do just that. "As long as my wife obeys me, she will not be denied."

His words were hardly reassuring, and Adrian saw the fire spark in Kendra's eyes, but she managed to *sound* demure when she spoke.

"I understand, my lord. I beg you to indulge me for tomorrow's ride." She smiled sweetly. "It's not as though your soldiers will not accompany me as well."

"Your two guards and myself will be ample protection," Adrian said. "Surely you will allow the lady the pleasure of a last ride on English soil?"

De Nogaret looked as though he wanted to argue, but the king was regarding him, as was Pembroke. "Three guards, then, since I will not be attending."

"As you wish." Adrian hid a smile. He'd already made plans with Pierre to take care of two guards. Three would not be a problem. He turned to Kendra. "I look forward to escorting you one final time tomorrow, my lady."

He hoped she understood what he was really saying.

****

Kendra quivered in excitement the next morning as she prepared for her ride, remembering yesterday how she'd hoped she had not misinterpreted Adrian's intent. A final ride could mean simply, with preparations for the Christ's Mass and her wedding only two days away, there would be no more time to ride. Or it could mean she would not be returning. She had prayed for the latter, and after dinner last night, her prayers had been answered. Adrian had managed only a minute of private conversation, but it had been enough. *Be ready tomorrow.*

She wore her braies and tunic under her split skirt and jacket. It felt bulky, but thankfully her cloak was loose enough to cover the pudginess. She couldn't very well pack a valise and, if she truly were escaping, she needed at least a change of clothes. Kendra picked up a small leather pouch that held a few coins and tucked it inside her braies, then she looked around her bedchamber as she opened her door. There wasn't anything else she wanted to take except her bow, but that would arouse suspicion.

Closing the door behind her, she felt a twinge of guilt as she passed her aunt's door, then hurried past it. The last thing she needed was to face Beatrice this morning and be delayed. Her aunt would no doubt be furious at her escape, and Kendra had no idea if she'd ever see her aunt and uncle again, but there was no other choice.

Adrian was waiting in the bailey with her mare and three of Gerard's guards. She wasn't sure how she'd get away from them, but she had to trust Adrian. Reality hit her like a horse's hoof in her stomach as he helped her to mount. This might be the last time she saw Adrian as well, for he would not be going with her, and she had no idea where he was sending her. He had only said Pierre would be waiting to escort her and that she would be going to a safe place. For all she knew, a ship might be waiting to take her to the Continent.

"I…" She started to speak and then stopped as Adrian subtly shook his head. She lifted her chin and blinked away tears that threatened to form. She must do absolutely nothing to cause the guards to be wary.

They rode through the castle gate and across the drawbridge without fanfare. Kendra looked back at the wall. The cage where Isobel had once lived was still empty. Kendra prayed the countess had been right and King Edward would not try to bring her back.

"I thought we might ride toward Duns and give you a chance to enjoy the countryside this morning," Adrian said to her as they passed through the village. "Is that acceptable?"

"It is, my lord."

"Mayhap we should go south instead," one of the guards said.

Adrian turned to him. "The men are hunting to the south. Do you want to put Lady Kendra in danger from a stray arrow? I doubt de Nogaret would thank you for that."

The guard looked flustered, but a second one spoke. "We have never been to Duns, so we don't know the terrain."

"As you can see, the road is wide and well-travelled." Adrian gestured with his hand. "There are also fewer trees, so less risk of an ambush, if that is what you are thinking."

The guards exchanged glances, and the second one nodded. "I suppose there is sense to that."

"There is. I rode into Berwick along this road," Adrian said. "I encountered no problems."

The third guard nodded. "Lead the way, then."

Kendra wanted to ride beside Adrian, but there was a guard on either side of her and one behind. She was baffled by why he had chosen this road, for the land was relatively flat and the trees a good distance away.

She saw no means for escape, but Adrian seemed unperturbed. Had she been wrong in assuming what he meant by a final ride?

As they rode, the land gradually became more hilly, and it wasn't until they crested one that she saw the road sloped down through rocky outcrops of whinstone.

"Halt!" one of the guards said.

Immediately a second one grabbed her mare's reins. "Why are we stopping?"

"I do not like narrow passes," the guard said.

Adrian turned his horse around. "The pass is not long. The road flattens out beyond it."

"We should turn back," the third guard said.

Kendra caught the subtle shift in Adrian's expression. Although she could see nothing out of the ordinary—Wales had lots of boulders scattered over the moors as well—she knew Adrian wanted to go through.

"We have not gone far enough for my horse to have sufficient exercise," she said. "Since I will not be riding for several days, I want to continue on."

"Lord de Nogaret will not—"

"Lord de Nogaret is not here." Kendra drew herself up in her saddle. "And might I remind you that I am not married to him yet and that I am a lady? And that my uncle is the Earl of Pembroke? I wish to continue."

Adrian raised a brow. "That is something to contemplate."

The guards didn't look happy, but finally their leader nodded.

"Good. We will have to go single file," Adrian said. "I will lead the way, Lady Kendra follows me, and the three of you will bring up the tail."

Save for the sound of the horses' hooves crunching the loose stone between the big rocks, all was still as they began to pass through, but her mare had barely cleared the final boulder when pandemonium erupted behind her. She twisted around to see nearly a dozen men emerge from behind crevices, hurling large rocks and wielding cutlasses at the three guards before jumping on the horses' backs and dragging the guards down. Adrian drew his sword and wheeled his mount.

"I have to make this look good," he said. "Ride around the bend. Pierre will be waiting for you." Then he gave her mare's rump a sharp slap. The startled animal galloped away from the chaos.

Kendra reached the bend before she got her horse under control. She looked back to make sure Adrian was all right and then nearly screamed when she saw him fall to the ground. She started to turn her horse, only to be stopped by a hand on the reins.

"You must come with me," Pierre said as he leaned over his horse.

"But Adrian's hurt!"

"Not seriously," Pierre answered. "I paid those men."

She stared at him incredulously. "To beat him?"

"It had to be done, Mademoiselle, to make sure it looked like a real abduction." He gave a tug on her mare's reins. "Now come. Quickly."

Kendra had no choice, since Pierre had not released the reins, but she turned one final time.

The four men on the ground lay still. She sobbed, praying Adrian was not dead.

****

"*Que diable enfer*... What the hell do you mean my

181

betrothed is gone?" Gerard glowered at the three guards standing in front of him in the king's receiving room that afternoon. "Imbeciles! *Stupide!*"

"Do not blame them. We were ambushed." Adrian held a cool cloth that Queen Isabella had ordered to the rather large bump on his forehead and winced. The men he'd hired certainly had taken his orders seriously that he not be spared.

"And *you…*" Gerard turned on him with a sneer. "Some bodyguard you turned out to be."

"He tried to protect the lady," one of the guards said.

"But a dozen of them attacked," another guard added.

"*Silence!*" Gerard roared. "I have no wish to hear your excuses. You should have been able to hold off a score of men!" He gave Adrian a menacing look. "She had her mighty *champion* there as well…and he was worthless."

"Have a caution," Gaveston warned. "His Majesty appointed Monsieur de Soules her champion himself."

"That We did," Edward replied. "And We do not like having Our decision questioned."

Lancaster snorted. "Maybe a *decision* should be made on bringing Robert Bruce to heel, Your Majesty."

Edward narrowed his eyes. "We will do so when We are ready."

"Meanwhile," Pembroke broke in, "my niece is missing. Since she was nowhere to be found when the men regained consciousness, I can only assume she was abducted." He turned to Adrian. "Were they Scots?"

Adrian started to shake his head, then stopped when the throbbing grew worse. "I do not think so.

They were dressed as seamen."

The earl's eyebrows rose. "Seamen?"

The idea of having the local ruffians dress as such had been Remy's idea to mislead rescue efforts. Adrian carefully avoided looking at his friend sitting beside him. "*Oui*. And they had cutlasses."

Gerard gave Adrian a suspicious look. "Why would seamen be hiding behind rocks on a road leading west?"

"And why would they abduct my niece?" Pembroke asked.

"It is no secret the king's court is wintering in Berwick. And you, Lord Pembroke, are well known for having aided Edward the First in battles both here and at Dunbar," Adrian answered. "Perhaps you were recognized on our journey to Bamburgh and were followed back."

The earl frowned. "Even so, how would someone seeking revenge know that Kendra was my niece and that she would be riding out this morning?"

"I suspect news of our party's arrival travelled amongst the servants at Bamburgh as fast as it does anywhere." Adrian shrugged. "It is no secret that Lady Kendra rides every morning, either."

"Then we should be receiving a ransom note soon," Gaveston said.

"There might not be a ransom note," Adrian said.

Pembroke frowned again. "What do you mean by that?"

He hesitated. "I could be entirely wrong, but if seamen abducted Lady Kendra, they might not be interested in ransoming her."

"Why on earth not?" Gaveston asked. "The earl is

wealthy, as everyone knows."

"Yes, yes. I can afford to pay." Pembroke waved him off. "But why…" He stopped and stared at Adrian. "Are you thinking… pirates?"

"It is a possibility. Barbary Coast corsairs have been known to come up the English Channel." Adrian paused again. "Fair-skinned English ladies bring a very good price from Middle-Eastern sultans."

"*Mon Dieu!*" Gerard exclaimed. "If the woman is sold… I cannot have spoiled goods."

Pembroke gave him a steady look. "Perhaps I should reconsider your proposal."

"Perhaps you should, my lord," Adrian said.

Gerard glared at him. "I only meant…"

"Are we not wasting time with talk?" Remy interrupted. "If pirates actually took Lady Kendra, then there is no time to lose in going after her. They will set sail as soon as they have her on board."

"But where is their boat?" Gaveston asked.

"If Lord Pembroke was sighted in Bamburgh and followed back, my guess would be the ship is near there," Adrian replied.

"Then I will lead a search party there immediately." The earl rose. "All who wish to accompany me, be ready to leave within a quarter hour."

Adrian rose too, still holding the cloth to his head. "I will be ready."

"You are wounded, Monsieur de Soules," Pembroke said. "You will slow us down."

"But I can—"

"You should rest," Queen Isabella said.

Adrian didn't look at Remy, but both knew it was

vital that one of them be with the group to lead it further south and away from the real trail.

"I will step in for Adrian," Remy offered.

Pembroke paused, then nodded before leaving to call for mounts. Adrian drew a breath of relief.

"I will retire to my chamber, then."

"Go," the king said.

"And I will order a bath for you," the queen said as she rose. "And you need another cold compress as well."

Adrian made his way to the kitchen for the compress and to secure a skin of wine to take to his chamber. The drink would help numb the pain. His stomach rumbled as he smelled the fresh bread one of the maids was removing from the oven, and he realized he hadn't eaten since early this morning. The cook must have heard it too, for she insisted he have a bowl of stew.

He heard the men leaving as he climbed the stairs a short time later, and he breathed a sigh of relief. With luck, Remy would keep the search party out a day or maybe two, and Pierre would have Kendra well out of danger by then.

He undid the laces of his tunic and pulled the dirty thing off. A hot bath, some wine… Opening the door to his chamber, he stepped inside and then stopped so abruptly he nearly tripped over his feet.

Queen Isabella sat propped against the headboard, an empty wine glass on the table beside the bed. The dim glow of two candles she had lit showed she was entirely naked.

"I've come to help you with your bath, *Monsieur*."

He stomped over to the bed and set the wine skin

down. Then he jerked at the blankets. "Get yourself dressed and get out."

"I don't think so." She gave him a coy smile. "I have waited so long to have you, and here you are, already half naked."

He started to put the shirt back on when she grabbed it with one hand and yanked on his braies with the other, pulling him closer. The jerking motion, along with his arms being momentarily stuck in the tunic, caused him to lose his balance, and he sprawled over her.

"Well, well. What have we here?"

Adrian froze at the sound of Lancaster's voice in the doorway. He sat up quickly and felt himself pale at the sight of the king beside the earl, along with the three guards from this morning.

"There is no need to hide the queen." Lancaster sounded amused.

Adrian started. Inadvertently, he was blocking her from the king's view. He jerked at the blankets again, hoping she had the decency to cover herself while he stood. "This isn't what it appears to be, Your Majesty."

Lancaster laughed. "Isn't that what they all say?"

"It's true," Adrian said. "I can explain—"

"I'm sure your lie will be priceless," Lancaster answered. "We were on our way up to question you further about why pirates might have been on that particular road this morning, but now *other* questions have risen. More interesting ones, mayhap. How long have you and the queen been consorting?"

"We have not."

"Oh, come. The queen has shown an interest in you at every turn," Lancaster said. "Although you needn't think to flatter yourself, since you are not the first lover she's had—"

"We are not lovers." Adrian turned to the queen. "Tell them."

She only stared at Edward, who stared back.

"You see? She does not deny it." Lancaster turned to Edward. "Finding your wife naked with her lover on top of her is something even you cannot ignore." He smirked. "Unless, of course, you want the realm to know you are a cuckolded king."

"I will handle my wife." For once, Edward did not use the imperial plural.

Lancaster arched a brow. "And your Scottish envoy? He has betrayed you."

The king gave Adrian a quick glance and turned away.

"He will hang tomorrow."

Chapter Seventeen

"You are sure that Adrian was not seriously hurt?" Kendra asked Pierre as she settled before the small campfire he had lit after they'd stopped for the night.

"The men were given strict instructions not to kill anyone." He carefully pulled a roasted rabbit off the makeshift spit and cut it into pieces with his knife. "Besides, Adrian has a hard head."

The two burly Scots who had joined them late that afternoon—and who had provided the rabbit—laughed. "The mon has taken worse than those Englishmen could dish out," the one called Cullum said.

"Aye, lass. Doona fash," Hammish, the other Scot, added.

She couldn't help but worry as she bit into her portion of the meat. Pierre had explained the entire ruse earlier that day. She understood that Adrian couldn't very well appear unscathed in order to be believable, but how hard had he been hit? Had he truly been unconscious? That would have left him vulnerable to real thieves.

"I hate that he had to be hurt on account of me."

Pierre gave her a slanted look. "It was his idea."

"The mon does have a sense of duty," Cullum said.

"Aye. 'Tis the Scottish half of him, nae doubt," Hammish answered.

Kendra was silent. Had Adrian only been acting

out of a sense of duty? Because he'd made a vow to help her escape her impending marriage? She had hoped—perhaps foolishly, but after their stolen kisses—that he'd *cared*. She wasn't naïve enough to think kisses made a man declare undying love, but his acceptance of her peculiar ability in seeing spirits had drawn her closer to him. She might never know, since he would have to stay at Edward's court until the king made a decision about a parley with Robert Bruce, and she had no idea where Pierre was actually taking her.

"I just wish we could have waited until I saw him move."

"We had no time for such a delay," Pierre said. "The whole point was to get you as far away as quickly as possible."

Kendra nodded. "I know. And I am most grateful, but—"

"I think the lass has a wee bit of feelin' for the mon." Hammish lifted a brow. "Is it like that, then?"

She felt her cheeks warm at the implication, but before she could ask what "it" was, precisely, Cullum cut in with a grin.

"If 'tis true, we might have sparks flyin' at the camp."

"Sparks? What do you mean?"

"Nothing," Pierre answered quickly and gave both of them a quelling look. "We are not even sure if you will be staying at the camp."

"Camp?" Kendra looked from one of the Scots to the other. Both had been waiting once they'd gotten across the border. Pierre had introduced them only as guides who knew little-used trails on the way north and west. He'd already explained earlier in the day that they would be taking no chances using main roads or staying at inns, in case secondary search parties were sent out in directions other than Bamburgh. As heavily muscled as the men were—and well armed with huge, deadly claymores across their backs along with an assortment of ferocious-looking knives attached to their belts—she suspected they were soldiers. Scottish soldiers. Her eyes suddenly widened.

"Are you talking about Robert the Bruce's camp? Is that where you are taking me?"

Pierre sighed. "We will stop *near* there. I cannot just ride in with you, since there was no time to get a message to Bruce about Adrian's plans."

She turned to Cullum. "Is that what you meant when you said sparks might fly? That your King Robert will be upset because I am English?"

Cullum grinned again. "It was nae Robert I was speakin' of."

She knit her brows. "Then who?"

"Never mind. That is a bridge we may not have to cross." Pierre poured wine for her from the skin and handed it to her. "I hope."

She realized the subject was closed for now, but if King Robert wouldn't be upset with her presence, she couldn't imagine anyone else who would be.

****

The irony of the situation wasn't lost on Adrian as the three guards whom he had ridden with this morning—and who had been beaten at his orders— were now the ones who had him firmly in tow on his way to the dungeon below Berwick castle.

He'd momentarily thought to break away, but common sense told him he wouldn't make it as far as

190

the front hall. And fighting would only make him appear guilty and exacerbate the situation. Better to wait until Edward had a chance to think things through and then request an audience.

Still, the sound of the heavy key turning in the cell grate was unnerving, as were the fading footsteps that left him alone in the dank, damp dungeon. One wall sconce near the stairs provided barely enough light to see, although a narrow slit through the rock near the ceiling also gave a bit. Adrian looked around the tiny cell, hardly large enough to pace more than three steps. A rat scurried across the floor, barely avoiding his boot. A mound of dirty straw lay heaped in one corner, no doubt infested with vermin, and the stench from the other corner told him no chamber pot had been in use.

He tested the strength of the iron bars, hoping they'd succumbed to rust, but all were sturdy. Then he listened for sounds of prisoners in the other cells. All was silent, save for the dripping of water seeping in from the river and down a stone wall. He was alone for now. At least he hadn't been thrown into an oubliette. Being so close to the bank of the Tweed, that would most likely have standing water in it, and who knew what else.

Adrian didn't know how much time had passed, but he'd grown tired of standing and slid down to sit against the bars, not wanting to disturb whatever nested in the squalid mass of straw.

Had Edward posted a guard? None had come down, but there was no need for someone to stand and watch him since the dungeon's bars and lock were sturdy. Besides, there was only one way out, and that was up a steep set of stairs secured by a heavy door. It would be much more comfortable duty for a guard to remain upstairs, where there was light and warmth.

Not having a guard down here posed a dilemma, though. How was he going to be able to request an audience with the king if no one would deliver the message? Then a secondary problem set in.

What if Isabella lied and claimed he'd forced her to his bed? The damn seductress would be capable of it. The way he had fallen, sprawled over the top of her, could look like he was holding her down. To avoid being sent to a convent, she would be desperate. He could almost hear her crying and begging the king to avenge her. Would he?

Adrian was fairly sure Edward had no warm feelings toward his wife. He also thought Edward had turned a blind eye to her indiscretions in the past, but this time was different. The Earl of Lancaster had been beside him.

For certes, there was no love lost between the cousins. Not only did Lancaster think the king an inadequate warlord, but Thomas needled Edward every chance he got. He had goaded him countless times during this visit for not being as ruthless as his father had been. Even if Edward were inclined to allow Adrian to present his side of the story, he might hesitate to grant leniency. The earl would only use it to point out how weak the king was.

For the first time since this bizarre confrontation had taken place, Adrian began to feel a sense of real worry. Pierre was well on his way west with Kendra. Remy was leading the search party southward and not expected back for at least two days. Pembroke, who might intervene and insist all sides be heard, was with

Remy.

Adrian stilled. Edward had said he would be hanged in the morning. If he wasn't able to secure the king's attention before then, he would be dead by the time his brethren returned.

****

By dawn, the weather had turned bitterly cold. Hoarfrost covered the ground, so that icy blades of grass crunched beneath the horses' hooves. Worse, the skies were low and leaden, promising snow.

Hammish pulled an extra tartan out of his pack and handed it to Kendra after she was mounted. As soon as she wrapped the wool around her shoulders, she felt instantly warmer. "This is wonderful."

"Aye. 'Tis better if ye make a hood and cover your head as well," he replied, showing her how with his own plaid. "And 'twill keep your face hidden."

"Do you think we will be encountering anyone?" Kendra asked.

"'Tis better to take nae chances."

As Pierre started out, leading Callum's horse, she turned around to see him scattering the ashes of their fire. "Is he not coming with us?"

"Aye, lass," Hammish answered. "He will meet us a wee bit down the trail."

Her brows furrowed. "Why doesn't he ride his horse?"

This time Pierre replied. "With the frost, it will be easy to see this place was recently used by horsemen. Callum will make sure the fire is cold and brush all hoof prints away so no one will know for sure."

"Then you do think we're being followed?"

"There is the possibility that your uncle ordered

two search parties—or even three—to go in different directions." Pierre shrugged. "At best, we have a day or two, but we may only have a few hours' lead."

She fell silent after that. If they were caught, not only would her three companions probably be hanged, but Adrian would be implicated as well, since Pierre was his man. It wouldn't matter if she told her uncle that fleeing was her idea. The enormity of the risk Adrian had taken for her settled like a brick in her stomach.

To add to her misery, snow began falling by midmorning. It was heavy and, with no wind, accumulated quickly. She heard Hammish say something in Gaelic that was undoubtedly cursing since he kept looking back at the hoof prints left in the snow. It wouldn't take a seasoned tracker to figure out four horses were making their way across the Lammermuir Hills.

"'Tis better we get back on the main road where our tracks will mingle," Callum said.

Pierre inhaled sharply. "It is too open."

He didn't need to add that if her uncle or the king had sent out more than one search party, English knights would be on that road. Her pulse quickened.

"We are in plaids. They'll think us simple Scotsmen." Callum looked at the braies Kendra was wearing. "If the lass keeps her head covered, no one will ken she's a woman."

"Perhaps not," Pierre replied, "but her horse will be recognized."

Kendra felt her blood chill, and it didn't have anything to do with the cold. Argenterie was silvery-white. That was why she'd given the mare the name.

Andalusian horses were rare in England, and hers was the only one at King Edward's court. Of course she'd be recognized. Then her blood felt like it had stopped flowing altogether. Would the men suggest she turn her horse loose to roam and she would ride with one of them? Instinctively, she patted the mare's neck.

Hammish's gaze followed her gesture. Her hands tightened on the reins, causing Argenterie to toss her head. Kendra relaxed her hold and gathered a handful of mane instead before forcing herself to look up. She loved her horse, but could she jeopardize the lives of three men?

"I…" She swallowed hard. "Do you want me to set her free?"

She was surprised at the sympathetic look on the Scot's face. "In the Highlands, a mon's fate sometimes depends on his horse getting him home," he said. "We'll nae be asking ye to do that."

A tear slid down her cheek, and she swiped it away, but not before Cullum noticed.

"Doona cry, lass," he said. "'Tis the one thing that brings down a decent man."

"I…I'm sorry." She wiped at another tear. "I… I don't want any of you getting caught. Maybe I should go back—"

"Nae!" both Scots said at once.

Pierre raised a brow. "You would have everything Adrian did for naught?"

She hadn't thought of it that way. Dear Lord. She shook her head. "I cannot do that either."

"We will speak no more about it." Pierre looked grim, then he turned to Hammish. "How far is it to Roslin?"

The man contemplated for a moment. "An hour by the main road. Mayhap a wee bit more."

Cullum gave him a curious look. "Ye ken the Baron of Roslin?"

Pierre hesitated, then nodded. "We met briefly several years ago."

"Well, St. Clair is a friend of the Bruce," Cullum replied.

"Will we be putting him at risk by staying there?" Kendra asked.

"He is careful to stay in Edward's favor," Hammish said. "If he claimed hospitality to strangers, the king would believe him."

She looked at Pierre. "How well do you know Baron St. Clair?"

He paused before he answered, "Well enough."

"Then we better ride," Hammish said.

They'd nearly reached the main road when they heard the thunder of horses' hooves. Quickly, they turned their horses back into the woods and then watched a contingent of English knights gallop past. Kendra swallowed hard.

"Were those Edward's?"

Pierre shook his head, but his face was pale. "They bore Lancaster's standard."

"Do you think they pursue me?"

He looked pensive. "They were in full armor. Hardly needed to chase down the ruffians who abducted you."

Kendra drew her brows together. "Why are they riding so hard, then?"

"I do not know," Pierre answered, "but the faster we can get you to Henri St. Clair, the quicker I can return to Berwick."

Fear stabbed her. "Do you think something is wrong at court?"

His jaw clenched as he kicked his horse forward. "I am almost certain of it."

****

Adrian looked at the narrow slit by the ceiling. It seemed the darkness had receded a bit, indicating dawn was not far away. No one had come to bring even bread and water, so he'd had no way to ask for an audience with the king. He supposed there was a possibility that Edward would be more receptive to listening after a night's sleep and might reconsider his sentence, but he couldn't take that chance at the last minute. He figured he had two or three hours before the hanging would occur since the king would want to break his fast first. Which meant he had to leave. *Now*.

He looked at the hairpin he held in his hand. Sometime during the night, he'd dozed enough to dream of the kiss he'd shared with Kendra at Guinevere's portrait. When he woke, he remembered he'd given her hairpins back, but he'd found one stuck to the cloth of his surcoat the next morning. He'd kept it as a token, never thinking it might save his life.

"I wonder," he whispered to himself, "if Lancelot didn't have something to do with that." For a moment, he stilled, half-expecting some ghostly voice to answer, but there was only silence.

Pushing his cell door open, he stepped out and listened for sounds from above. He'd heard only one set of boots throughout the night, and no conversation. Was the guard still there? Adrian had already checked every corner and crevice of the dungeon—once he'd picked the lock—for a means of escape, but there was none. He'd then returned to his cell, hoping to surprise and overpower whoever came down to check on him. But no one had.

He only had one choice left. Climb the stairs and attempt to pick the lock on the heavy door at the top without alerting the guard. The footsteps had stopped, so he hoped the man had fallen asleep.

Ascending the stairs seemed to take an eternity since he placed his weight slowly on each one to keep them from creaking. When he finally reached the top, he put his ear to the door. He heard snoring. Carefully, he slipped the pin into the lock and began to wiggle it. This lock was more rusted than the cell one had been, and he breathed a sigh of relief when it gave without too much effort.

Then he froze.

Another guard had arrived.

"It's about time someone relieved me," the original guard grunted as he woke. "I've been sitting on my arse all night on a cold floor."

"At least you were out of the king's sight," the second one said. "He's been in a rage since the Frenchman was thrown in here."

"No man wants to be cuckolded."

"True enough. The queen's personal guard have all been flogged, right in the Grand Hall, and His Majesty knocked one of his pages down for grinning about it."

So much for appealing to the king's good will. Adrian was pretty sure his appearance would have the effect of stepping on a bear's wounded paw. The only thing he could do now was wait for the first guard to leave and take his chance on surprising the second one.

He stepped back.

The rusted lock dropped to the floor with a crash.

"What the…"

Adrian didn't give the guard a chance to finish the sentence. He picked up the iron piece, yanked open the door and swung. The metal made a satisfying thud on impact, but in the next instant, a fist flew at Adrian's jaw. He managed to duck, but it struck his shoulder, throwing him off balance. More fists pounded his head. He was able to block some of the blows, but fending off two armed guards with only a bit of metal wasn't good odds. He already tasted his own blood.

Thank God the dungeon was at the far end of the castle near the garderobe, where no one ventured, or the commotion would be drawing more men. Reeling from another blow, he spun, pivoting on one foot, and slammed into the first guard, throwing him against the stone wall. The man hit hard and slumped to the floor. Adrian caught sight of the blade in the second guard's hand and started to crouch, but not before the knife sliced his forearm. He staggered and bent to grab the other man's knife when he heard a loud whack, followed by a thump. He straightened, ready to do battle.

Gaveston held up both hands. On the floor beside him was a silver tray with what appeared to be a bowl of spilled porridge. Adrian slowly looked up.

"What are you doing here?"

"I came to help you escape."

"Why?"

Gaveston grimaced. "I don't believe in men dying because of some harlot."

"I don't either." Adrian tore a piece of his tunic off

to wrap around his bleeding arm. "Not that I don't appreciate it, but how were you going to help?"

"The guard's porridge was laced with laudanum."

"Ah." Adrian stuck the loose end of the cloth inside his makeshift bandage. "Won't the king be furious when he finds out?"

"I doubt he will investigate much." Gaveston shrugged. "Lancaster can't blame your escape on him, can he?"

"I suppose not." Adrian finished arming himself with the guard's weapons. "I owe you more than thanks."

"Perhaps some good will come of this," Gaveston answered. "Now go. Your horse is already saddled."

Adrian nodded. "I'll not forget."

A Templar never forgot who did him favors.

Chapter Eighteen

Henri St. Clair did not look particularly surprised to see them as they crossed the stone bridge over the River Usk and came to a stop at the front door to his home. He did look askance at Kendra when Pierre introduced her, but made no remark, simply telling a lad to be sure their horses were kept inside the stables.

Kendra welcomed the warmth of the fire blazing from the hearth in the receiving room across from the Great Hall. Although the plaid had kept her warm and the ride itself kept her blood circulating, her fingers and toes felt numb from the cold.

Once they were all seated near the hearth and a serving wench had brought warm, mulled wine, the baron turned to Kendra.

"You are fleeing a betrothal you do not want?"

She started, wondering for a moment if the man possessed a peculiar skill to read minds. The St. Clair name was well known in France. They were descendants of the marauding Viking Rollo, who eventually had married the Frankish King Clovis' daughter and signed a peace treaty near the well of Sanctus Clarus, from whence came their name. The first Henri de St. Clair had gone on Crusade. Another had fought beside William of Normandy in the Battle of Hastings and been given lands in Scotland. But she'd never heard that any of them had any otherworldly abilities, though.

"How did you know that, my lord?"

"Lancaster rode through here not more than an hour ago," he answered.

Kendra looked at Pierre. "So the earl was looking for me."

"No," Henri answered. "That information came out in passing. Lancaster was searching for Adrian de Soules."

Her warming fingers suddenly grew numb again, and she nearly dropped her goblet. Had someone found out he'd assisted in her escape? What had gone wrong? "Is Monsieur de Soules not at Berwick?"

"Apparently not." Henri turned to Pierre. "According to Lancaster, he was caught *in flagrante delicto* with the queen."

"The queen?" Stunned, Kendra's voice came out as a squeak. She'd known Isabella had flirted outrageously with Adrian. There was no doubt the queen wanted to be Adrian's lover, but why would he acquiesce? "I don't believe that."

Henri gave her a long, steady look. "I will not ask, mademoiselle, why you think that."

Kendra felt her face heat, and it wasn't because of the fire. Dear Lord. Did Henri St. Clair think Adrian was her lover? The thought—which should have been shocking—had the effect of warming her all over. "I...just meant...Monsieur de Soules never seemed to show interest in the queen."

"Lady Kendra is right," Pierre said. "Adrian would never seek her out."

Henri lifted a brow. "I think we all know Queen Isabella has rather low scruples."

"She doesn't have any at all!" Kendra said.

He studied her again. "A lack of morals does make it easier for her, does it not?"

"Lancaster has his own reasons for accusing Adrian," Pierre said.

"Perhaps. Unfortunately, Lancaster was with Edward when the queen was found with Adrian in his chamber."

Kendra felt as though a bucket of icy water had been thrown on her head. It couldn't be true! The queen was deceitful. Somehow, she must have connived...

"The result," Henri continued, "was that Edward had no choice but to declare Adrian a traitor and sentence him to hanging."

Kendra's wine goblet tumbled to the floor from her lifeless fingers as the word sank in. *Hanging.* Edward had ordered Adrian to be *hanged.* And her uncle wasn't there to try to make the king see reason, since he was chasing down her imaginary abductors. *Mon Dieu!* "We have to do something! We do!"

"There is nothing to be done at the moment." Pierre looked grim. "I assume Adrian managed to escape or Lancaster would not be looking for him?"

Henri nodded. "It seems Adrian was able to break out of his cell somehow and overpower one guard. The other was hit from behind and didn't see who it was."

A very tiny feeling of relief swept over Kendra. Adrian had managed to get away. Then another thought intruded. "Remy will be in trouble for helping him. I hope he got away too."

Pierre shook his head. "Remy was to lead the search party. I doubt he'd come back by then. Someone else must have decided to step in."

"But who?"

"I don't know."

A clatter of hooves on the stone bridge stopped their conversation. Kendra froze. "Do you think Lancaster came back?"

"Doubtful. I gave him permission to search my stables before he moved on," Henri said as he rose and then glanced at Kendra. "I suspect this is someone you will be glad to see."

She started to follow, but Pierre held her back. "No one can know you are here. You must stay hidden until we know for sure who it is."

Kendra knew he was right, but a second later she heard a familiar voice. Breaking away, she rushed into the hall as Adrian, beaten and bloody, stumbled through the door and fell to the floor.

****

Adrian drifted in a foggy haze, listening to what sounded like the melodic voice of an angel and wondered if perhaps he had gone to heaven after all. The place where he was seemed warm, but not hot, so it surely wasn't hell. He was lying on something soft enough to be a cloud, and he caught the light scent of primrose. *Her* scent. His wood nymph. He sighed contentedly in his dreamlike state. Had God blessed him with his mate for eternity?

But Kendra hadn't died. She had gotten safely away. Hadn't she? He stirred and then groaned as something sharp pricked his arm numerous times. He realized he wasn't dead either. Someone was stitching his arm. His eyes flew open.

Kendra leaned over him. For a moment, his fuzzy mind thought she was going to kiss him, but she only bent down to bite off the thread she'd been using.

"I hoped you'd stay unconscious until I finished," she said as she wrapped a clean bandage around the wound. "How are you feeling?"

"I am fine." He started to sit up, then flopped back as dizziness overcame him.

She smiled at him. "I don't think *fine* is the right word."

"Better then."

"You've lost quite a bit of blood. Lord St. Clair said you needed to rest."

"I made it to Roslin?"

"Yes." She looked at him quizzically. "Was this where you were headed?"

His head was clearing, and he realized he needed to be careful in replying. St. Clair could not be connected to the Templars in any way. "St. Clair is known for his hospitality. Every summer he allows the gypsies to camp on his land, so I figured he might grant me sanctuary for a night." He frowned. "But why are you here? Pierre was supposed to have taken you to Stirling."

"The snow. He thought we were too easy to track, and Roslin was close." Kendra tilted her head to study him. "One of the guards who rode with us said the baron is a friend of Robert the Bruce."

Adrian breathed a small sigh of relief. Better she make that connection than any other. "It is something best not spoken of. Lord St. Clair walks a fine line."

"I already figured that out," Kendra replied. "My uncle once said even Robert the Bruce had to side with the English years ago in order to keep Annandale and his title as Earl of Carrick."

"That is true, but when Edward the First captured William St. Clair at Dunbar and imprisoned him in the Tower, everything changed. Henri must be careful not to show his hatred toward the English."

"I did not like the intrigue at the French court, and I like it even less in England. Everything is about power and control. Why should an English king tell Scots how to live?"

Adrian realized his feeling of relief also came because his trust in Kendra had grown. If she still felt any loyalty toward her uncle, he was sure, after what she'd just said, that she wouldn't betray the Scottish cause.

"It relieves me to hear you say that."

Her eyes widened. "Did you doubt me?"

He flinched. "I do not want to doubt you."

'Then do not." Kendra sighed. "I suppose I can understand why you say that, though. You are taking a big risk helping me."

"A risk I think worth taking."

Kendra searched his face as if she were looking for more meaning, but Adrian wasn't sure what to say. He had no idea what the future held for him or her. Everything really hinged on what Robert's reaction to all this would be. The thought had hardly cleared his mind when she spoke almost the same words.

"I hope your king agrees with you."

"I am sure he will." Adrian hoped he sounded more confident than he felt. Sending her to Bruce for sanctuary while he stayed at the English court was one thing. His becoming a fugitive because of the queen's plotting was quite another. The plan to mislead her uncle, the king, and her betrothed as to where she had gone by convincing them that pirates abducted her wouldn't seem as palatable now. And if Gaveston were wrong and Edward decided to launch a thorough search for him, everyone would be in jeopardy.

Every single one of them.

****

"Please forgive the humble setting," Henri said as they entered a room near the kitchens that evening for dinner. "Under the circumstances, I thought it best that the fewer people who know you are here, the better."

"This will suit our needs just fine," Adrian answered and pulled a chair for Kendra with his good arm.

She looked around the room. It was minimally furnished with a long oak table and straight-backed chairs that had worn but comfortable cushions. No pictures or tapestries adorned the walls, although a cheerful fire blazed in the hearth. It was in stark contrast to the extravagance of Edward's private dining room at Berwick. She suspected this might be where the servants ate.

After the crowds and noise at the English court, she welcomed the peace and quiet of a country estate. Lord St. Clair's manor was relatively small, although she'd been told earlier that plans were in the making to build a stone castle farther into the glen. As yet, the barony was a simple, timbered structure, which was perhaps why it felt so warm and comforting.

Or perhaps it was because Queen Isabella was not here. After Adrian had told her what had happened, Kendra wasn't sure she'd be able to resist the urge to slap the woman silly. Or worse. The "worse" kept getting nastier each time she allowed herself to think on what might have happened to Adrian because of the queen.

"Pierre took his leave this morning," Henri said as soon as the same maid who'd served them lunch had gone. "He said he was going to find Robert."

"Bruce needs to know what happened as quickly as possible." Adrian grimaced. "I doubt there is any chance to broker a peace treaty now, even if another envoy were sent."

"I suspect you are right," Henri answered, "although with Lancaster wintering in Berwick and a thorn in Edward's side, I don't think the king would be inclined to parley anyhow."

"That's true," Kendra said. "My uncle mentioned he didn't think it would happen."

Henri turned his gaze on her. "I'm told your uncle is Pembroke?"

"Yes. He…" Kendra faltered as she saw the look of speculation on the baron's face.

"The earl is a powerful man." Henri turned back to Adrian. "He will not let her abduction rest. He will search for her."

He didn't have to add *she is putting everyone in danger* for Kendra to know that was what he meant. She'd been harboring that fear herself.

Adrian gave him a grim look. "I hope to have us in Bruce's camp by then."

Henri's brows rose. "You're taking her directly to Robert?"

Again, he didn't have to add *are you sure you can trust her*. It was in his tone of voice.

"No one has ever found the camp," Adrian said. "Kendra will be safe there."

But will we? The baron might as well have spoken the words. Kendra lifted her chin. "Perhaps it would be better if I took passage to the Continent…or to Ireland. No one would think to look for me there."

Henri nodded. "I can arrange either of those. I have a ship that can be readied in a day or two—"

"No," Adrian said.

Kendra and Henri both looked at him.

"No," he said again. "It is too risky for Kendra to remain here while such arrangements are made." He took a deep breath. "If Lancaster doubles back and finds her here, your head will roll."

"Robert might well be livid if you take her to him."

"That is why I sent Pierre ahead. If Bruce refuses her refuge, I will take her elsewhere. I will not stand by and allow Kendra to marry de Nogaret." A muscle twitched in Adrian's jaw. "I will not let that happen."

In that moment, Kendra realized that she loved Adrian. Totally.

"We ride in the morning," Adrian said.

And she couldn't wait to ride by his side.

****

"I am sorry Henri embarrassed you," Adrian said later that evening as he escorted her to her chamber door.

"He didn't say anything I hadn't expected," Kendra answered. "He has a right to be suspicious. Pierre brought a stranger—one who is the niece of an English earl and hunted by mayhap the king himself—into his house. That puts Lord St. Clair in danger."

Adrian had to admire her for being so astute and for not taking insult like many women would have done. She hadn't minded eating in the servants' room either.

"*Oui*, it does put him in danger, but my presence does also, which is why we ride at dawn tomorrow." His arm hurt like blazes, but he wasn't going to let that stop them. "Hopefully, Gaveston will have a chance to reason with Edward soon."

"But what about Lancaster?" she asked. "I doubt the king ordered him to hunt you down."

He almost smiled at how quickly her mind put things together. "No, but if Lancaster captures me, it will demonstrate his shrewdness and skill over Edward's."

"Does Lancaster want the Crown, then?"

"That would not surprise me, since Edward has no heir yet." A *coup* would be total disaster, since the earl was eager for French support and suspicious of Templars hiding in Scotland, but Adrian kept those thoughts to himself. "For certes, there is no love lost between them."

"Mayhap when my uncle returns, he can reason with both of them."

Adrian gave her a skeptical look. "When your uncle returns empty-handed, he will launch a massive search for you."

Kendra's eyes widened. "You don't think he'll believe pirates sailed away with me?"

"I do not know," Adrian answered. "Remy will most likely try to encourage him to confiscate an English brig to follow, but once Pembroke finds out I am gone as well, he will be suspicious."

"But my disappearance and yours are not related."

"It would seem not, at least on the surface, but de Nogaret knows of my interest in you..." Adrian stopped. He didn't want Kendra to feel obligated to him. "I mean, I am your champion."

But she was smiling, a rather flirtatious smile at that. One he hadn't seen before.

"*Are* you interested in me? Not as my champion, but personally?"

Any other woman asking that question would have sounded coy as if fishing for a compliment. But as Adrian gazed into Kendra's eyes, he saw only a question, as if she wanted an honest answer. He swallowed and studied the wall above her head.

"I am. I have been since we first met. But you have my word, I do not expect anything from you."

One brow arched. "Like what?"

Now that question didn't sound entirely innocent or naïve. He looked at her again. Her eyes had darkened, her breathing had become shallow, and her tongue darted out to lick her lips. *Was* she flirting with him? He felt desire swelling in his groin.

"Do you want to be kissed, my lady?"

She smiled, and it was naturally seductive. "I would like that very much."

He took a step closer and started to lower his head, but she backed away, opening the door to her bedchamber as she did. "Come inside," she whispered as one small hand grabbed his shirt and tugged him toward her.

Caught off balance, he stumbled through the doorway. He wasn't sure where this was going to lead, but he wanted to find out.

****

Kendra closed the door and threw the bolt, a little surprised at her own brazen behavior. Ever since they'd shared the kiss in front of Guinevere's portrait, her body had desired Adrian, but the monumental realization earlier that she *loved* him was like adding kindling to long-simmering embers. Fire had ignited in her soul. She wanted him with every fiber in her being.

She just wasn't sure what to do next. She squeezed her eyes shut, tilted her face up, and waited. And waited.

Just when she thought Adrian wasn't going to kiss her at all, she felt his lips, feathery soft and light, brush across hers. Her arms wound around his neck as she rose on tiptoe to press herself closer. She remembered what his tongue had done during their last kiss and, tentatively, gave a little lick.

That brought the action she wanted. He circled her waist, drew her tight against his chest, and deepened the kiss, his tongue skillfully exploring her mouth, encouraging hers to do the same. When he finally broke the kiss, they were both shaking.

He held her away. "What is it you want, Kendra?"

She blinked. "Is it not obvious? I want you to make love to me."

He made a sound, something between choking and a growl. "Do you know what you ask?"

"I know I like your touch. I like the way you feel, the way you make *me* feel. I am tingling all over." She glanced toward the bed. "I'm sure everything would feel much better if we lie down."

That strange sound came again from his throat.

"Well, wouldn't it?" she asked.

"*Oui*. That it would, *ma chère*." His voice sounded strangled. "But it would be very difficult to stop with kisses and caresses if we were to lie down."

"Then we do not have to stop."

"I cannot promise you anything since we don't know what the future holds for either of us," he said hoarsely.

Now he was going to be logical? She sighed. "That is the point, isn't it? We are both fugitives at the moment. If I am caught, I will be forced into a marriage I do not want."

Adrian frowned. "I am not going to let that happen."

"I believe you, but just in case the inevitable happens, I want to experience real lovemaking with you."

"I don't have the right to take your virginity."

"You aren't *taking* it. I'm *giving* it to you." Kendra smiled and put her hand on his shoulder. "Tomorrow, we'll be on the road with Callum and Hammish. We may not get a chance to share a bed in private again."

He glanced at the bed. "We should not—"

"We *should*." Was seduction supposed to be this hard? Then another thought hit her like a horse's hoof. "Do I not have the type of body you like?"

The sound this time was definitely a growl. And the next thing she knew, she was flat on her back with Adrian looming over her.

"Your body is perfect." And those were the last words spoken for a long while.

Adrian rained kisses across her forehead, feathered them across her eyelids, then followed the curve of her cheek to claim her mouth once more. Vaguely she was aware of his undoing of the laces on the simple gown she wore and then cool air brushing her breasts. Her nipples hardened against the chill. In the next moment, she gasped as his hot mouth covered one of them and he began to suckle while he kneaded the other tight bud between his thumb and forefinger. The sensation was exquisite and sent heat pooling low in her belly.

She nearly cried out in anguish as his lips moved away from such delicious torture, but then he nipped his way up her neck to take her mouth again. She wrapped her arms around his neck to pull him down on top of her, wanting more friction against her sensitive peaks. His body moved in rhythm with hers, rubbing, agitating, and soothing the need all at one time while his hands slowly pulled the gown off her shoulders.

In another moment, she lay bare before him. Instinctively, she tried to bring her knees together, but he'd managed to settle between her legs when he removed her clothes. Now he lifted her calf to his shoulder and began to nibble the inside of her thigh. She inhaled sharply. The awareness of how close his mouth was to her private area caused a strange sort of ache to begin, followed by a slow pulsing between her legs that she had never felt before.

Adrian settled her other calf on his other shoulder, leaving her splayed open to him. Before she had time to be embarrassed, he dipped his head and she felt his tongue. *There*. Right where the pulsation was. She gasped.

He spread her slick folds with his thumbs and began to lick in long, slow strokes, each time stopping just short of the little nub that was now throbbing. Her hips began to gyrate against his mouth, her body desperately seeking *more*. Kendra wasn't sure exactly what *more* was, but she knew she wanted it. Something was building inside her. She began to writhe in earnest.

"Please…"

He looked up and smiled, then resumed his ministrations. On her second plea, he inserted a finger into her core, moving it in a circular motion. Her hips arched up in anticipation as a second finger joined the first. She began to tremble as she felt something deep inside her begin to spasm and then, just when she thought she might lose her sanity, his mouth closed on the pulsing nib and she convulsed.

The world went black, and she blinked it into existence seconds later, her breathing still fast and shallow. Adrian came back into focus, still sitting on his knees between her legs.

"You're still dressed."

"That I am."

"Why?"

He managed a smile. "Because I should not take your virginity."

She frowned. "Are we going to have that argument again? I do not claim to be a seductress—"

"You have seduced me, *ma chère*. Quite thoroughly."

"*Non.* You have given me pleasure, but you have not taken yours."

"It is…not necessary."

The tight set of his jaw told her otherwise. "I have observed a maid or two coupling with stable boys when no one thought I was about. We are not finished, my lord."

"We are."

"We are *not*." Instinctively, she arched her hips again, wantonly exposing her still swollen, wet core to him. "I want to feel you *inside* me."

He growled again, his golden eyes turning wolfish. A tiny tinge of thrilling fear raced through her at his feral look, but she held his regard, this time letting her own hand stray close to where his mouth had been. His gaze shifted down, and he groaned.

Then, with lightning speed, he pulled his tunic off his head, slipped his braies down, and settled the length of his body against hers. The hard ridge of his manhood pressed into her belly and then the rounded tip probed at her entrance. It felt much bigger than she had thought, and she must have flinched, because Adrian raised to his elbows.

"Are you sure this is what you want?"

She wiggled against him. "I'm sure."

He lowered to take her mouth in a deep kiss. She felt herself being stretched and then a sharp pain, followed by a feeling of fullness as he filled her. He held still for a few seconds, giving her time to adjust, and then began a slow, steady thrusting.

Kendra felt the urge and the need start to build again, this time stronger than before. Her body undulated of its own accord. Adrian drove into her now, the thrusts deeper and faster. Wildfire spread through her body like a blaze through dry timber. With a cry, Adrian gave one last, hard thrust that touched the wall of her womb, and her body exploded like an inferno as she screamed her ecstasy. He smothered the sound with a kiss and then collapsed beside her.

Kendra lay in silence then, eyes closed, trying to recall every single wonderful second. Then she heard a slight rattling sound beside her and opened her eyes. Adrian was sound asleep.

She smiled into the darkness. She was a fugitive

and might never see Wales again, but in Adrian's arms, she was home. And she always would be.

Chapter Nineteen

Although neither Callum nor Hammish seemed to notice anything different as they set out the next morning in the pre-dawn light, Kendra could hardly keep from smiling every time she looked at Adrian on his stallion next to her. They'd made love twice more last night and again this morning. She had sore muscles where she didn't even know she had muscles, and the area between her legs was tender, but both only served to remind her of what had taken place to make that happen. Surprisingly, the impact of sitting astride her horse created a pleasant friction that made her want to grin again. And so she did.

"Will we stop at an inn tonight?"

Adrian's mouth quirked as though he knew why she was asking the question, but he shook his head. "We can't afford to leave a trail."

"But are we not far enough away from the searchers to be safe?"

"I doubt that Edward will agree to stop looking for me, with Lancaster at Berwick," he answered, "and once your uncle returns, he will probably lead additional searches as well. Better that no one has a description of us."

Cullum turned in his saddle to look at them. "We doona want to lead anyone to Bruce's camp, either."

"I thought we were not going to Robert Bruce's

218

camp."

"We are not, at least not directly," Adrian answered. "We will stop near Stirling and await orders."

"Stirling? That is still one of Edward's strongholds." Kendra frowned. "Will that be safe?"

Hammish laughed. "Sometimes 'tis better to hide in the middle of the enemy's army than from it."

She widened her eyes. "You don't mean to go inside the walls of the castle, do you?"

"Not quite," Adrian replied, "but Robert has had men watching Stirling for a year, reporting the comings and goings of the English garrison. One of the safest places to camp is just north of there where a scouting party raided a village and left it in ruins."

"How horrible!" Kendra said. "The peasants aren't involved in this war. Why should they be burned out?"

Hammish sobered. "'Tis nothing compared to Dunbar, lass."

"Or Berwick either," Cullum added.

She knew of the massacres that had taken place under Edward I, although she was sure she'd been spared a lot of details. "Those were bad enough that my uncle favors a peace treaty."

Adrian gave her a side glance. "With no envoy, that's unlikely to happen now."

"This is my fault." Although neither Cullum nor Hammish replied, she caught the look they exchanged before turning their attention back to the road. "If you hadn't arranged for my escape, you wouldn't have been hurt, so the queen wouldn't have gone to your room—"

"Do not blame yourself," Adrian interrupted. "The queen would have found some excuse eventually to waylay me somewhere. She was determined to make me a conquest."

"It is too bad she didn't get caught with one of her real conquests," Kendra said.

Adrian grimaced. "You'll not get any argument from me on that count."

"Let's hope Gaveston can convince the king it was Isabella's fault, not yours."

"I think Edward already knows that." He shrugged. "It's Lancaster that's the problem."

"And Lancaster dislikes Gaveston." Kendra gave Adrian a sideways glance. "Is it because Gaveston has the king's ear?"

"Perhaps. Lancaster resents that," Adrian answered. "The earl wants to be the most powerful man in England, but to attempt a *coup d'ètat* would be treasonous. The best route to power is to be able to influence the king."

"So he uses intimidation."

Adrian nodded. "Edward does not share the bloodlust of his father, which makes him look inherently weak."

"He knows that?" Kendra asked.

"He knows." Adrian paused. "And that is why he will continue to hunt me."

"And if a connection is made between us, it will be doubly bad," Kendra said.

Adrian looked grim. "I am afraid you are right."

She felt a shiver of fear slide down her spine, but then she lifted her chin. "In that case, we had better not get caught."

The last thing she expected was for all three men to laugh, but in a moment, she joined in. What other option did they really have?

****

The snow had stopped, but the weather remained cold, not allowing it to melt. Adrian debated whether to stick to the trails, where their shod horses' hooves might be spotted, or to stay to the main roads, which were travelled enough to leave no individual hoof prints. In the end, he decided to stick to the trails since Kendra's Andalusian mare and his own black stallion would stand out.

It also took longer.

By the time they stopped in the shelter of a copse of oak trees for the night, his arm had begun to throb. He tried not to wince when he removed his horse's saddle, but Kendra noticed immediately.

"Your arm? Is it worse?"

"It will be fine."

She lifted her chin in a way that he was beginning to recognize as determined. *Very* determined. It was much the same gesture she'd used just before she'd spread her legs wide for him to take her fully the night before. The recall of that image made his groin tighten painfully, but he ignored it. There was no way they would be able to couple while on the road. Even if they were quiet—and Kendra was *not*, another thought that made him tighten more—he was not about to divulge their relationship to Callum and Hammish.

"Let me see it."

For a moment he thought she meant his wayward part and he gave himself a mental shake back to reality. He couldn't keep thinking about Kendra in his bed. He should not have allowed himself to take her virginity in the first place.

He set the saddle down and offered his arm. Kendra unwrapped the bandage and then squinted at it. "I do not like that it is red and swollen."

"Most likely because you just sewed it up yesterday."

"Mayhap. But it looks angry."

He smiled. "How can my arm look *angry*?"

"Your *wound* does." Her brow furrowed. "The only thing I know to do is pour whisky on it."

Hammish must have heard her because he brought a flask over. "Here ye go."

"Wouldn't it make me feel better if I drank it instead?" Adrian tried to keep his tone light even as the liquid stung like a hundred bees. "It seems like a waste of good liquor."

"Mayhap you are right." Kendra lifted the flask and tipped it back to take a swallow, then squeezed her eyes shut as the whisky slid down. "It is certainly not claret."

Adrian laughed and took a swallow himself, then handed the flask back. "It does its job of lessening the pain, though."

She frowned. "So you *are* in pain."

He could have bitten his tongue. Not because he wanted to appear manly in front of her—Templars were taught to withstand pain a lot worse than a simple knife slice—but the comment brought a look of consternation to Hammish's face as well. And Cullum had wandered over to look at his arm too. He felt like a lad still in short pants. "Really, it is nothing."

"I just wish I knew what else to do," Kendra ignored his words as she re-bandaged his arm. "But I am no healer."

"There is a healer at Bruce's camp," Callum said as

he and Hammish exchanged glances.

"She's taken care of Adrian before," Hammish added.

"Good," Kendra said, "then she'll know what to do."

"Aye, that she will."

"You said the camp was near Stirling?" Kendra asked. "How long will it take to get there?"

"A day or two, lass," Hammish said.

Adrian gave the Scots a warning look. "That is, if Bruce wants us to go there."

Kendra shrugged. "Does it matter what he wants now? Adrian has a wound that needs tending. You say there is a healer at the camp. The sooner she sees Adrian the better."

Hammish made a sound that quickly turned into a cough while Cullum chewed on his lip.

Adrian glared at them both. "We will await a message from Robert, as planned."

Kendra shook her head. "But—"

"As planned," Adrian repeated. "It will be safer that way."

He was in no hurry to have all hell break loose. And he was pretty sure it would.

****

After two nights of sleeping on cold, hard ground, Kendra had never been so glad to see buildings finally appear, even if they were mostly burned-out shells. She was tired, stiff and sore, but worse, she worried about Adrian's arm.

It remained red and swollen, although he insisted he was not in pain. She'd nearly snorted at that since she could feel his arm muscles tense when she poured

223

whisky on the wound again last night. *Men*. He'd probably be willing to lose his arm rather than admit it hurt.

But then her attitude softened as she recalled how truly *manly* he had been in bed the night they'd spent at Lord St. Clair's. Some of the soreness left as her body remembered how he had filled her.

She sighed. She had hoped they'd share the one tent each night on the ride here, but he'd insisted she take it, loading her down with so many tartans she could barely move. He'd slept outside by the small fire with the Scots. He said it was to protect her virtue. She *had* inwardly snorted at that. Her virtue was gone, and she didn't much care if Hammish and Cullum knew it. She had liked losing her virtue. She was eager to have him take her again, and she was eager to learn how to please him as he pleased her. Why wouldn't he want to do that?

Which brought her back to her original worry. His arm was hurting more than he would admit.

She hoped they wouldn't have to wait very long for a message to arrive from wherever Robert Bruce's camp was.

"Will Pierre know where to find us?" They had stabled the horses in what was left of the village stable and taken shelter in a building that had a partial roof and two walls standing. Being within two miles of Stirling Castle, they didn't light a fire that could draw attention from a mounted watch that might be riding nearby.

"This place is a rendezvous point." Adrian broke off a hunk of bread and handed it to her. "He'll know where to look."

"He might not be expecting us for a day or two, though," Hammish said.

"A day or two?" Kendra looked at the bandage on Adrian's arm. "That wound needs to be seen by the healer."

"It will be fine." He used his dirk to slice off some cheese for her.

She knew from his tight-lipped look that it was not *fine*. Although she had cleansed the wound with whisky every day and torn her chemise into strips for clean bandages, his arm remained swollen and hot to the touch. She was almost sure infection had set in. But she knew it would be useless to argue the point. She was fast finding Adrian was as stubborn as she was.

Callum gave Adrian a subtle look. "Pierre willna have heard what happened to ye, so he willna be in any hurry to get here, just to wait for us to bring the lass."

"That will not do." Kendra sensed the Scots were as worried as she. "Why don't one of you ride ahead with Adrian? I can wait here."

"*No*." Adrian's jaw set. "We wait together."

Kendra frowned. Stubborn, stubborn man. If they were alone, she would soon tell him what she thought of his willfulness, but she'd also sensed that the Scotsmen had a hardy resilience not found with English courtiers. Adrian would not appreciate her making him appear less hardy than they were. Stubborn man.

Without a fire, quick work was made of their dinner. It was sometime later, after she'd fallen asleep curled into the corner of the two adjoining walls, that she woke to the sound of stealthy footsteps. Already, Adrian and the Scots were on their feet, swords drawn.

A minute later, she heard pebbles hitting the side of

the building. Adrian sheathed his sword. "In here."

In another moment, Pierre appeared in the burned-out doorway, silhouetted by the light of a waxing moon. "I was hoping you'd arrived. Do you think you were followed?"

"I don't think so. We were careful to stick to the deer trails and avoid the road," Adrian replied. "What message do you have from Robert?"

"Well, that is a bit interesting." Pierre stepped back and gave three owl hoots, then returned. "You can ask him yourself."

Adrian frowned. "Robert is—"

"Here." Another figure filled the doorway.

Even if Hammish and Cullum hadn't started to drop a knee, Kendra had no doubt she was looking at the Scottish king. Although his face was only half-visible in the moonlight, the angles and planes were hardened. He looked imposing.

"Your Majesty," Adrian said with a short bow. "We were not expecting that you would come yourself."

"I wished to interview Pembroke's niece myself before I make any decisions."

Although his voice was strong and held authority, he did not use the imperial "we" as Edward loved to do. He'd also gestured to the Scots to rise before their knees had actually touched the ground. He didn't act like he expected such. In spite of his stern countenance, she was already warming to him.

"Where is she?"

Kendra rose from her corner, wishing for once she was actually wearing a gown instead of braies and tunic. She stepped forward, attempting to curtsey, and tripped on the tartan she had wrapped around her.

Adrian leapt forward to catch her. Bruce's attention turned to his arm.

"You've been wounded?"

"It is nothing—"

"It *is* something, Your Majesty," Kendra interrupted, ignoring Adrian's glare. "The wound is festered, and he needs the attention of your healer." The king raised a brow, and she could have sworn he looked amused, but she hurried on. "I understand your camp is undisclosed. I can wait here for you to make a decision on where I am to go. But send Adrian back. *Now*." She paused for breath, suddenly aware from the incredulous looks on the Scotsmen's faces, that she had just given orders to their king. She swallowed. She'd be lucky if he didn't return her to Berwick immediately. "I meant to say *please*."

Robert gave her a long look, and then he laughed. "The lady reminds me of the Countess of Buchan."

Adrian smiled. "I will vouch for her honesty, Your Majesty."

The king gave him a long look too. "And you wish to bring her to the camp?"

His smile faded. "I do."

"I see." Robert studied both of them and finally nodded. "So be it. As soon as you get your horses saddled, we will be gone."

"Thank you, Your Majesty," Adrian said.

Kendra took a step forward, then stopped to stare. As the king turned away, a lingering shadow remained. The figure wore a purple cloak, thrown back over one shoulder to expose leather mail such as Lancelot had worn. A magnificent sword protruded from a rune-engraved sheath, a huge ruby winking in its hilt. In the dim, silvery light, a gold crown glinted on the spectre's head. He turned slightly to look at her, and Kendra gasped. She'd seen his face before in another portrait at Bamburgh, hung not that far from Guinevere's. Now she knew who he was.

She blinked and the image was gone, but she suspected the fetch of King Arthur had just lent his support to Robert Bruce's cause.

****

Kendra was surprised to find that the Scottish king had come so close to Stirling with only half a dozen men, but she figured one of the reasons the king had eluded Edward I for so many years was because of his ability to move with small bands and not huge armies. And then she realized, as night turned into dawn, that an unusual number of what appeared to be peasants were travelling the road north as well. She began to suspect that, beneath their mantles, they may very well have been armed. So Robert Bruce had an army after all.

When they stopped to water their horses, Adrian approached her holding a strip of linen. "I am sorry, but for the next few hours you will need to wear a blindfold so you don't see where we are going."

He looked so abject that she couldn't even be indignant. She simply nodded. "I understand."

She could feel from the movement of the horse that the terrain grew more rugged as the hours passed. It wasn't until the heat of the afternoon sun began to fade that they stopped again and she was told she could remove the blindfold. She blinked as her eyes adjusted.

Below them, a burn meandered like a silver thread

through a small glen where sheep grazed. Beyond that, two steep hills rose with a narrow pass between them.

Bruce nudged his horse down the trail to the glen, his mounted men following him while the peasants who'd shared the road started dissipating, blending into the trees on either side.

Kendra glanced at Adrian. He didn't look like he thought it unusual for scores of cloaked serfs—if that's what they were—to suddenly begin to disappear. Nor did he survey his surroundings with much interest, which told her he'd been here before. Still, when she caught a glimpse of metal flashing in the sun from atop one of the hills, she pointed.

"There's someone watching us from up there."

He smiled. "*Oui*. A guard."

"Is Robert Bruce's camp close, then?"

"Just through the pass."

They slowed their horses in order to progress single file. It reminded Kendra of the pass on the road near Berwick where her escape had taken place, only this one was longer, narrower, and its rock walls high, not just jutting boulders. Halfway through, she realized what a perfect, natural trap it was. She'd seen castles that had outer and inner curtain walls with a portcullis in each that could be used to effectively trap the enemy while hot oil was poured from the battlements or arrows shot from murder holes. She felt Adrian watching her.

"I can see why Robert Bruce chose this spot. It is highly defensible."

Adrian nodded. "There is another glen on the other side. The burn widens into a river along one edge and the tree line is distant on the other, which makes an enemy approach highly visible."

"And the far end of the glen?" Kendra asked.

"A munro blocks that." Seeing her confusion, he added, "A mountain that is high and hard to climb."

"I am beginning to see why both Edwards have been thwarted," Kendra said. "Your king is clever to find such hiding spots."

"It seems Scotland is full of such natural defenses." Adrian paused. "But perhaps you should begin to regard Robert as your king too."

Kendra blinked. She hadn't given that much thought, but Adrian was right. If she were going to be living in the Scottish camp, she didn't want to be thought the enemy. Then another thought struck her, one she didn't want to think about. "Do you think he will let me stay?"

"I suspect so." Adrian gave her a contemplative look. "You have been to his camp now."

The elation she'd felt spring up—she'd be staying with Adrian!—deflated like a knife driven into a sheep's bladder at his second remark. She knew, more or less, the secret location, and she was still the niece of a powerful English earl. She might very well be more prisoner than guest.

But the worrisome thought disappeared like fog in front of a gale wind when she exited the pass and rode into the clearing beyond. The area bustled with activity, tents were erected everywhere and, in the distance, she saw a herd of horses as well.

Adrian dismounted and started to walk toward her mare when a distinctive female voice called out. Kendra looked up to see a beautiful woman with long hair the color of copper running toward them. She threw her arms around Adrian's neck, pressed her curvaceous body along the length of his, and kissed him.

"My love!" she said. "Ye have returned!"

Chapter Twenty

Adrian tried to extricate himself from Greer's arms as inconspicuously as he could. He was only too aware of Kendra's shocked face before she turned away. Now he wished he'd explained the situation to her beforehand, but he'd hardly expected such an immediate reception from his former paramour. They'd had an argument about their relationship before he left and he'd assumed, given the fact that she had been raised in the ancient Celtic matriarchal ways of thigh freedom that still existed in the far north, that she'd taken another lover by now. He certainly had not been her first since her arrival at Bruce's camp.

He stepped back. "You are looking well."

She looked him over brazenly, but her coyness stopped when she saw the bandage on his arm. "Ye have been wounded!" Before he could answer, she'd unwrapped it from his arm and frowned. "'Tis infected."

"Yes," Pierre said as he came to stand with them. "It happened as he was escaping Edward's dungeon."

Greer looked at Adrian in surprise. "How did ye come to be in the dungeon?"

He'd rather not go into that either, but Pierre answered for him.

"From what I gather," he said as he helped Kendra dismount, "Queen Isabella took a fancy to him."

Greer's eyes narrowed. "Ye were caught with that French whore?"

"It wasn't what it appeared to be," he answered, "but Lancaster was with the king—"

"I care not for those details," she answered. "What were ye doing in the queen's chambers?"

"I was not in her chambers. She was waiting in mine." Belatedly, he remembered Greer's tendency to be jealous, and it irritated him now just as it had done before. It was another reason they'd argued. "That is the end of this conversation."

She arched one brow slightly, then turned to look at Kendra. "And who is this that you bring here?"

Kendra lifted her chin slightly. "I am Kendra de Claremont."

"Another French wh—"

"Lady," Adrian said before Greer could complete her sentence. "*Lady* Kendra de Claremont of Pembroke."

"Pembroke?" she echoed. "The English are our enemy, in case ye've forgotten."

"I have not forgotten." He decided to change the subject. "I need for you to see to my arm."

She turned her attention back to it. "Who did the stitching?"

"I did," Kendra paused. "You...are the healer?"

"Aye." Greer gave her a long look. "And ye did nae tend to the wound after?"

"I...tried. I poured whisky on it every night."

"Every night?" Greer repeated, her eyes narrowing again as she turned to Adrian. "Ye were unfaithful to me?"

His temper flared. "I have not been *unfaithful* to

anyone, and I have no desire to follow this conversation further. Right now I need my arm attended."

She looked about to argue, then seemed to think better of it. "Ye need a salve of mistletoe berries to draw the fever out." She suddenly smiled at him. "I have some powder in my tent."

He wanted to tell her he'd wait right here, but they'd already begun to draw a crowd of interested onlookers, so it would be better just to go with her and have done. The pain in his arm had definitely gotten worse over the past two days.

"I'll see Lady Kendra to her quarters," Pierre said.

Adrian wasn't sure if he was trying to be helpful or not. His tone was noncommittal, but there was a hint of amusement in his eyes. Adrian almost scowled at him, but managed to nod instead. "Lady Kendra, I am sure you would like to rest after the journey." Then he turned to Greer. "Lead the way."

****

Kendra stared after them. No one, least of all Adrian, had mentioned that the healer was a beautiful young woman with fiery red hair and vivid blue eyes. No one, *especially* not Adrian, had bothered to mention that the healer was obviously his leman as well. He certainly had not denied it. Just now, he'd even been abrupt in his dismissal of her in order to follow Greer to her tent.

Tears stung the back of her eyes. No wonder he had tried to resist seduction at Roslin. *I don't have the right to take your virginity.* At the time, she thought he was only concerned for her virtue. Now she knew why he'd said it. Anger started to well up and then quickly subsided. She'd all but thrown herself at him. ...*I should not take your virginity.* He'd said it twice. She hadn't listened. Her face heated when she recalled how wanton she had been. How she had spread her legs wide and lifted her womanhood to him. He'd only taken what she insisted he take.

Now she understood those strange looks the Scots had exchanged when she'd mentioned the healer needing to see to his arm. Her face flushed again.

Pierre touched her elbow. "This way."

Kendra followed him, trying to ignore the fact that nearly everyone was staring at her. The women—who did not appear to be camp-followers—eyed her warily and some with curiosity. Among the men, she saw more than one smirk and in her peripheral view she even saw several whispering and pulling out coin. No doubt they were wagering on what her relationship with Adrian was and the outcome of the meeting she'd just had with his leman.

She was tempted to tell them all to save their money. She had no intention of throwing herself at him again. Kendra touched Pierre's arm briefly, and he stopped.

"I…would appreciate your support that I am only seeking temporary sanctuary here."

"Temporary?"

"Yes." Dear Lord. She couldn't stay in the same camp with Adrian and his woman. "I am sure Robert Bruce will not want me underfoot for long, since I am English."

A muscle tensed in Pierre's jaw. "It is precisely *because* you are English that you will not be allowed to leave."

Kendra felt her eyes widen. "You mean I am a

hostage?" *Mon Dieu!* Could that possibly have been Adrian's plan all along? That he thought her uncle could exert enough influence over Edward to get him to sign a peace treaty in exchange for her return? But it could be true. Adrian had not been eager to repeat their bedroom encounter while on the road, even though she slept in his tent. The thought made her feel ill.

"I did not use that term," Pierre said.

Maybe not yet, but she'd already seen the campsite. If she stayed long enough to hear anything of real significance, her fate would be truly sealed. "Couldn't the king just send me to some remote place in the Highlands or even the Hebrides? Surely, he wouldn't think I would pose a danger there."

"That would be his decision." Pierre studied her. "But your sudden wanting to leave has to do about Adrian, does it not?"

She felt her face warm again and looked down. "Monsieur de Soules has been gallant enough to save me from a marriage I did not want. I expect no more favors from him."

"Gallant? Do you think he got himself hit on the head because he was gallant?"

She winced, recalling him lying on the road. "Honor, then. He gave me his word he would help me escape. The wedding was upon us. He did what he had to do because he is honorable."

"Honorable, yes." Pierre paused. "Remy and I tried to talk him out of it."

She looked up. "Was it because you considered me a spy for my uncle or because of his leman?"

He hesitated again. "Perhaps both."

"Then the healer *is* his leman?" She sounded pitiful

and hated it. Why was she clinging to any sense of hope when she'd seen with her own eyes what had just happened?

"That is a question you will have to ask him," Pierre replied.

As if she would *ask*. She was suddenly furious with Adrian. He *should* have told her he had a woman waiting for him. She was equally angry at herself for being so naïve as to think he cared about her. Men tumbled women for sport, and she had been all too willing to let him. She would not be stupid enough to make that mistake again. She lifted her chin.

"Such a question will not be necessary. I only seek sanctuary for as long as the Scottish king allows it."

****

Adrian kept looking for Kendra over the heads of the men seated around him under the large tent that served as both dining hall and barracks. By the time Greer had finished applying the poultice—and offering to see to his other needs, which he'd declined—Pierre had taken her to the tent shared by the women who cooked, laundered, and repaired clothing. When he'd asked him how she was doing, Pierre had only shaken his head and given Adrian a sympathetic look.

A look that didn't bode well.

Hellfire and damnation. Why had Greer not taken up with someone else by now? She could certainly have her pick of soldiers, even most of the one hundred Templars who were part of this camp. They were Bruce's elite force, and they'd all given up any vows of chastity after they'd left France.

He glanced to where she was seated next to Robert on a makeshift dais of raised wooden planks. As the camp's healer, it was expected she sit at what amounted to the head table, so at least he didn't have to make excuses not to sit beside her.

Unfortunately, because of her healing skills, she'd also been awarded an unofficial rank and was accorded due respect, so he couldn't simply ask that she be removed from camp. Besides, the men—including himself at present—relied on her ability to use herbs.

Would Kendra understand? He'd never been in the position of having to explain anything to a woman. After the disastrous affair with Angelique, he made sure the women he took to his bed knew to expect nothing more than to be pleasured. A few evenings at most was all he lingered. He thought he'd made that clear when Greer first approached him, but he realized his mistake had been in allowing her to keep his bed warm overlong.

"You look like you have been ordered to hold the weight of the world on your shoulders," Pierre said as he set a trencher down and slid onto the bench next to Adrian.

Adrian gave him a side glance. "It was the sky, not the world."

"Pardon?"

"The sky," Adrian repeated, glad to get his mind off Kendra. "Zeus ordered Atlas to hold up the sky after the Titans were defeated."

A corner of Pierre's mouth lifted. "Sometimes I think you should never have taken up reading Greek mythology. So where has this burden come from?"

Adrian shot him a dark look.

"I doubt that Bruce gave you such an edict," Pierre went on as though he were not aware of Adrian's ill humor. "So I surmise the problem is a woman. Or *women*."

Adrian dropped any pretense of being subtle. "What did Kendra say?"

"Ah." Pierre shrugged. "She thinks Greer is your leman."

"The healer is not my leman!" Adrian lowered his voice. "I'll be glad to tell Kendra so if she asks."

"The lady has too much pride to ask," Pierre answered.

"I have pride too," Adrian said. "I cannot just go around offering explanations of my personal affairs."

"You may want to reconsider that." Pierre nodded toward the tent flap.

Adrian turned to see what he meant and then bit back a curse. While they had been talking, Kendra had entered the tent and taken an empty seat at the far end, but she was not alone.

"What is Dion doing over there?"

"It looks like he is conversing with her."

"I can *see* that." Adrian hid his irritation, knowing it would only encourage Pierre to egg him on. Dion Arnoux was a Templar brother and a thorn in Adrian's side for nearly a decade. He was the one who'd made the other Templars aware of Adrian's ill-fated relationship with Angelique. Afterwards—in jest, he said—he'd offered to tup any woman Adrian did to make sure there wasn't another traitor in the midst. Only the jest had often become a reality. Too often. He started to rise, but Pierre put a restraining hand on his arm.

"Do you mean to claim Kendra as your woman?"

"What if I am?"

Pierre shrugged again. "Given her temperament—and what her perception of your relationship with Greer is—I suspect she will not appreciate you storming over there like a Viking marauder claiming her as your property."

Adrian frowned at him and then sank back down on the bench. He hated when his friend was right, but Pierre *was* right. Even without the misconception of Greer being his leman, Kendra would not take kindly to being ordered to do anything. Least of all, succumb submissively to being his woman. *Mon Dieu.* He couldn't even offer that since he'd not had a chance to talk with Robert about what her—or his—future held.

His frown deepened as Dion sat down next to Kendra, a smile on his face. When she smiled back, Adrian was hard-pressed not to ram his clenched fist through a plank in the table.

"Easy, *mon ami*," Pierre said. "Do not let your irritation show."

Pierre was right again. For now, all Dion knew was that Robert had granted Kendra refuge. If he caught wind of any interest on Adrian's part, he would assume the gauntlet thrown. It would be too easy for history to repeat itself.

Adrian couldn't let that happen. Not this time. And, if he hadn't realized it fully before, he did so now. He wanted Kendra to be his woman. But before he could persuade his willful nymph of that, he had to contend with both his king and his former lover.

Maybe Pierre was right on one more thing. He did feel like he was holding the weight of the world on his shoulders.

****

Kendra tried not to let her eyes search the large, crowded room for Adrian, instead concentrating on the man who'd introduced himself as Dion and asked permission to sit beside her. Perhaps she could learn more about Adrian's leman.

"Of course you may sit, my lord."

"No 'lord,' mademoiselle." Dion smiled as he slid in beside her. "Robert prefers we not use titles."

"Is that why he does not use 'We' in his personal speech?"

"*Certainement.* He does not want to mimic the English king in any way, but he also relies on the common people to build his armies."

"And if they can identify with him they will follow him?" Kendra asked.

Dion studied her. "You are very astute."

She smiled, thinking he probably wanted to add *for a woman* yet didn't. But she didn't want to tell him she learned much from listening to her uncle's discussion of strategies. The fewer people in the camp who knew she was the Earl of Pembroke's niece, the better. "I spent some time at the French court. Intrigue runs rampant there, as I am sure you know."

He lifted a brow. "What makes you think that?"

"Your voice bespeaks education, as do your actions. Only people who have dealings with the court display such."

He seemed to consider, then nodded. "My grandfather had been a courtier for King Philippe the Third, so I was able to attend the Université de Paris."

"Did Monsieur de Soules also attend?"

"I believe so." He shrugged. "He is several years older than I am."

"How did you meet, then?"

He hesitated again. "When the current king acknowledged Robert the Bruce's right to the Scottish crown, a number of landless knights decided to sail across the channel and offer our services."

"You are mercenaries?" She didn't want to think of Adrian being a sword-for-hire, but she'd seen his warrior skills, and she'd just found out he was a knight.

"More like knights errant." Dion smiled. "Looking for an honorable quest to support."

"And you think the war for Scottish independence is that?"

His smile widened. "France is no friend of England."

Kendra became thoughtful. Would the French king send more soldiers when Gerard returned home with the news that she'd managed to escape from Edward's court?

They could very well assume she was hiding in Scotland once they found no trace of Barbary corsairs in English waters. France could easily switch its alliance if Gerard managed to capture both the king's and the pope's ears. Robert had been excommunicated, after all, so support was tenuous at best. Had she brought more trouble to the Scottish king? Then again, she was also English, which made her no friend of Scotland either.

"How many of you came here to search for your Holy Grail?" Dion's eyes widened at her mention of it, and she felt her face warm. "I did not mean literally, of course. I meant how many landless knights thought to seek their fortune here?"

"You ask many questions, mademoiselle." He

studied her. "I would like to ask you one."

Kendra felt herself tense, but she could hardly refuse. "Of course."

"Why did de Soules bring you here?"

She blinked, not sure she was relieved that he hadn't wanted to know why she asked so many questions or whether to be worried about him finding out her relationship with Adrian. Not that she had one anymore.

"I wished to avoid a betrothal, and Monsieur de Soules was gallant enough to provide escort here."

Dion eyed her. "He would not bring you into the heart of Bruce's camp simply because he is gallant."

Her face heated again. "It is somewhat complicated."

"It usually is with de Soules," he said dryly.

Kendra frowned. What did that mean? "It was imperative that I be gone. Monsieur de Soules realized the gravity of the situation."

"I imagine he did. He was always one to help a damsel in distress." He let his gaze drift to the makeshift dais and then back. "I understand you have already met Greer."

She was sure most of the camp had. "Your healer hardly seems like a damsel in distress, Sir Dion."

He laughed. "She hardly is that. When de Soules found her, she was wielding a knife and fending off a small mob of women who'd accused her of witchcraft after a child had been stillborn."

Kendra swallowed. So Adrian *had* rescued Greer. And she, no doubt, had pledged her undying loyalty to him. "And so he brought her here for safety—"

"Among other things."

The implication he left unsaid hung in the air. Adrian had gone straight to the woman's tent. Kendra swallowed again, trying to keep her composure. Perhaps it was better to change the subject.

"I am very grateful to both Monsieur de Soules and to Robert Bruce for allowing me refuge," she said in as even a tone as she could muster. "But I am not a helpless damsel either. I will prove my worth."

"I am sure you will." A corner of Dion's mouth lifted as he rose to leave. "Meanwhile, I am at your beck and call, mademoiselle. I offer my support."

"*Merci*," she said and then had the feeling she was being watched. Turning her head slightly, she met Adrian's gaze across the emptying tent. For a moment, his eyes blazed, burning into hers. And then she saw Greer walking toward him.

Kendra turned back to Dion, offering both a smile and her hand. "*Merci, Monsieur.* I accept your offer."

Chapter Twenty-One

The morning of the fourth day after they'd gotten to Bruce's camp, Remy rode a tired horse through the pass. Robert had immediately asked Adrian and Kendra to come to his tent. Adrian felt a twinge of impatience as they waited for Pierre to join them. That Remy had made such haste from Berwick could be either good or bad.

"What is the climate at the English court?" Robert asked as soon as Pierre had closed the tent's flap.

"Is King Edward pursuing Adrian?" Kendra asked.

Adrian cast her a glance. Since their arrival, she had maintained an aloof attitude, only answering politely when he inquired after her. He understood that she needed to appear virtuous and not be seen as his English mistress, especially since she thought Greer was his leman. He had tried several times to seek Kendra out to explain Greer's possessive tendencies, but Dion always seemed to appear from nowhere whenever the opportunity arose. That she inquired after his own safety before her own gave hope that her coolness was just an act.

"The atmosphere is tenuous," Remy replied. "When I returned from Bamburgh, the castle was in an uproar. The queen was confined to her chambers, Lancaster kept goading Edward that he'd allowed you to escape, and Gaveston fired back that none of it was the earl's business."

"Lancaster thundered past us when we were near Roslin," Adrian said. "He'd already stopped at St. Clair's."

Remy nodded. "I stopped there too. Lancaster has not been back."

"But does that mean Adrian is safe?" Kendra asked.

"For the moment, perhaps." Remy shrugged. "The more Lancaster insists Adrian be found, the more Gaveston encourages the king to dig his heels in."

Kendra frowned. "It is all Queen Isabella's fault anyway. It was obvious the queen saw Monsieur de Soules as a conquest she wanted to make."

Robert gave Adrian a wry smile. "You seem to have a champion."

Adrian saw Kendra blush before she cast her eyes down. It gave him hope that if she understood the queen's motivations, she would also understand Greer's. But he didn't want to embarrass Kendra. "Perhaps it is fitting, since I was declared her champion at court."

She looked up, the impassive mask she'd assumed the last few days back in place. "And I thank you. You fulfilled your obligation by bringing me here."

Robert glanced from one to the other and then turned back to Remy. "What about Lady Kendra? Did her uncle believe she'd been abducted by pirates?"

"I am not sure." Remy grew thoughtful. "Pembroke ordered a group of his men to track down the English coast to determine if any corsairs have been seen. He also told them to stop at each harbor all the way to London and find out which foreign ships have put into port since she disappeared."

"He is suspicious, then," Adrian said.

"I would say that is likely an understatement," Robert answered. "The Earl of Pembroke didn't become a powerful lord by accepting rumor and not getting to the truth."

"It is only a matter of time before he comes searching for me, then," Kendra said. "If he finds me here—"

"He won't find you," Adrian interrupted. "We are well-defended."

"As protected as this glen is..." Kendra gave Adrian a quick glance before she took a deep breath. "As safe a place as this is, I am still putting the rest of you in danger. Perhaps I should be moved elsewhere."

"*Non!*" Adrian said before Robert could answer.

The king lifted an eyebrow and gave him a mild look.

Kendra's gaze was more penetrating. "Why do you want me to stay?"

The question caught him off guard, especially since he had just now usurped the king. "I...think it is in the best interests of everyone."

"You think I will betray you?" She glared at him now. "Or am I a hostage?"

Adrian felt himself glower. "I never said that."

"If I might have a word?" Robert asked.

Kendra's face turned an interesting shade of pink. "I am sorry. My aunt always tells me my mouth gets ahead of my thoughts."

Adrian bowed his head since he was already sitting. "I beg your forgiveness as well, Your Majesty."

Bruce waved his hand in dismissal. "You know I

do not stand on formality here." He looked at one and then the other again. "It would seem you have some personal issues to discuss, but that is not my concern. I agree that, for the present, I want to keep Lady Kendra here." He paused. "However, the possibility that either Lancaster or Edward will hunt Adrian down *is* my concern. The only way to keep them from doing that—and Pembroke from looking for his niece—is to distract them."

"What do you have in mind?" Adrian asked.

"I have been patient while you were at the English court trying to arrange a truce. Edward chose to drag his heels." The king grinned. "Now it's time for action. We will begin raiding again."

****

If she lived a century, Kendra would never understand why men enjoyed fighting. After Robert Bruce's announcement that raids would begin again, they were almost gleeful. She said as much to Fiona, a young woman who had befriended her from the first day she'd arrived.

"Och, aye, they do." Fiona looked up from the pot of stew she was stirring in the kitchen tent. "Mostly they are bored from sittin' around while we waited for a possible truce."

Kendra chewed her lip. "That truce might have happened if Adrian hadn't helped me escape."

"Doona fash yourself," Fiona replied. "He could nae let ye marry that bastard mon the bitch queen betrothed ye to."

Kendra smiled at her, partly because she had no hesitation in giving her opinion on most subjects and partly because of the colorful language she often used.

But then, her father was a soldier, and her mother and she had followed him when he'd joined Robert Bruce's army as a captain several years ago. "The bitch queen was just as nasty."

She found she rather enjoyed using the word too. She could just imagine her aunt's reaction if she'd used it at Edward's court. She'd probably have been restricted to bread and water for a month. But Beatrice wasn't here. "Damn the bitch," she added for emphasis.

Fiona grinned at her. "One of these days, I'll start teachin' ye to curse in Gaelic." Then she sobered. "But 'tis true. Her crawlin' into his bed near cost him his life."

Kendra nodded, hoping her face wasn't the same shade as the turnips waiting to be chopped. She had acted like a wanton too, luring Adrian to her bed. She hadn't shared that fact with her new friend. "It was selfish of her to take such a risk."

"From what I heard, the English queen is nothing more than a whore."

"She is a whore." It rolled off her tongue, the accumulation of all the loathing she felt toward Isabella rolled into one word. Her aunt would no doubt faint. "How do you say it in Gaelic?"

"*Seòrsa siùrsach.*" Fiona tilted her head to one side. "Do ye want me to tell ye what to call your lover?"

"*Non!*" Kendra was sure her face was now the color of those turnips. Had Fiona guessed how she felt about Adrian, even though she'd tried so hard to ignore him? As much as she liked the girl, it wouldn't do to have *that* rumor spreading all over camp. Better to return to the original subject.

"How much danger is there to the men when they raid?"

Fiona gave her a speculative look that said she wasn't through with her questioning, though she let it go for now. "'Tis rather like reiving."

"Reiving?"

"Aye. Sneakin' onto a neighbor's land and borrowing a few cattle or sheep."

"Borrowing? They return them?"

"Och, well, nae." Fiona grinned again. "Takin', then."

"You mean stealing."

Fiona shrugged. "The clans have been doing it since anyone can remember. 'Tis almost an honor-bound tradition."

"Ummm. King Edward probably won't think there is anything honorable about stealing...I mean reiving...any English property."

Fiona shook her head. "Ye were right with the first word. The men plan to steal, plunder, and destroy as much as they can and then get away."

"But if they get caught—"

"They are careful. 'Tis why it's called a raid. The men move quickly and are gone before the English can attack."

"But I've been at the English court. Edward will make examples out of anyone who is caught."

"My father says this king is not as bloodthirsty as his father."

"That's true." Kendra thought of Lancaster goading him constantly. "But that doesn't mean he will not hang them and then put their heads on pikes."

Fiona looked thoughtful. "Robert Bruce was told

that the earl from Wales has the king's ear and does nae want to repeat the Hammer's massacres."

The earl from Wales? That would be her uncle, Pembroke. The hair at her nape rose. "Did Adrian tell your king that?"

"Aye. My father says he learned much while at the English court."

"Adrian was an envoy, so I suppose he did hear some things."

Fiona shrugged again. "Being an envoy was partly a ruse."

"A ruse?"

"Aye. Robert Bruce didn't really think the English king would sign a peace treaty."

"He didn't?" Kendra frowned. "Then why did he send Adrian there?"

"To spy, of course."

"To spy?" Kendra felt like she was beginning to sound like a parrot. And then her hair bristled again. All those conversations they'd had...she thought Adrian was interested in her. But, given that he had a leman waiting, had he only been using her for information?

And was he *still* using her? Her need to escape her betrothal was a perfect opportunity for him to "help" and bring her here... She had played perfectly into his plans.

Maybe she really was a hostage after all.

****

By the time the evening meal was over—Kendra had hardly tasted the stew—she was seething with both anger and disappointment. Had she been used? Maybe he'd intended to bring her to Bruce's camp all along, but not for personal reasons. He certainly had made no attempt to make love to her again.

The subject of her emotional soul-searching was seated at the high table next to Robert this evening. Greer was not in attendance, but one of the men out hunting this afternoon had been gored by a boar, so she was probably seeing to him.

As much as Kendra didn't want to admit it, the other woman had healing skills. The poultice she'd applied to Adrian's arm had taken the swelling down in little more than a day. If she'd known about the medicinal properties of mistletoe, she could have done it the first night they'd stopped in the copse of oak trees. The branches had been full of mistletoe.

"You are not hungry this eve?" Dion asked from his seat across the table from her.

"I... I helped out in the kitchens today, so I've already had a sample."

He frowned. "Why are you working in the kitchens?"

"I have the feeling your king expects each person to do his or her share of work."

"But you are a guest."

A guest or a hostage? But Kendra didn't voice that thought. "I do not want to be seen as idle."

"You are also a lady."

Kendra smiled. "Not one who expects to be waited on, though. I believe in sparing servants what I can do for myself."

"That makes you an unusual lady, *mademoiselle*." He gave her a thoughtful look. "I would be honored to stroll with you if you have finished dining."

"I... Actually, I am a little tired, so I think I will just go back to the women's tent." It wasn't a total lie.

She was *tired* of thinking about Adrian. *Tired* of trying to second-guess his motives. But she also didn't wish to encourage Dion. They'd already strolled one evening, and often he was nearby.

"In that case, may I escort you to your tent?"

She wanted to say it was perfectly safe for her to walk the short distance, but he looked so disappointed, she hated to refuse. Besides, there would be a number of women already there. She smiled at him. "Thank you."

He was perfectly polite and proper on the short walk across the camp, keeping the conversation casual and impersonal. Kendra gave herself a mental shake. Dion was simply being courtly. She was probably being silly to think he was interested in her. She'd already made that mistake with Adrian, hadn't she?

"Thank you," she said again as they reached the tent. "It was kind of you to escort me."

"I am at your service, *mademoiselle*." He bowed slightly. "I look forward to the pleasure of seeing you in the morning."

Now why couldn't Adrian say something like that? Kendra thought as Dion left. Of course, he didn't have reason to when they were on the trail, and they'd only had public exchanges since they'd gotten here, but it didn't help her feeling out of sorts.

Nor could she sleep once she lay down on her pallet. This far north, even though the sun had set, it was still early. The women returning to the tent were chattering and moving about as well. Sleep would be a long time coming and, restless as she was, it might not come at all.

She needed answers. Before they left Berwick, she

was sure Adrian had come to care for her. He'd taken a blow to the head to help her escape look real. But he hadn't said anything about following her. That he'd been caught in Queen Isabella's trap and had to escape himself had been a fluke.

Adrian had tried to dissuade her from making love, too, but once he changed his mind, the night had been wonderful. Although *wonderful* didn't even begin to describe everything she'd felt. And she *knew* he'd felt something too. But she didn't know if was simply male lust or something stronger.

They hadn't had a chance to talk privately since they'd arrived. Perhaps that was her fault. She'd been so upset about Greer that she had purposely kept her distance. But now that she thought about it, Adrian had not danced attendance on Greer at all. The times she'd seen them together, Greer had advanced on him, not the other way around. Maybe, just *maybe*, things weren't what she'd assumed they were.

Kendra sat up. There was only one way to find out. She had to ask him.

She made her way outside and paused to make sure the path was clear. Sounds of the men gathered around the campfires on the other side of the large tent drifted across the way. They would probably be dicing and drinking for several more hours, anticipating the raids. Based on her observations at Berwick, she knew Adrian only indulged lightly in drink, so she doubted he'd be partaking in the revelry.

She turned away from the noise. Adrian's uncle, as Bruce's special envoy, had been given his own tent when he traveled with Robert Bruce, and Adrian, as envoy, had inherited it. The tent stood near the edge of the camp, near the meadow where the horses grazed. She could see an oil lamp burning through the partially pulled-back flap. Kendra looked around once more, then quickly hurried toward it.

As she approached, she heard his voice, and she slowed. She hadn't anticipated someone might be with him. And then she heard Greer's voice as well. Her heart thudded to a near stop. She thought the woman was attending the wounded soldier. She should leave. Right now. But, as Kendra started to turn, she paused. She was already here. Maybe if she heard what they were saying, she would have her answer.

Quietly, she angled around to the side of his tent, then crouched low, not wanting to take the chance on being seen. Thankfully, she could hear quite clearly.

"You promised me it would not come to this," Adrian said.

"I believe I said I would be careful." Greer's voice was soft.

"You said you took precautions." His voice was louder, almost angry.

"Potions do not always work." She sounded nonchalant.

"This was not what we agreed to." Most definitely, there was anger in his voice.

"Perhaps not, but the gods sometimes have other plans."

"Do not bring your old-world religion into this." He paused. "Are you sure?"

"Sure?" Greer laughed. "My courses have not come, so the logical conclusion is that I am with child. *Your* child, my love."

Kendra didn't wait to hear any more. She nearly

stumbled getting up and hit her ankle on a wood tent peg. She put a hand to her mouth to keep from gasping aloud at the pain, and then she was running.

Running, with tears streaming down her face.

Chapter Twenty-Two

Adrian's head snapped up as he thought he heard a noise outside his tent. He listened intently, but Greer's voice drowned out any sound of footsteps. Pushing past her, he swept aside the entrance flap and peered into the darkness. Nothing moved, and the only sound was from the men celebrating by the campfires.

Greer came up behind him and put a hand on his arm. "What is it?"

"Nothing." He wanted to shake her hand off, but instead he stepped away. "You had better go."

She slanted him a sultry look. "Why? You know how good we are together in bed."

"*Were*." He tried to keep the annoyance out of his voice. "I told you before I left that our time together was over."

"But that was before we knew I carried your child."

His jaw tightened. He had been a true fool to believe her when she swore she would take the potion of motherswort and angelica that would keep her from getting with child. He was even more the fool that he hadn't thought to connect the word "angelica" to Angelique as an omen. That woman had played him false as well. He narrowed his eyes. If Greer had lied about the potion, what else had she lied about?

"You told me you are descended from ancient

Celts whose women were allowed thigh freedom. How do I have proof the babe is mine?"

Instead of being insulted, she just shrugged. "You can ask around. I have not lain with another man."

"Not even Dion?" The man was already proving himself an irritant where Kendra was concerned, sitting at sup with her near every night, and he had no way of knowing how Adrian felt about her. But the man *was* very aware that Greer had warmed Adrian's bed frequently. In truth, he had fully expected Greer to be Dion's leman by the time he returned.

"Not even Dion." She gave Adrian another sideways glance. "Although he does seem to be very interested in that English tart you brought back."

He clenched his jaw again. "Lady Kendra is not a tart."

This time it was Greer who narrowed her eyes. "Is *she* the reason you do not want me in your bed?"

Suddenly it seemed overly warm and stifling in the tent. "She has nothing to do with my decision."

"No?" Greer studied him. "I think she has *everything* to do with your rejecting me. You spent nights on the road without a chaperone—"

"Hammish and Cullum were with us. We were not alone."

Her mouth curled, not in a pleasant way. "They're soldiers. You are their commander. Why would they try to stop you?"

They wouldn't have. Although Bruce had a steadfast rule that raids didn't include rape, he didn't stand in the way of his men taking their ease of willing wenches whenever the opportunity arose. Adrian had stumbled upon too many of them coupling in the bushes during celebrations to know that privacy wasn't an issue. Hammish and Cullum would just have pretended nothing untoward had occurred, had Adrian visited Kendra's tent. But it was her reputation he wanted to protect.

"She is a lady and was treated as such."

"We both know *ladies* take lovers." Greer's eyes turned to slits. "Were you really rescuing her from a marriage she didn't want? Or because you wanted her yourself?"

"Your jealousy is uncalled for."

"Jealous? I only seek to protect what is mine. *You* are *mine*."

"I was never *yours*. I cannot be owned." Adrian shook his head. "Your possessive nature is not attractive. It's what killed anything between us."

Her eyes opened and she smiled. "There. You just admitted there is something between us."

"What *was* between us was only lust. When you first came to my bed and offered yourself, I told you that physical pleasure was all I would give."

She laid a hand on his shoulder. "And we can have that physical pleasure again. Right now."

"No." He shook her hand off this time. "Whatever we had is done. It is *over*."

"What of the child?"

Adrian ran a hand through his hair. "I will provide for it."

"And me?"

"And you. Find a cottage in a village you like, and I will make sure all of your needs are met."

Greer smiled again. "*All* my needs, my lord?"

He sighed. "All of your financial needs."

"But I don't want your coin." She moved closer. "I want *you*."

"I have already given you that answer."

"Have you? I think not." Raising on tiptoe, she grasped his face with both hands and kissed him. "Let me show you the real answer."

"*No*." He pulled her hands down and stepped away. "You need to leave."

"Leave?" Her eyes narrowed again. "Are you waiting for that bitch to come to you?"

"That's enough."

"Really?" Her eyes became slits once more. "Was that the noise you heard? Your paramour was waiting outside your tent?"

Adrian pulled back the flap. "I said *go*."

Greer hesitated, then she flounced past him. "We'll see how she feels when she finds out I'll be the mother of your child."

He stared after her as she left. He had no reason to believe—or hope—that Kendra would have come to see him. But when he'd heard the sound, the hair at his nape had prickled like it always did when something was about to go wrong.

Mon Dieu! What if she had heard what Greer had said? He let the flap close and slumped onto his cot. Nothing in that conversation would be construed as positive, although if he were given a chance to explain the entire set of circumstances, perhaps Kendra would understand. Or not.

He could hardly ask if she'd been lurking outside his tent. He knew for sure how she'd react to such an accusation. And, given that Dion was acting like Sir Galahad around her, Adrian didn't want to appear like the conniver Modred.

But what to do? He wished he knew the answer.

****

The atmosphere at the camp turned quite animated and jovial over the next few days. The entire place bustled. Some of the women laundered and mended every piece of clothing the men would take on their raiding, and others were baking dozens of oatcakes and drying strips of game that came from the morning hunting expeditions. In the afternoons, the men sharpened swords and prepared their other weapons. Provisions, not only for the men leaving but for everyone remaining behind, were piled up everywhere. It was almost as if they were preparing for a siege.

But the horsemen were the ones who drew Kendra's attention. She stood at the fence separating the pasture from the rest of the camp to observe. There were nearly a hundred of them—Adrian commanded a score-and-five—and they seemed to be an elite group. They practiced what appeared to be jousts of sorts, although she got the impression it was more of an exercise to train the horses at close-combat battle than to actually unseat anyone. A quintain had also been set up at one end of the field for tilting, although they used swords instead of lances to strike the wooden shield that served as the target.

"He is wonderful to behold, isn't he?"

Kendra didn't have to turn around to know who spoke nor did she have to ask who "he" was. Greer seemed to be everywhere she was the past few days.

"The men are highly trained."

Greer laughed. "Of course they are."

As much as she would prefer to have no

conversation with Adrian's leman, at least the topic seemed safe enough. "I never heard that Robert Bruce commanded an actual cavalry."

Greer gave her a long look. "He doesn't."

"What do you mean? It is obvious they know how to fight on horseback."

"That's because many of them were impoverished knights in France who decided to seek their fortunes over here."

Kendra remembered that the countess had referred to Adrian as a knight, although he didn't say so himself. Why would he not? She felt her eyes widen. "Are they mercenaries?"

"I suppose you could call them that." Greer shrugged. "No one has really ever said."

She hated to ask, but she had to know. "Are they actually going into battle this time instead of just raiding?"

"I don't know." Greer slanted a sly glance at her. "Adrian and I have more interesting things to discuss."

She knew she shouldn't let the barb sting her, but it did, just the same. Although Greer hadn't actually announced she was with child, she managed to caress her stomach and smile contentedly whenever she was near, which had been often the past few days. Kendra had started to avoid taking her meals in the large tent because she didn't want to watch Adrian sharing his trencher with his leman. Just the thought of it made her lose her own appetite and made her feel slightly nauseous.

"I am sure you do." She turned away from the fence. "I have dallied long enough. I need to join the women at the river laundering clothes."

"Don't let me keep you, then."

From anyone else, it would have been a reply of accord, but Kendra knew full well coming from Greer it was a dismissal. Not that she cared. Any excuse to put distance between them was a good one.

"Ye should nae let the witch bother ye," Fiona said a couple of hours later after they'd taken down clothing that had been drying.

"Why do you think that I do?" Kendra asked as she folded linens.

"Ye are as easy to read as a book once I learned my letters."

Embarrassment seeped over her. What if Adrian could tell too? "You are saying my expressions give me away?"

Fionna grinned. "We Scots can be a dour lot, but ye French are not."

She supposed she did cling to some of her French ways in spite of living in England for the past several years. She certainly had never learned to be stoic. Maybe if she had, this whole business with Adrian and Greer wouldn't bother her so much. But better to steer away from that.

"I watched the horsemen practicing. Did your father mention anything about an actual battle this time?"

Fiona shook her head. "The horsemen always practice, but they doona ride out in armor."

Kendra raised a brow. "Why not? They'd be better protected."

"I heard my father tell my mother once that Robert Bruce wants to keep them a secret until he needs them to force the English from our land."

"I suppose that makes sense. I am almost certain King Edward knows nothing of a Scottish cavalry."

"And our king took a risk on allowing ye to come here." Fiona studied her. "If ye actually need proof that Adrian cares about ye, that is it."

Kendra forced a smile. She hadn't told Fiona what she'd overheard. Even if he did care—even a little—nothing would change between them. And even if he had sounded angry over the news, Greer was going to be the mother of his child. He wouldn't abandon her.

"There ye go again."

"What?"

"Ye look like a thundercloud about to burst open."

"I do not!"

"Then stop your frowning." Fiona picked up some linens and thrust them into Kendra's arms. "Why do ye nae take these to Adrian's tent? 'Tis well known he likes to wash after practice." She winked. "Mayhap ye can get a nice glimpse of him."

Kendra felt herself color. "Fiona!"

"What?" The girl gave her an innocent look.

"I…shouldn't—"

"Why nae?" Fiona asked.

"What if Greer is already there?" Lord, the last thing she needed was to overhear another conversation like the last one.

"Fie! Are ye just going to let the witch win, then?"

"No, but—"

"Then 'tis settled." Fiona suddenly made a dire face and clutched her stomach. "I feel an ague coming on and need to find the healer."

Kendra shook her head, trying not to smile at her friend's antics. But…if Fiona could distract Greer, perhaps it *was* time she had a talk with Adrian. It was what she had intended to do several nights ago. She couldn't hear any worse news than she already had. Besides, the men were supposed to leave tomorrow. She didn't want to wait to talk until they got back. "You're sure you can keep her away?"

"Have faith." Fiona gave her a little push. "Be gone with ye."

Kendra held the stack of linens close as she made her way across camp. She didn't want to look too obvious about where she was heading nor did she want to be intercepted. The horses were back in the pasture, and most of the knights were walking back to the tents they shared. She didn't see Adrian, so maybe he was already in his. If not, she would wait for him. They would have this conversation.

Still, as she approached, she listened for any strain of conversation. It was silent save for some rustling around that he was doing inside. Perhaps he was getting clean clothing out of a trunk? The thought that he might be partially unrobed made her think of the night they spent together completely naked. Her entire body heated, and she pushed back the flap to step inside and then stopped so abruptly she almost tripped over her feet.

Adrian was wrapped only in a towel, his naked back to her, but he had been delving into the trunk by the foot of his bed. Only he was not fetching clean clothing. Instead he held a white mantle with a large red cross emblazoned on it. As a child in France, she'd seen the familiar garment often.

Templar.

****

Adrain whipped his head around at the sound of the tent flap opening and pushed the mantle into the trunk at the same time. He looked as guilty as a child trying to conceal stolen scones. He straightened, silent.

She felt her face pale as she looked at the closed trunk. Her gaze finally shifted to his face.

"You are a Knight Templar."

It wasn't a question, but he nodded anyway. "*Oui.*"

"*Pourquoi?*"

He raised one brow. "Why? Why am I a Templar?"

She shook her head. "Why did you not tell me?" When he didn't answer immediately, she asked, "Were you *ever* going to tell me?"

"Ah…Yes. Eventually." He hesitated, then shrugged helplessly. "I don't know. Maybe."

Her eyes burned. "I *trusted* you."

"I knew how much you hated Templars because of your father. You felt very strongly that the Templars were the cause of your father's downfall." He looked miserable. "I didn't want to lose you."

She opened her mouth. Closed it. Frowned. He had a point. She had been vocal about her feelings. More than once. Often. But…after getting to know Adrian— and not just in the carnal sense—she couldn't hold him accountable. And, she realized, she couldn't hold *any* of the Templars accountable. They may have lent her father money, but no one had forced him to wager it away. That was her father's weakness. Not that she could actually blame her father either. He had loved her mother. He'd been lost without her.

"You're angry. I don't blame you."

Blame again. She blinked. She couldn't blame the Templars. She couldn't blame her father. Why should she blame Adrian? He'd withheld information from her, true. But he'd also known how she'd react. Suddenly, it felt like a great weight had been she lifted from her shoulders.

"It's true that I did hate Templars, but I realize I was wrong." She gave him a tentative smile. "I don't want to lose you either."

He grinned, a relieved expression crossing his face. "That is good to hear."

"Hmmm, well." She was still trying to sort out her feelings. Changing the subject might be best. "Are all the horsemen Templars?"

Adrian hesitated. He looked like he didn't want to answer that question. She supposed she might not either, if she were in his shoes. Even though Edward had declined to take orders from either the Pope or the French king in rounding up exiled Templars, if he found out they were supporting Robert Bruce, the king might well change his mind.

"Not all of them," he finally said.

"I suppose Remy and Pierre are." She considered. "And Dion?"

"Why do you ask about him?"

She was a little surprised because of the vehemence in his tone. Was he jealous?

He sighed. "Unfortunately, yes."

She felt amusement flicker in her eyes and tried not to notice as he adjusted the towel to hide his increasing arousal...which she was very aware of, at the moment.

"There is a past history that has nothing to do with you." That sounded a bit petulant. "Just because we are brethren doesn't mean we have to like each other."

"So I gathered." She looked at the closed trunk. "I

assume Robert Bruce knows?"

"He does."

She paused. "Does Greer know?" she finally asked.

"No. She thinks we are only knights errant."

"You never..." She felt her cheeks color. "...told her?"

"It was never her business."

Kendra stared at him. "But she is going to have your child!"

****

Adrian almost choked at her words. So she had heard the conversation. Or at least, a part of it. Why had she been lurking outside his tent? Had she actually been coming to see him? The thought made his groin swell instantly, but he managed to quell his spontaneous lust. Kendra needed an answer.

"When Greer first came to me, I told her we would only share bed sport. That she would have no claims on me. She agreed, and I was fool enough to believe her when she said she would take a potion that would prevent getting with child. She obviously lied." He took a deep breath. "I will provide for the child, of course."

She nodded, but she looked down. "I would expect you to."

He put a hand under her chin and lifted it. "I care about you, Kendra."

Her eyes searched his face. "I care about you too."

"Let me show you how much I want you." He moved closer. "My bed is comfortable enough."

Shaking her head, she stepped back. "I will not be another leman."

"You mean more to me than that."

"I cannot share your bed when another woman is

bearing your child." She set the linens down and turned. "I should go."

"Wait." He caught her arm and then released it when she stiffened. "I meant what I said. I would not have taken the chance on bringing you here if I didn't care greatly."

"And I am grateful." She focused on his face. "There are a number of men here who don't think an Englishwoman can be trusted, even if she is fleeing Edward's court."

"I don't care what they think." He smiled a little. "Besides, Robert allowed it."

She studied him again. "You do know you can trust me? I would never, ever betray you."

"I believe you." He looked deep into her eyes. "To prove how much—and how much you mean to me—I will tell you a carefully guarded secret."

"A secret?" Kendra looked intrigued.

For just a moment, he questioned his own wisdom in revealing it, but he had to convince her, somehow, that she was more important to him than Greer.

"You have heard of the treasure that was taken when the Templars fled France three years ago?"

"*Oui.* It was one of the reasons Philippe sent the edict to Edward to capture you." Her eyes widened. "Is it here?"

He shook his head. "Henri St. Clair met us in Orkney. He has guarded the treasure ever since."

"I thought there might be a reason for Pierre to stop at Roslin on our way here. And you came there too." She frowned. "Are you telling me the Earl of Orkney and Baron of Roslin is a Templar too?"

"*Non.*" He hesitated. The St. Clair connection to

269

the Templars was not his to divulge. "Henri's ancestors fought alongside the Conqueror. He still has family in Normandy who are...were...related to one of the original Templars. So we sought refuge with him."

"I see." She pondered for a moment and then smiled. "Thank you for trusting me with your secret."

He smiled too. "That is not the whole tale."

She gave him a surprised look. "What else?"

He paused for a fleeting second, then went on. "One of the pieces of treasure is a relic we consider sacred. Legend says if it is carried into battle, the bearer will be the victor."

Kendra smiled again. "Kind of like King Arthur wielding Excalibur?"

"Something like that." He tilted his head to the side. "In a way, Robert Bruce is much like Arthur. He wants to unite all of Scotland and live in peace."

"I know," she replied. "I think King Arthur agrees with him."

Adrian grinned. "You do?"

She shrugged. "I saw the shadow of a king behind him the first time we met."

His grin widened. "Why am I not surprised?" Then he sobered and looked around. "There aren't any ghosts in here now, are there?"

"Of course not. Why would you ask?"

"Because I don't want anyone—living or dead— watching what we do next."

She finally glanced down at his towel and then gave him a wary look. "Which is?"

"Come here and find out."

Chapter Twenty-Three

She should not obey. She should leave. Turn around and walk—maybe run—out of the tent. He could offer her no more than a few minutes' pleasure. There certainly was no future for them, that was clear. Even as those thoughts flitted through her head, her feet were moving toward him. Then he closed the distance in two strides, and she was in his arms. And she nearly wept with relief.

Nothing had ever felt so good—so *right*—as being in Adrian's embrace. Her hands slid across his bare, muscled chest to wind around his neck as she turned her face upward to receive his kiss. There was nothing gentle or tentative about it. His mouth was as hard and demanding as his manhood pressed against her hip. She shifted so could rub her belly across it and was rewarded with a raw moan.

"Forget the bed," Adrian growled as he dropped the towel and delved into her mouth to deepen the kiss.

Her tongue frantically did battle with his. She felt his hands hike her skirts before he lifted her and wrapped her legs around his waist. The thick head of his shaft swept her wetness once, slicking her folds, and then he drove inside her, filling her completely.

Kendra cried out in joy and clutched him as he ground into her, his thrusts hard, fast and deep. Her climax built like a rogue wave out of nowhere, its intensity rising as every fiber in her being responded to the plundering between her legs. The room began to swim, even though her eyes were closed, and then the wave crested, flooding her with pure ecstasy just as his hot seed spurted into her.

For a long moment, they clung to each other, and then she felt his hold lessen as he gently slid her legs to the ground. She mewled her discontentment and heard him chuckle.

"I am not through with you yet, *ma chérie*."

Kendra heard the words through her fog-filled mind. "You aren't?"

"Not by the length of a bow shot," he answered and led her to his bed. "I want to pleasure you until there is no doubt in your mind that I care."

"That may take some time, my lord."

"It that a challenge?"

"Perhaps."

He grinned and laid her on the bed, spreading her legs wide as he settled between them. "Then we had better begin."

She was already convinced, but then, who was she to argue?

****

Adrian ignored Greer's sullen looks the next morning as he sat down with Pierre and Remy to break his fast. Neither he nor Kendra had made an appearance at sup the night before, and no doubt their absence had been noted.

He probably should have used a bit more discretion and insisted they take their meal, but Kendra had been reluctant to leave his bed, and he had been equally reluctant to allow her to do so, since Robert was ready to ride this morning.

Remy smirked at him. "You have the look of a man satisfied."

"And by the look on Greer's face, I would wager she wasn't the one who did it," Pierre added with his own grin.

"How could she be," Remy went on when Adrian remained silent, "when Fiona insisted she'd eaten bad food and needed Greer to stay beside her all night?"

Adrian almost choked on the piece of meat he'd been chewing. *Mon Dieu!* He had not even given a thought to Greer last night. If she had come to his tent, she would have made Kendra's life miserable the entire time they'd be gone. Which might be weeks, since Robert intended to prove to Edward the practicality of signing a truce.

He looked around for Fiona but didn't see her. "How ill is the girl?"

Remy shrugged. "She seemed fine yesterday afternoon."

He was getting a sneaking suspicion that Kendra's arrival at his tent might have been more planned than he'd thought. Not that he minded the outcome. Still, if there was bad food had, some of the men might be getting sick as well.

"Are you sure? It is not like Greer to spend hours attending someone."

"You can thank Robert for that," Pierre said.

Luckily, Adrian hadn't taken another bite or he surely would have choked. It was quite possible the king had figured out there was something between them, but he'd never known him to play matchmaker. "Robert made Greer stay?"

"In a roundabout way," Pierre answered. "Fiona was carrying on, and her mother got hysterical, insisting she was not having her husband ride off to raid and leave his possibly dying daughter behind."

Remy nodded. "And Bruce needs all his captains, so he ordered Greer not to leave Fiona's side."

"Ah." It seemed Adrian owed Fiona—and her mother—a great deal of thanks. "I hope she is recovered, then."

"Greer wouldn't be here if she were not." Pierre looked around. "But I do not see Kendra."

Remy grinned. "Is she recovering too?"

He felt his face warm even as another part of his anatomy stirred. Kendra probably was sore after the entire night spent making love. But that wasn't why she was absent from the tent. When she'd left him just before dawn, she'd told him she didn't like goodbyes, and she'd rather remember their last moments as private. Not that he was going to share that information with his two friends.

"She is probably checking on Fiona." It would be a good guess that the two were probably chortling over how successful their subterfuge had been.

"So you are not going to admit Kendra spent the night with you?" Remy gave him a speculative look. "Not that we need your confession."

"I have no comment."

"But have a care," Pierre said.

Adrian frowned. "What is that supposed to mean?"

"Do not forget that she is Pembroke's niece, which makes her English as well as French." He paused. "And that she hates Templars."

"Pierre is right. If she found out who we are…"

Remy let the sentence drift.

Adrian hoped it wasn't a question, since he didn't want to answer it. Kendra had discovered the fact by accident, but in truth, he had admitted to it as well. He trusted her, but he knew many in the camp did not. "Our identity has been kept secret for over three years. It will remain so."

And then, miraculously, he was saved from further inquisition by the sound of the horn calling the men to arms. He pushed back his plate and rose. "Bruce is ready to ride."

A short time later, the men began to ride out, flanked on either side by soldiers left to guard the camp and by women—wives waving teary farewells and camp followers shouting bawdy comments—but Kendra was not among them.

Adrian was about to ride through the pass when he looked back one final time. Kendra stood at the entrance of the great tent, watching him, but just as he raised his hand to wave, she stepped inside and disappeared from his sight.

He dropped his hand, feeling strangely unsettled as he rode on.

****

The camp seemed empty with Adrian gone, although a good two score soldiers remained. Many of the camp followers had trailed after the army, but some of them remained. After a week or two, arguments began to break out between the harlots and the wives, the latter accusing the former of not helping with any of the chores that they'd been assigned while the king was in attendance. Everyone was expected to share the workload.

Kendra made sure she did her part. She helped prepare food, and every Wednesday, she joined several of the women who did laundry. Since it was easier to clean the clothes by brushing them over rocks, they usually went outside the pass to where the brook had not yet widened into a river. It gave her an opportunity to walk through the village. Since Adrian left, the camp enclosure had felt too confining.

But what she enjoyed most was joining the two men who did the hunting in the nearby woods. At first, they'd simply laughed at her, but that stopped once she'd demonstrated her archery skills. In one morning, they could easily bring in enough meat to feed what was left of the camp for a week.

"'Tis hard to believe the men have been gone nearly two months," one of the women said one day as they gathered dirty utensils after the midday meal. "I wonder how much longer they'll be."

"The last report we had said Robert Bruce was bedeviling Edward by striking from Dumfermline to Dundee." Kendra had to smile as she recalled the tidings—delivered by a Scottish lad whose whiskers had not grown in yet, but who was puffed up with importance at delivering the news—that the raids happening simultaneously in different areas would make Edward think the Scottish army was much bigger than it was, thanks to the small groups of mounted Templars being able to cover ground quickly.

"My mother is afraid the king means to continue north, maybe all the way to Aberdeen, before he returns," Fiona replied. "If that is so, they may be gone for another two or three months."

"Surely not so long." Greer patted her rounded

belly. "Adrian will return for the birth of his child."

Kendra forced herself to keep her expression impassive. It was a skill she was learning to perfect since Greer took every opportunity to remind her that she was carrying Adrian's child. And, with her belly becoming more pronounced each day, Kendra could no longer deny the fact. It actually made her slightly nauseous whenever she saw it.

They'd just finished tidying the large tent when the clatter of horses' hooves could be heard coming through the pass. Since neither of the guards posted on top of the tall rocks signaled a warning, Kendra assumed it was probably another messenger. She hurried outside along with the rest of the women.

She didn't recognize the messenger, but his accent didn't have the heavy burr of the Highlands. He sounded more like a Lowlander, which wasn't surprising since Robert himself came from Arrandale. She moved as close as she could to the men already gathered around him.

"News from Bruce?" Hammish asked.

"News of a different sort." The man looked around, his gaze lingering on Kendra long enough that she became uneasy. "English scouts have been roaming the hills to the east and south of here."

"'Tis nae that unusual, is it? They hold Stirling Castle."

The rider shook his head. "They do not wear the king's uniform."

Hammish frowned. "Whose then?"

The man looked around the group again. "They wore the red and blue of the Earl of Pembroke."

Kendra's blood suddenly ran cold. So her uncle

was looking for her after all.

****

Ever since the messenger left nearly a week ago, Kendra had felt she was living on borrowed time. Her uncle probably was methodically combing the area from Edinburgh westward. She didn't know how many men Edward had given him leave to take, but how long would it be before they were in this very area?

"Doona fash so," Fiona said as they chopped vegetables for stew. "Ye will nae be found here."

"I hope not." The camp would be hard to find, but not impossible. "I know everyone blames me for them being in the area." She had tried to ignore the accusatory stares of some of the women as well as some of the soldiers.

"Robert Bruce himself gave ye sanctuary here," Fiona said stubbornly.

"But he is not here right now." That was her other big concern. "Only forty soldiers have remained to defend the camp."

"Forty-one," Fiona gave her a smile. "Ye are right good with a bow."

Kendra knew her friend was trying to make her feel better, so she forced a smile. She was no soldier. But she had put her bow to good use. The hunters were going out daily now to ensure enough meat could be cured and salted to allow them to stay inside the camp once the English soldiers were closer.

The women had been going out as well, to gather herbs and berries that grew in the woods. Greer was busy mixing potions and salves to take to the villagers since she wouldn't be able to leave the camp either. One thing Kendra was grateful for was the healer spending many of the afternoons in the village, most likely instructing the women how to use her remedies.

She feared for the villagers. Every last one of them was loyal to Robert Bruce and would not give away their location, but her uncle's men might ransack the place in retaliation for no information.

By the following Wednesday morning, supplies had been gathered and food stored. The women met near the camp entrance carrying more loads of laundry than usual. Hammish had told them this would be the last week they'd be going beyond the pass to wash clothing. Greer joined them late, holding two huge sacks.

As they walked toward the village and the brook, Kendra tried not to notice how much Greer was increasing. The baby would be due in less than two moons, and how she was going to cope with seeing Adrian's child, she didn't know.

She wished Fiona had come with them, since she could usually distract Kendra from such maudlin thoughts, but her mother had come down with a malady this morning, and Fiona had stayed behind to help cook.

Once they reached the burn, Kendra put her sack on the ground, not surprised when the other women moved farther downstream from her. Since the word had come of English troops having been seen, most of the women had taken to avoiding her. Only Greer remained close, and that was probably so she could talk about her child. Kendra was about to open her laundry sack when Greer placed a hand on her arm.

"This needs to be taken to Widow Murray." She handed Kendra one of the sacks. "I doona feel like walking that far."

"But I need to wash Fiona's and her mother's clothing as well as mine," Kendra said.

"I will take care of their clothing." Greer actually gave her a rare smile. "Ye do tend to tear holes in things."

Kendra felt her face warm because, unfortunately, Greer was right. Most of her own clothes had rips and tears because she hadn't managed the art of using the rocks properly. Fiona and her mother would probably be grateful to get theirs back intact.

"All right. Where does the widow live?"

"She is the last house past the stables."

Kendra took the sack and started walking. As she approached the village, she thought it a bit odd that no children were about, but their parents were probably keeping them busy hiding their own stores, should the English scouting parties come.

The house, at least, was easy to find. There was no missing the stench of the stables that housed livestock as well as horses. She walked past two that were tied to the hitching rail and up the short path to the widow's cottage. The door was opened immediately upon her knock by a small gray-haired woman leaning on a cane.

Kendra held out the bag. "Greer told me you were needing this."

"I do." She gestured with her free hand. "Would you mind putting it on the table right there?"

"Of course." Kendra stepped inside, blinded temporarily by the dimness after the bright sunshine outside. "I will—"

The rest of her words were cut off as someone grabbed her from behind and held a foul-smelling cloth to her nose. She clawed at the arm around her throat, but the hold was too strong, and the fumes overcame her as the world turned dark.

Chapter Twenty-Four

Adrian didn't think he'd ever been so glad to see Robert's camp as he did a week later when they rode through the pass as the sun was setting. They'd been raiding a little over two months, and he looked forward to not having to sleep on hard ground and keep a constant vigil.

But more importantly, he looked forward to seeing Kendra. Their night of lovemaking at the camp had only made him insatiable for more. All the while he'd been gone, he thought of her. Dreamt of her. Waited impatiently for this moment. All he needed was a bath first. He grinned. Why wait? Kendra could join him for his bath.

Women burst out of several tents as the horses clopped to a stop in the middle of the yard. He glanced over them quickly, looking for Kendra. Where was she?

Dismounting, he gave his stallion a pat and turned the reins over to a stable lad as he made his way toward the big tent. She was probably helping get the evening meal ready. Hammish stepped out just as he reached it.

"Is Kendra inside?"

Hammish took a deep breath. "The lass is gone."

Adrian stared at him. "Gone? What do you mean, *gone*? Is she in the village?"

Hammish shook his head. "She left."

He wasn't sure he heard correctly. "She left?

Where did she go?"

"We think she went home to Wales."

"Home? Wales?" Adrian repeated the words, but not understanding.

"Pembroke was looking for her. There were English soldiers everywhere."

"The soldiers came *here*?" He looked around quickly. Everything seemed to be normal. When Hammish shook his head again, Adrian nearly panicked. "They abducted her? *Mon Dieu*, I will get a fresh horse and—"

"They have more than a week's start on ye." Hammish paused. "We think she went willingly."

"*What*? Explain!"

"'Tis a long story. Perhaps we should have a dram or two—"

"Whisky later. Talk now."

Hammish sighed. "The women went to do the laundry. Kendra told Greer she had to take something to Widow Murray in the village. A short time later, two men were seen galloping away with the lass."

The hair at his nape began to prickle. "This is Greer's account? Did anyone question the widow?"

"I did, but she said two men she didn't know barged into her cottage earlier that day and told her they were expecting to meet someone. Gave her a coin for her trouble."

Adrian frowned. Something wasn't right. "Did Fiona go to the village with her?"

"No. Her mother woke up with a malady, so Fiona stayed here to do the cooking."

Fiona's mother was normally healthy as a horse. "What kind of malady?"

"'Twas something she ate the night before, she thought."

Something was really not right. His hair was practically standing on end. "No one else got sick?"

Hammish furrowed his brows. "Now that I think on it, nae."

He was beginning to suspect Greer had something to do with it. She had plenty of potions. And she resented Kendra... "Did you question anyone else?"

"Aye, I asked around. The other women doing laundry were too far away to hear anything, but they did see the lass leaving." Hammish hesitated again. "There is something else."

"What, for God's sake?"

"Lady Kendra took all her belongings."

Adrian nearly gaped at him, not quite comprehending. "Someone could have cleaned up afterwards."

"Some of the women went to her pallet right after they got back. There was nothing there." The Scot gave him a sympathetic look. "She probably put her things in one of the laundry sacks."

He ran a hand through his hair, not wanting to believe that Kendra left on her own accord, not after the night they'd spent together. Why would she? His nape began to prickle again. Had Greer made life so miserable for her while he was gone? If she did, she'd answer to him, babe or not. He narrowed his eyes. She hadn't come running out to greet him either. Was she fearing his wrath?

"Where is Greer?"

"In her tent, most likely abed," Hammish answered.

"With a lover?" He could only hope.

"Nae. Greer was the one who suggested they check for Lady Kendra's belongings and led the way to the women's tent. One of the ground pegs had come loose, and she tripped over it." Hammish gave Adrian a wary look. "She lost the babe the next morning."

****

Kendra's head pounded to a strange rhythm…one, two, *three*: one, two, *three*. Slowly she became aware of a sound accompanying the pattern. As her mind began to clear, she realized she was astride a horse, its hooves pounding the road at a steady pace.

She opened her eyes slowly, then quickly closed them as the scenery around her spun, the dizziness making her feel nauseous. A man she didn't know had her braced in front of him, and another horseman galloped alongside. *Mon Dieu*! Who had abducted her? And why? She decided to feign unconsciousness to find out what she could learn.

Unfortunately, the fast pace didn't encourage the men to talk. The jostling was getting uncomfortable too, since her thighs were hanging over the man's legs and she had no way to grip anything. She was about to give up her pretense when, what seemed like hours later, the horses finally slowed to a walk and then stopped.

"The lass is still out?" one of the men asked.

"Aye," the other answered. "She should be awake by now."

They were Scots, but what did they want with her? They couldn't have been from the village, for everyone there knew Robert Bruce had granted her sanctuary. Kendra kept her eyes closed, forcing herself to stay limp as the man dismounted and dragged her off the horse. She slumped to the ground, only to be pulled by her arms across grass and then propped up against what felt like tree bark.

"We canna just leave her here," the second man said.

The first one grunted. "Do ye want to be caught by the English patrol, then? This is where the lady witch said to bring her."

The lady witch? They must mean Greer. They'd obviously been waiting for her, and Greer was the one who'd told her to go the Widow Murray's.

"I doona like leaving a woman out here alone."

"We were nae paid to wait. The sooner the lass is back in English hands, the sooner the Welsh earl will call off his men."

"There is that," the second man seemed to agree. "Avoiding the regular redcoats 'tis difficult enough."

If they would just *leave*. Kendra didn't know where she was, but as soon as they were gone, she'd follow the road in the opposite direction and somehow make her way back to the camp.

The first one yanked her to a better sitting position, and as he did, a sharp stone pricked her leg. A loud groan escaped her lips before she could catch herself.

"She's waking up."

"Aye. Well, we canna leave her to wander about."

Something made a whooshing sound, and Kendra felt a rope being wrapped around her. Her eyes sprang open as she instinctively tried to fight off the bonds, but the man holding the rope only tightened it.

"How long have ye been awake?" the other one asked.

"Just…just now." Kendra looked from one to the

other, trying to note any special features, but they both had beards and the light brownish-red hair that was common in Scotland. Their clothing was nondescript as well...tattered braies, rather dirty muslin tunics with weathered leather vests. No distinguishing plaids to tell who they were. "Why are you doing this?"

"We mean ye nae harm, but ye put our king in danger with yer presence." The kinder man tossed the sack she'd originally taken to the widow's house on the ground. "Ye will find all your things in there."

"Enough blethering," the first one said and cocked an ear. "I hear hoof beats. We must be gone."

"But wait!" Kendra called out to no avail. The men had already rushed to their horses and in another moment, they were galloping away. She struggled against the rope that kept her bound to the tree. If she could only get away...

But it was too late. Her captors had barely disappeared around a bend when a half-score of English soldiers came into sight. Maybe she could concoct some sort of story and escape them as well.

Whatever hope she harbored for that disappeared as they drew closer. To her dismay, they wore the red and blue of her uncle's livery, although her uncle was not among them. One of them slid from his saddle.

"We have found her!" he said.

****

After talking with Hammish, Adrian approached Greer's tent with a mixture of anger and trepidation. He was sorry for the loss of the babe. Even if Greer had tricked him, the child would still have been his. But he was also angry because he suspected she had arranged Kendra's disappearance.

Greer turned from the small table in her tent that held an assortment of small jars as well as a mortar and pestle. She put the utensil down and smiled. "So you have finally returned."

"And too late, it seems, to have stopped Kendra's abduction."

The smile faded. "'Twas no abduction, my lord. She took all her things when we went to launder garments at the burn. Two men lay in wait to help her escape."

"So I've been told."

She arched a brow. "'Tis true. Ask any of the women who were with us."

"Hammish already did. All of them were too far away to hear what was said between you."

The brow went higher. "Ye think I lie?"

"I think you have cause to." Adrian glanced at her herbal jars. "I find it very suspicious that Fiona's mother took ill that morning so Fiona had to stay behind to help with the cooking."

Greer shrugged. "Perhaps a piece of meat was tainted."

"Yet no one else was affected?" He paused. "I find that very strange as well."

"I do not prepare the meals." Greer turned toward the table to arrange some jars. "She told me she was leaving because her uncle's troops were too close and she didn't want to risk the camp being found. Rather noble of her, I must say."

Adrian started. Was Greer telling the truth? He couldn't see her face as she spoke. It was possible that Kendra would do something like that to protect him. Them. All of them. It was also quite possible—and more likely, given her possessiveness—that Greer had made the arrangements to get rid of Kendra.

"Aren't you going to ask after the babe?"

He probably should offer condolences, but he found he couldn't do it. Not once he'd realized that Greer was as conniving as Queen Isabella. "Hammish told me you lost the child."

"I tripped over a tent peg. It had probably come loose in Kendra's haste to get away." She picked up one of the jars and turned to him. "But I have potions that can help me quicken again, my lord."

He grimaced. "Potions you used the first time too?"

She put the jar down and came closer. "I didn't have to." Smiling, she caressed his cheek. "Do you remember how much pleasure we shared? We can do so again."

Adrian stepped back from her touch. "As I told you before I left for Berwick, our affair is over."

"But it doesn't have to be."

"It *is*."

Greer's eyes turned to slits. "That English bitch is gone. For all we know, *she* lied to *me* and will turn traitor once she reaches her uncle—"

"Enough!" Her words had the impact of his stallion's hind hooves striking him. He would swear on his life that Kendra would never betray them, but what if her uncle managed to coerce the information from her? Adrian threw back the flap and strode from the tent.

She'd worn a blindfold for the closest part of the journey, so she didn't know precisely how to get to their camp. The village itself was obscure, with no name, as were many set among the hills, but Pembroke had a commander's well-honed instincts. Would he be able to find them?

Then again, Adrian didn't know how keen Pembroke was to continue the brutal war that Edward I had begun. The earl was part of a growing number of nobles who thought too much power was invested in the king, and he had, on several occasions, played the part of middleman between Edward II and Lancaster. Perhaps Greer had told the truth and Kendra had left of her own accord. With her return, her uncle might let things be.

But it would drive him mad if he didn't know for sure that was the case. Greer could have arranged for Kendra to be taken to the far Hebrides or sent to Orkney.

He ran a hand through his hair. It would take a good fortnight to ride to the southwestern tip of Wales where Pembroke Castle was situated, and another returning. He was captain of the right flank of Bruce's cavalry. Bruce would never give him leave for that long.

But Kendra was literate, and so was he. He could post a letter from the coaching inn that they used for their contacts. He would write in French for security reasons and ask her what her motivation had been. Adrian took a deep breath to quell the touch of panic he felt. He would also tell her he loved her and wanted her to be his woman forever…and, if she loved him too, he would make arrangements to bring her back.

Writing that letter would be the most courageous thing he'd ever done. But he had to know. He *had* to.

****

As much as Kendra had longed to ride her horse

across the moors of western Wales once more, this wasn't the homecoming she'd wanted.

She looked out her bedchamber window at Pembroke Castle to Cleddau Estuary below. Although the water here was tranquil, in the far distance she could hear the pounding of the sea as it crashed on rocky shores. She grimaced, thinking how much the two bodies of water reflected herself. Outwardly, she gave the appearance of being calm. Inwardly, her soul seethed with a restlessness that could not be stilled.

She had been back nearly two months. The English soldiers had taken her to Stirling Castle when they'd found her. Her uncle and aunt arrived a day later, and she remembered the entire conversation.

"Do you have any idea of how you disgraced us by running away?" her aunt had asked.

"I told you I would not marry Gerard de Nogaret," she'd answered.

Her uncle had waved a dismissive hand. "That is no longer of concern. He went back to France."

Before Kendra could breathe a sigh of relief, he'd also added, "Who helped you?"

"Helped me?"

Pembroke had given an exasperated sigh. "If there is one thing you aren't, it's stupid. You could not have left Berwick on your own and found your way past Stirling without help. Was it de Soules?"

"We were accosted on the road and Adrian was injured. How could he have helped me?"

Her uncle looked like he didn't believe her, but he let the question go.

"Where have you been?"

She'd lifted her chin. "At Robert Bruce's camp."

That had piqued her uncle's interest. "Where is it?"

"I do not know. I was blindfolded on the way there." That was at least true.

"Why were you taken there?"

"To be used as a hostage, probably." A small lie, perhaps.

Pembroke looked suspicious. "Why did we never receive a ransom note then?"

She'd raised her chin a little higher. "Because I begged him to let me stay."

"You did what?" Her aunt reached for smelling salts. "And why?"

"I already told you. I wouldn't marry Gerard. Nobody would listen to me."

Her uncle considered her thoughtfully. "How then did you come to be tied to a tree along an English patrol route weeks later?"

She'd paused. "Someone obviously didn't want an Englishwoman lingering at the camp. I was betrayed."

"By whom?"

"I don't know."

But she did know. Greer had planned the whole thing, right down to packing all of Kendra's things in the sack she'd so unwittingly taken with her to Widow Murray's.

What had Adrian thought when he returned? Would he believe she'd left on her own?

On the entire journey to Wales, she'd hoped he'd somehow magically appear like one of King Arthur's knights to rescue her from her escort. Her mind told her that was impossible since he didn't even know what had happened, but her heart held hope.

Once she'd arrived home, she foolishly wished and prayed for a messenger to arrive with some word from him. The night they'd spent making love had also been the night he admitted he was a Templar. He had trusted her with his secrets. Surely, he would not have done that if he didn't care?

Another thought struck her numb. Did he think she might turn traitor? Use her knowledge that the Templars still survived? That it was the reason she left...to inform Edward—or worse, send word to King Philippe? If Adrian thought that, he'd hate her now.

The idea made her nauseous and she hurried over to the chamber pot to cast up the contents of her breakfast. Then she sank onto a chair, feeling vaguely fatigued.

She needed to face the truth. By now, Adrian would have returned to camp. Word would have spread that Kendra had arranged for two men to escort her back to England. Greer would be about to deliver his child to him. And that was the truth Kendra did not want to face. Adrian owed his allegiance to the woman who bore his child, regardless of his affections for her. More importantly, Adrian would want to raise his son.

He would not be coming for her.

But there was another truth she could not put off any longer. Her listlessness could no longer be attributed to feeling depressed. There had been too many mornings that she had been ill, and her courses had not come since she'd returned home.

She suspected she was about to bear Adrian a child too.

Chapter Twenty-Five

London
Spring, 1314

"Leave the candle burning, Mama," four-year-old Owen mumbled sleepily.

Kendra patted her son's downy curls, the same raven color as his father's. "I will, sweetheart."

"Can you read me a story too?"

"Not tonight." She tucked the blanket under his small chin. "Queen Isabella insists I attend her."

He pouted. "I don't like the queen."

I don't either, she thought as she stepped into the hall and closed the door to the small chamber she shared with Owen. Edward had been tolerant enough to allow her son to stay with her, but the queen had made clear motherhood was not to interfere with Kendra's duties as one of her attendants.

Not that she wanted that role, although her aunt reminded her frequently how grateful she should be to have the position. She hated London with its noise and crowded, dirty streets, but since Lancaster had abducted and subsequently executed Piers Gaveston while he had been in her uncle's custody two years ago, the earl had become a staunch supporter of the king. Hence their move to London.

Kendra missed the freedom she'd had in Wales. To

prevent scandal, her aunt had quickly spread the word—before the fact she was with child became visible—that she had married a minor Border lord who'd been killed in battling the Scots. Thankfully, the Welsh had a tendency to mind their own business and had not questioned the story. For good measure, her uncle had suggested she give the child a solid Welsh name as well. Owen had not been quite a year old when she took him for his first ride across the moors, and he'd squealed with delight. She'd hoped to give him his own pony for this fourth birthday, but the move to London had cancelled that.

The only good thing about being at the English court was that she could keep informed as to what was happening in Scotland. Robert Bruce had gained more followers—and land—over the past three years. There had been several missives from Scottish envoys, including one from Adrian, offering peace treaties, but Edward, not willing to relinquish any more power than had already been taken away by the Ordinances of 1311, refused to meet with any of them.

Other than Adrian's missive, which she hadn't actually seen, she'd had no word of him. Shortly after Owen was born, she'd written to tell him he had a child, much to her aunt's dismay, but she'd received no reply. The hurt had eventually given way to resignation. She was the niece and ward of one of the most powerful earls in England, and by now Robert Bruce would have learned of Pembroke's reinforced allegiance to the king. There would be no way he'd allow her back into his camp even if she could find it.

And the cold, hard truth was that Adrian probably had several children with Greer. Kendra's own night of lovemaking with him would be just a distant memory by now.

As she made her way toward the stairs that led to the queen's chambers, she became aware of the din of noise from the hall below. It was louder than the usual after-dinner lingering that took place. Had a messenger arrived? Perhaps with news of Scotland? In spite of her resolve to accept her circumstances, she still didn't want to miss any word of Adrian.

In her free time, she'd explored much of the Tower with Owen and discovered a number of hidey-holes where she could eavesdrop on conversations. She felt no qualms about doing so as she hurried to the nearest one.

"Roxburgh Castle has been taken?" King Edward sounded both incredulous and angry. "It was impregnable and well-guarded! How in thunder did it happen?"

She couldn't see the messenger, but she heard the quiver in his voice.

"Cows, Your Majesty."

"Cows?" The king's voice rose nearly an octave. "Cows?"

There was a slight hesitation as if the other man was collecting himself. "Sir James Douglas and Walter Stewart disguised some of their soldiers as cows and were able to approach the walls without notice."

A longer pause ensued before the king spoke again.

"You are telling me a handful of soldiers captured Roxburgh?"

"They did have the element of surprise, Your Majesty. Once the walls were breached, the gates were flung open, and the rest of the Scottish army rushed in."

"English casualties?" That question came from her uncle.

"Hundreds, I was told, my lord."

"Hundreds?" Edward thundered again. "According to my information, Douglas and Stewart don't have hundreds of men between them. How could they inflect so much damage?"

More silence. Then, "I was told a band of well-trained cavalry rode with them."

The voices faded away as Kendra's ears began to buzz. Or maybe it was her head. *Well-trained cavalry.* The French knights—she still suspected they were all Templars—at Bruce's camp were well-trained cavalry. Had Adrian ridden with them?

And how much danger had they put themselves in by razing a nearly undefeatable castle? How much more would Edward take before he decided to march north again?

****

"You did well!" Robert handed a tankard of ale to James Douglas and another to Adrian, then held up his own in toast. "Roxburgh stands no more."

"Aye!" The chorus went up from the men surrounding them in the camp's main tent. "To the Black Douglas!"

Adrian quaffed his ale, wishing he felt as ecstatic over the recent victory as the rest of Bruce's men. It had been nothing short of miraculous, given the strong garrison quartered at Roxburgh. Douglas' plan had been brilliant. They'd lost few men, overall, and none of the elite cavalry that had distracted the archers on the battlements.

But the thrill of victory—even the highly likely

Scottish independence that loomed closer with each battle won—didn't fill the emptiness that he felt inside. He knew he was being foolish to keep thinking about Kendra. He'd lost count of the times he'd cursed himself for caring. Nearly four years had passed. She'd never answered his letter. After all this time, he no longer expected it, but the memory of the first time he'd seen her at Berwick, looking like an ethereal forest nymph, stayed with him.

"'Tis nae every day we bring a castle down, and ye are nae even smiling," Hammish remarked under the din of voices as he gave Adrian a sideways glance. "And here I thought we Scots were the stoic ones."

Adrian shrugged. "I am glad all went well."

"Now ye sound as if ye were discussing reiving a cow or two instead of the most important battle in two years. If it had not been for your horsemen—"

"The accolades go to the Douglas. The disguise was his idea."

"I am nae talking about that, although I doona deny it. I saw how close ye rode to the wall. 'Twas like ye were darin' the devil himself."

He shrugged again. "The closer I rode, the more the English focused on me."

"Aye, but ye could have as easily been killed, had the devil won." Hammish finished his ale. "Sometimes I think ye doona care if he does win."

He forced a smile. "I wouldn't be much good to Bruce dead, would I?"

Hammish shook his head, although Adrian wasn't sure whether it was in agreement or in reprimand. Over the last three years, he'd spent hours honing his already excellent skills with knife and sword and lance until no one—even Robert—could best him. He'd taken more risks than he'd allowed his men to do, as well. He'd dismounted in battle to take part in hand-to-hand combat, willingly taking on two or three English soldiers at a time. His weapons were an extension of his body, and he moved with the efficient ferocity of a predator. The men had taken to calling him "the wolf," but maybe that was because he preferred to be alone these days, like a lobo.

"I think ye need a woman," Hammish said.

"And I think you need more ale."

Hammish gave him an intent look before he nodded and turned away. That was another thing men did these days. Not engage him in idle conversation. And no one, except for the stubborn Scot, gave him advice.

Unfortunately, Adrian had discovered months ago that taking a woman to bed didn't fix what was wrong with him. Greer had moved away from the camp once she realized he would not fall prey to her twice, but there were plenty of others who let him know they were available. He'd initially been attracted to two or three that had long, reddish-blonde hair and green eyes, but he'd soon found the looks didn't matter. These days, to keep up appearances—or to keep from maiming half of Bruce's army for insinuations that something was *wrong* with him—he invited a harlot to his tent where he poured her wine, gave her a coin, and had her leave an hour later.

Oddly enough, after he'd done that once or twice, he had even more women waiting for him.

"De Soules!"

He snapped out of his miserable reverie at the

sound of the Douglas' voice. The man motioned him over, then clapped him on the back. "The king and I were discussing Edinburgh. Do ye think we can take it?"

"The Rock? That would be as difficult as trying to take Stirling."

"That's the point," Robert said. "Those two castles are the last ones standing in our way. If we can take the Rock, Stirling would be next."

"And we will send the English running with their tails between their legs," James added.

"Umm." Adrian looked from one man to the other. "If you attack Edinburgh, you will force Edward to re-engage in the war."

Bruce waved a hand dismissively, somehow managing not to spill his ale. "We've offered him enough opportunities to treaty. I want to end this."

"Aye!" Voices rose again. "To Edinburgh!"

"To Stirling!"

"To Scotland!"

"And to our true king," Douglas said. "Robert Bruce."

Adrian nodded as he looked at the jubilant men around him. Edward moving north would mean Pembroke would march beside him. Would there somehow be a chance for him to meet with the man and inquire… He cursed silently.

Damn him for caring about Kendra.

Scotland had a war to win.

****

From beneath her lashes, Kendra watched Queen Isabella lounging on her chaise in the solar, a small smile playing on her lips. She definitely looked like a cat who'd found an open door to the creamery. It was also an expression that usually meant she had found something to goad Kendra about while the other ladies looked on and twittered.

It didn't take long for her to find out what it was. The queen produced a letter from the folds of her skirt which clearly showed the broken seal of the king of France. She held it up.

"I am thinking of visiting my father in France, since Edward is getting ready for another dreary march north to fight the barbarians again. I should like all my ladies to attend me."

While there were excited exclamations from the others, Kendra's heart sank. Going to France would mean leaving Owen behind, since the queen had made it abundantly clear she would not tolerate the interruption of small children amongst her ladies. And, as the Earl of Pembroke's niece, Kendra couldn't refuse to attend the queen without creating a scandal of epic proportions.

Word had arrived just yesterday that Edinburgh Castle had been captured by an elite band of thirty men scaling the north face of the rock—Kendra suspected Adrian might have been involved—so who knew how long Edward would be gone. Without the king at court, Isabella couldn't very well entertain and might quite easily decide to spend months in Paris until the Scottish war was finally won.

That meant months of leaving her son in the custody of her aunt, who had little patience with curious children. Noting the queen's smirk of satisfaction about her plight, Kendra masked her own dismay.

Isabella unfolded the single piece of vellum. "My

father writes that Jacques de Molay, the Grand Master of those heretical Templars, was finally burned at the stake a fortnight ago."

"Good riddance!" one of her ladies exclaimed while several others nodded vigorously.

Kendra bit her lip to keep from responding. Had that news reached the Scottish camp? How would Adrian and the others react? She tried to keep her expression as impassive as she could.

Apparently, the queen wasn't quite finished, though.

"My father has also written Edward to finish flushing out any of the heretics that crossed the Channel."

One of the ladies' rounded her eyes. "Does he think we have *Templars* living in our midst?"

"Here? In London?" another asked.

"I hardly think in London," Isabella answered, "but these recent Scottish victories in which small, specialized bands of men were able to defeat large garrisons has piqued my husband's interest...and his anger."

"That doesn't prove anything," Kendra said. "All armies have specialized groups of men. My uncle has said so many times."

"Perhaps." The queen narrowed her eyes slightly. "However, I recall that Adrian de Soules and his two companions were highly skilled in weaponry. And, they were *French*. A coincidence, do you think?"

Kendra's heart plummeted to her feet and for a second, she felt like she couldn't breathe. She'd known the queen was vindictive and had probably never forgiven Adrian for not succumbing to her, but Kendra hadn't thought the woman would trouble herself with factions of war. "Monsieur de Soules came to Scotland to fill his uncle's position."

"Hmm. Most envoys are men of letters, not warriors. The Templars were both." The queen refolded the vellum. "Perhaps I shall speak to Edward about my suspicions."

Kendra felt the room start to spin, but somehow she managed to remain upright until the sensation stopped. Edward had not been especially interested in following the mandates of a French king in rounding up Templars, but that was before these recent battles. Kendra knew who Robert Bruce's elite army was. Edward would be more than happy to collect any and all Templars at this point. From what her uncle had said just this morning, even Stirling Castle, still in English hands, was under siege, which was why the English were marching north.

Kendra could hardly wait until the queen was dressed for dinner and had descended the stairs to the hall. She had nearly a half hour to tend to her own ablutions before she'd be expected to reappear. She was going to use that time to try and find out from her uncle what she could about Edward's response to the French king's request.

The door to the suite of rooms her uncle and aunt had been assigned stood slightly ajar. As she approached to knock, she heard them talking. At the mention of Adrian's name, she dropped her hand and stepped closer to listen.

"There is always the chance he has returned to France," her aunt said.

"Doubtful," her uncle answered. "He is still

Bruce's envoy."

"You won't seek Monsieur de Soules out, will you?"

A pause ensued. "I think the man has the right to know he has a child."

"We have been over this before," her aunt said. "It was easy enough for me to keep Kendra's letter to him from being posted, but it was divine intervention that I intercepted the one he sent shortly after her return. We cannot afford to be seen as consorting with the enemy. Especially not now."

Kendra didn't hear her uncle's response because of the buzzing in her ears. She steadied herself against the wall for a moment before silently backing away. Thankful that her satin slippers made no sound on the stone floor, she squelched the urge to run until she turned the corner. By the time she reached her own chamber two floors above, she was out of breath, although whether from racing up the stairs or from shock, she wasn't sure.

Adrian had written! Her aunt had kept the letter from her. All this time, she had thought he didn't care… Then another thought settled like a rock on top of the first one. *He* had not gotten *her* letter either.

"Mama, what's wrong?" Owen's small face looked up at her in concern.

Kendra forced a smile and patted his head. "Nothing, sweetheart. Mama is just late in getting down to dinner."

"When you get back, will you read me a story about adventure?" he asked. "I like the one you tell about the knight who rescued the princess in Scotland."

That was the story of Adrian rescuing *her,* with the

names changed and a happy ending added. As she looked at her son, an idea began to form. She knelt down. "Instead of telling you the story again, would you like me to take you there?"

His eyes grew huge as he nodded.

She smiled, genuinely this time. "But it must be our secret for now."

Owen nodded again, placing two fingers across his lips.

Kendra rose, feeling more lighthearted than she had in more than three years. She was going back to Scotland.

Chapter Twenty-Six

Not quite a sennight later, the army had mobilized and begun its march north. The thousands of men Edward had gathered formed a line stretching nearly a mile long. Behind the cavalry and foot soldiers came the heavy wagons, loaded with everything from ammunition to cooking utensils, and behind those came the women. Although a few of them followed to provide night pleasure, some were married to soldiers while others were to help with the cooking, laundry, and mending that was always needed.

It was this last group to which Kendra had attached herself and her son. She'd bribed her maid out of sturdy walking shoes, two serviceable dresses, and a plain woolen shawl. Luckily the maid also had a son about Owen's size and was only too happy to accept an additional coin for similar clothing for him. Thankfully, Owen thought it was all a great adventure and was soon frolicking with the half-dozen other children in the entourage.

While many of the women vied for the opportunity to serve the king and his commanders each evening, Kendra was careful to stay well in the background when they made camp. Even though she'd applied soot to her hair, making it darker, she didn't want to take the chance on her uncle possibly spotting her if he decided to walk the grounds.

"Mama, when are we going to get there?" Owen asked one night after they'd been on the road for nearly a fortnight.

"Soon, baby." At least, she hoped it was. The landscape had changed from gently rolling hills to steeper terrain and, even though the children rode in whatever spaces they could find in the wagons, they were becoming fretful on this long journey.

"I want my own bed."

She stroked his curls. The idea of a soft, warm bed was something she yearned for too—to say nothing of a hot, fragrant bath—but neither would be happening any time soon. But how could she explain that to a four-year-old?

"Pretty soon we'll come to a castle, and you'll have another adventure."

He looked at her with wide eyes. "The castle where the knight rescued the princess?"

"The very one." She smiled, remembering how Adrian had indeed arranged her rescue from Berwick, although it was actually an escape.

"Will the knight be there?"

"He doesn't live there anymore, but you will meet him soon." At least, she hoped he would.

Over the days of the long journey northward, she'd considered several options. From what she'd overheard from her uncle, the plan was to move the huge army to Berwick, and quarter there only long enough to rest horses and men, perhaps a sennight at most. Edward planned to march north toward Edinburgh, then westward, gathering more forces along the way, until he reached Stirling Castle. Since the Scots were outnumbered nearly four to one, the king didn't think it would take long to relieve his soldiers and declare victory.

The obvious choice would be for Kendra to remain with the army and follow them to Stirling, but she didn't want Owen anywhere near an actual battle. The other problem with that choice was that Bruce no doubt would have received word the English were approaching, and she didn't have a way to get to Adrian first.

The more difficult, but hopefully safer, choice was to fall away from the army as it passed the road to Roslin. She hoped the baron would remember her, but even if he did not, she could ask him for refuge for her son as well as ask him to take her to Bruce's camp. The two of them riding alone on trails the English army couldn't use would get her to the camp—and Adrian—ahead of Edward.

The plan had to work. It simply had to.

They approached Berwick late in the afternoon two days later. It had misted most of the day, making clothing damp and everyone miserable. The empty cage that still hung over the castle looked dark and dismal as well. Kendra felt tears welling in her eyes as she looked at it. The Countess of Buchan had died two years ago, but at least she hadn't spent her last years imprisoned.

As they passed through the city gates, Kendra felt a shiver slide down her spine, and she looked up once more. What appeared to be tendrils of fog swirled through the bars of the cage and, as she watched, the fog pulled itself together, a face seeming to form in the midst of it. Her breathing hitched. It was the same face she'd seen that night so long ago when she'd stood in burned out ruins and met Robert the Bruce for the first time… and seen the fetch of King Arthur.

She blinked. When she opened her eyes, the image was gone and only fog was beginning to settle in. She hadn't had an encounter with a ghost since she'd returned to Wales, but she was nearly back in Scotland now. Had Arthur been waiting all this time?

Kendra was so absorbed in her thoughts she didn't realize the vast army had fallen away to set up tents outside the city walls. Only the women had followed Edward and his commanders into the castle bailey. Too late, Kendra realized she was highly visible in the much smaller group. She knew the continuous mist had rinsed the coal soot from her hair, leaving it lighter, as well. Quickly, she reached for her shawl to cover her head, but a familiar figure was already approaching.

"What in Hades are you doing here?" the Earl of Pembroke asked.

****

From the battlements, Kendra watched the English army move out several days later and twitched with impatience. Since her ill-fated discovery—she'd given the excuse she didn't want to go to France with the queen—her uncle had hardly spoken with her other than to let her know, in most emphatic terms, that he was not pleased she had followed him north. His first inclination had been to send her back to London immediately, but Humphrey de Bohun, Earl of Hereford, and another of Edward's commanders, had told her uncle not to waste the number of men it would take to escort her. After Edward had added that she would be perfectly safe—he meant *guarded*—at Berwick until they returned, her uncle had reluctantly agreed.

So now, all she had to do was escape the castle. Without Adrian's help this time.

One of the first things she'd done after being separated from the group of serving women was to take Owen to the stable to see the horses. He didn't need any coaxing since he loved the animals, but her main reason was finding someone she could trust to turn a blind eye while she "borrowed" a mount—not that one more horse would be missed with the number of extras the cavalry had taken. Luckily, there were several stable hands still there who remembered her, and a few coins persuaded them to have a horse ready for her as soon as the army was out of sight.

Kendra hurried down to the small room she'd been given and smiled at Owen, sitting on the edge of the bed. "I see you're ready."

His lower lip stuck out. "I have been waiting and *waiting*."

"I know you have, sweetheart, but I had to wait until the army disappeared."

"Can we go now?" He jumped up, eager to be off.

"Yes, but we can't act too much in a hurry. Remember our secret?"

"We are running away."

"But no one can know that. They think we are just going for a little ride."

He studied her. "But we aren't coming back, are we?"

She shook her head. "We're going to find the knight who rescued the princess in the story."

Her son's eyes rounded. "Do you really know where he is?"

"Not exactly, but I know a man who will help us

look for him." She held out her hand to Owen.

At least, she hoped the Baron of Roslin would agree.

****

"Are you sure?" Adrian stared intently at Callum's younger brother Cameron as he drained his tankard of ale in the king's private tent. He'd arrived at Bruce's camp half an hour ago on a horse that was nearly winded. That had drawn Robert's ire, although perhaps not as much as the news that Cameron brought. Edward had already arrived at Berwick.

"Aye."

Cameron was one of Bruce's spies at Berwick and worked as a groom. English knights seldom noticed stable hands, and Cameron gleaned lots of information listening to their conversations. He usually sent the news with a trusted Scotsman, but this time he'd come himself.

"Is it true that Edward has nearly twenty thousand men?" Bruce asked.

"It looked like it," Cameron answered. "There were tents as far as the eye could see."

Adrian exchanged a look with Pierre and Remy. They all knew that capturing Edinburgh and laying siege to Stirling would bring Edward north, but they had thought the rumors of such a huge number were exaggeration.

"That is four times as many men as we have," one of the other commanders said.

Bruce looked thoughtful. "Sometimes size can be a disadvantage." Several sets of eyes focused on him, and he raised his hand, signaling silence. After a moment, he continued. "Think of the terrain. He will have to use the Falkirk-Stirling road since it is the only firm ground for his cavalry."

"You are thinking of an ambush?" someone asked.

'Of sorts."

"The road is on an open plain, so that would be hard to do."

"We would wait at the western edge of New Park, which is heavily wooded."

"They would still outnumber us."

"True, but if we dig pits containing caltrops along the left side of the road and then cover them, the English army cannot fight its way across the open space. They will veer to the right, not aware how treacherous Bannock Burn and its marshes are." The king smiled. "Horses do not do well in boggy ground and heavily armored knights even less so."

Pierre nodded. "Putting their cavalry in such a quagmire will certainly even the odds of our schiltrons against their foot soldiers."

"I agree," Remy said. "The spearmen are more than ready, not to mention the plain folk who want to free their land."

"Exactly." Bruce looked at Adrian. "And then, you will bring in our elite force to attack from behind. The English will have no place to go, and this war will finally be over."

Adrian nodded. The timing could not have been better. If Edward were already on the road to Stirling, the army should arrive sometime late on June 23rd, which meant battle would commence at dawn on St. John's day, June 24th, a date held sacred—and considered lucky—by Templars. Besides that, the exiled Templars had not been able to save their Grand

Master from his horrible death. They were more than eager to prove their worth in Scotland. He glanced at Remy and Pierre. "We will not leave the battlefield while one of us is still standing." It was an old Templar vow.

Cameron cleared his throat. "But there is something else to consider."

Bruce turned to him. "What is that?"

"Lady Kendra, sire." He stole a look at Adrian. "Lady Kendra rides with Edward."

Adrian kept his expression impassive, refusing to give in to any emotion. She had left him over four years ago. He certainly wasn't going to allow anyone—especially not Robert Bruce—to know how he felt. "Why would Pembroke bring his niece along?"

Cameron hesitated, then took a deep breath. "There was talk that she might lead the English to this camp."

Adrian felt like a sword had just pierced him. She'd been living amongst the English for three years, to say nothing of her uncle being one of Edward's top commanders. Had she been persuaded to lead Edward's men to this secret hideaway? Granted, she didn't know *exactly* where it was, but with twenty thousand English soldiers able to spread out, it could very well be Bruce's men who were surrounded before the battle even began.

Evidently, the king had similar thoughts. "We break camp at dawn," he said as he rose and left the tent.

No one said a word as everyone except Remy and Pierre followed him. Adrian looked at his friends. "She wouldn't do it," he said, but he wasn't sure he wasn't trying to convince himself instead of them.

Was it possible Kendra had turned traitor?

****

Kendra arrived at Bruce's camp with Henri St. Clair as the sun dipped low behind the hills. As they rode through the narrow rocky pass, she saw that it was nearly empty, and her heart sank.

"Where has everyone gone?"

St. Clair looked grim. "Perhaps the battle has already engaged."

"Edward's army couldn't possibly have gotten here before us." She paused. "Could they?"

"Doubtful, but I'll have a look around to see if there are tracks to show they've gone by. I'll return in a few minutes." He wheeled his horse and rode back through the pass.

Kendra frowned as she took in the scene. Obviously, the men had left in somewhat of a hurry, since much of the camp remained intact. Had Edward managed to get here before her?

She had arrived at Roslin the same day the army left, and it hadn't taken her long to convince Henri to take her—and a particular piece of Templar treasure— to Bruce's camp. They'd left Owen in the safe, capable arms of the baron's staff and struck out on horseback along mountain trails familiar to St. Clair. Edward's army should be hours behind them.

Just then, Hammish emerged from one of the smaller tents and made his way to her. She smiled in relief.

"What are you doing here?"

The smile faded at his abrupt tone. "I came to warn Adrian…I mean, Robert the Bruce. Edward's army will be at Stirling very soon."

He peered around her. "Or did you bring them to us?"

"What?"

"You are English. When word came that you rode with your uncle, Bruce thought you were leading them to us."

She stared at Hammish in disbelief. Had Adrian thought the same thing? "I would never betray you."

He gave her skeptical look. "You left four years ago, and you never replied to Adrian's letter."

Oh, Lord. "My aunt intercepted it and I never got it. I wrote him, too, about..." Her voice trailed off. Owen was her secret until she could see Adrian. "My aunt intercepted that one as well."

He remained suspicious. "So you just rode here by yourself? I doubt your uncle allowed that."

She shook her head. "I'm supposed to be at Berwick. I escaped after the army left and went to Roslin to get Baron St. Clair to bring me here."

Hammish raised an eyebrow. "And where is he?"

"He went to check..." She didn't finish the sentence as she heard horse's hooves, and a minute later, Henri came back through the pass. She almost felt giddy. "There he is! Now do you believe me?"

The Scot's expression changed when he saw the baron. He said something in Gaelic to which Henri replied. She couldn't understand a word of what they said, but a few minutes later, St. Clair turned back to her.

"Hammish is waiting for the locals to arrive. Bruce and the Tem...the others have already gone to await Edward."

Kendra eyed the saddlebag in which the treasure

resided. "I thought you said they all should drink from the cup before the battle."

He gave her a warning look, since Hammish was not a Templar. "They will. I should be able to reach them before dawn."

"I am going with you."

"Battlefields are no place for women. You will be much safer here."

If he thought she was going to remain behind, he was sorely mistaken. She had pondered why King Arthur's ghost had appeared at Berwick, but when St. Clair had brought out the silver cup—the actual Holy Grail hidden in the Temple of Solomon—everything had fallen into place. Arthur had beaten the Saxons and united his kingdom five hundred years ago. Now it was time for Robert the Bruce to do the same.

"I am going."

St. Clair grimaced. "I suspect you're going to be a bigger challenge to Adrian than tomorrow's battle."

"Well, let's fight one battle at a time, shall we?"

He sighed. "I'm not going to win this one, am I?"

"No. I would suggest we not waste time debating that." Kendra nudged her horse forward. "Dawn comes early to these parts."

****

Kendra couldn't remember when she had been this angry. Angry at herself, especially, for having been duped. From where she sat, bound to a chair, she looked around the tiny crofter's cottage, its sole inhabitant smiling benignly at her.

"Ye should nae fash yourself, lass," the old man said. "'Tis safe ye are."

Safe. Sunlight streamed through the open door, and

she could hear the distant sounds of a battle already engaged. Why, oh, why, hadn't she been suspicious when St. Clair had stopped at the cottage last night? He'd said it was to water the horses and ask for a bit of bread and cheese. Since it had been dark, she'd had no idea they were on the very edge of the battlefield.

She forced a smile. "I think Lord St. Clair called you Donald. May I do so?"

"Aye."

"Thank you, Donald. I must say, having my hands bound is very uncomfortable."

He gave her a calculating look. "'Tis the baron's orders."

Kendra silently cursed St. Clair as she tugged at the rope. "He is not here."

Donald jutted his chin. "He gave me a coin to keep ye tied."

She would gladly have offered him two coins to release her, except her money pouch was in the small bag secured to her horse, and the baron had taken her mount along with his. Of course, they were both his horses, but she had the sneaking suspicion he wanted to make sure she couldn't follow him, even if she got away. She twisted her wrist and felt the rope give just the slightest bit.

"I understand you wish to do the honorable thing, but surely the baron didn't mean for you to keep me tied until he returns?" Donald grunted, and Kendra forced another smile, although it felt more like baring her teeth. "I am hardly going to go running off on foot, not even knowing where I am."

He grunted again, and she wondered if he knew that was exactly what she planned to do. St. Clair had not thought about the sturdy boots she wore. Tugging again, she felt a little give of the bonds. "I'm sure the baron didn't mean for you to leave me in a painful situation."

Donald drew his brows together. "The baron said nae to be taken in by what ye say."

Blast the man to Hades. She tried a different tactic. "What about if I need to attend to...*personal* needs?"

He looked startled, then slightly horrified, as though the idea had not occurred to him. Which it probably hadn't. "You wouldn't want me to humiliate myself, would you?"

"Will ye quit your blethering?" Donald frowned. "A mon canna think with the noise."

"Noise?" Kendra cocked her head, listening. "It does seem the battle sounds closer, doesn't it?"

His head lifted, and his gaze sharpened. She could have sworn his ears even perked. And then she realized that the *noise* really had gotten much louder. She could hear men shouting and the shrill whinny of horses and, faintly, the clash of steel on steel. She twisted her wrists again, managing to free one finger. "It sounds like they're coming this way!"

Donald sprang to his feet, surprisingly spry for his age, and grabbed the stout shepherd's staff by the door. "'Tis time I joined them, then."

Kendra managed to free one hand as he ran out the door. It didn't take long to free the other hand. She quickly crossed the small room and hefted herself onto the window ledge at the back of the cottage, glancing toward the door once to be sure Donald wasn't in sight. Then she pushed herself through, landing with a soft thud in the dirt.

Picking herself up, she made her way to the side of the cottage and stood still in shock at the chaotic scene in front of her. English foot soldiers were fleeing across the field, Scots spearmen in pursuit. From the nearby marsh, horses were struggling to gain footing, a few making it out of the boggy ground onto firmer ground. She heard the thundering of hooves as a group of cavalry galloped along the road on the other side of the field. She couldn't tell if they were English or Scots, but this was not the place to stand and find out. The tree line framing the field wasn't that far away. If she ran, it would only take a few minutes to get to the safety of cover.

Kendra bolted from the side of the cottage, praying no one would notice one person running in the opposite direction from the rest. Once she reached the shelter of the trees, she could wait until the battle faded and then proceed to find Bruce's camp and, more importantly, Adrian. She refused to think that he might be injured or even dead. She'd come too far and waited too long…

A horse thundered toward her from the woods, and before she could turn to run, a gauntleted arm reached down to grab her and fling her across the saddle like a sack of grain. As her head made contact with the chausson covering the horseman's thigh, her last thought before the world dimmed was that it was *English* armor.

Chapter Twenty-Seven

Robert's plan had worked, Adrian thought as he galloped alongside his Templar brothers. The Earls of Gloucester and Hereford had been driven back at the south end of New Park. To the north, de Beaumont and Clifford had been beaten down by the Earl of Moray and, thanks to the pits dug along the road, the remainder of English cavalry had to turn right, straight into the marsh where the Bannock Burn surrounded them on three sides. A perfect trap. Chaos and disruption of the English ranks ensued, with Edward fleeing the scene with the knights who'd managed to avoid the bog.

Scotland's war with England was effectively over.

As his cavalry unit moved to round up the foot soldiers trying to escape, movement in his periphery caught Adrian's attention. Across the field, someone was running in the opposite direction, like a salmon swimming upstream. It took a moment for his mind to register that the figure was wearing a skirt. And then he knew who it was.

Kendra. Even though St. Clair had assured him he had her safely and securely trussed in a crofter's cottage, Adrian should have known she would somehow manage to slip away. Not that he was totally surprised. She had, after all, managed to get to Roslin to warn St. Clair about the English army. The baron had told him he was sure she would have followed him to the battle site if he had simply refused to let her accompany him. Adrian had no doubt that was true, but he'd also thought she would be safe with Donald. He'd been looking forward to riding there once this last group of soldiers was caught. He grimaced. Of course, she wouldn't think about *waiting* for him to do that.

The grimace turned into a frown as an English knight shot out of the woods, heading straight for her. In one fell swoop, without the horse breaking stride, the man had pulled her up in front of him. Adrian cursed and signaled Pierre to take charge of the men as he fell away from them to give chase.

The knight glanced behind him and then spurred his horse on. Rather than follow through a churned-up field muddied with both blood and water, Adrian stayed on the road, knowing he could stop the man where the road took a sharp turn and cut across his path. What he hadn't known, though, was another peat bog lay ahead.

As soon as the charger's front hooves sank into the soggy ground, it jerked to a stop, unseating the knight as Kendra slipped upside down into the mire. Adrian flung himself off his horse before it slid to its own stop. He spared a quick glance at the knight as he rushed to Kendra. The acute angle of the man's head told him the neck had broken when he landed.

Kendra lay on her stomach, not moving, her face buried in the mud. Adrian plunged in, ignoring the sucking pull of the bog on his boots, and bent to clasp her waist and pull her up against him. Knowing the effort of turning around would only cause his feet to sink deeper, he slogged his way backward, thankful the horse hadn't gotten farther than it did.

After what seemed a small eternity, he felt his feet

finally making contact with firm ground. Another step or two and he knelt to lay Kendra on the ground, wiping the mud away from her mouth and nose and willing her to breathe.

"*Je t'aime! Ne me laisse pas!*" He brushed her wet hair away from her face. "Do not leave me!" When she didn't stir, he felt frantically for a pulse but couldn't find it. His eyes stung with unshed tears. He hadn't cried since he'd been a babe, but he hadn't felt helpless as a babe either. "*Mon Dieu! Si'l vous plait!* Do not let her die! Do not let her die!"

A calm settled over him then and, as if he were being guided, he bent and placed his mouth over hers and gave her his breath. Her chest lifted slightly, and he did it again. And again. He felt for a pulse once more and, very faintly, felt it. And then her chest rose on its own as she inhaled.

And he cried.

****

Something was jostling her, lolling her side to side. Sounds vibrated around her...the creak of wood, the sound of metal grating on stone, the clop of horses' hooves. Slowly, the darkness around her shifted to a gray hue and then to light. Kendra opened her eyes to see blue sky as the scents of straw and leather assailed her.

She was in a wagon, tucked rather snugly between the side board and a stack of saddles. Even without moving a muscle, she hurt all over, a soreness that couldn't have come from lying in a wagon, however much it bounced.

A horse sidled alongside, and Adrian peered over, an anxious expression on his face that quickly changed into relief.

"You're awake!"

"*Oui*." She tried to sit up, only to have him lean down and push her gently back.

"Don't try to get up yet."

It was probably just as well, since a wave of dizziness had washed over her. "What's happened? Why am I here?"

"What do you remember?"

"I saw part of the battle. I thought I would be safe in the forest. I remember running…" She winced. It even hurt to think. "…and then nothing."

"An English knight captured you, only his horse hit a bog and threw both of you. You have quite a nasty bump on your head."

She lifted her hand to feel it, then winced again.

"You need to rest now," Adrian said. "We will be back at Roslin soon, and St. Clair will get a physician."

Roslin. Owen. Lord, she hadn't had a chance to tell Adrian about his son. "There is something you should know—"

"If it's about the letters, Hammish already told me." Adrian frowned. "I should have suspected they were intercepted."

"It isn't that. Well, it *is*, but there's more—"

"Which can wait." He broke into a smile. "All that matters right now is that I have my woman back. The woman that I love. We can discuss the details once we get to Roslin and the physician has checked you over."

"But I want—"

"Hush now. Don't use your energy to talk right now. Just rest." He put his fingers to his lips, then bent down to brush them across her mouth. "*Je t'aime, mi amoureux, je t'aime,"* he said as he spurred his horse forward.

"Je t'aime," she whispered back, tears of happiness spilling down her face. "I love you too."

****

By the time they reached Roslin, Kendra felt much better. Adrian had ridden alongside the wagon, although he insisted she stay lying flat and save her strength by not talking. Not that she had much opportunity. She'd wanted desperately to tell him about Owen, but one or another of his Templar brothers usually rode beside him. They either relived the victory or, in more hushed tones, spoke of the Holy Grail that they were carrying back. If news got back to Edward that the sacred relic was in Scottish possession, he would stop at nothing—including seeking help from King Philippe and Pope Clement—to get it. That, in turn, would also lead to the discovery of several hundred Templars still alive and well in Scotland…and both the French king and the Pope wanted them dead.

From what she could gather, St. Clair had plans to dig a special vault not too far from where he intended to build his stone castle. Far enough away that if the castle were raided, the Grail would not be found, but close enough to keep an eye on its surroundings.

Now, as the wagon rolled to a stop in front of the current residence, Kendra held her breath. Owen would come flying out the door any moment, and she'd had no time to prepare Adrian.

However, instead of her son appearing in the doorway, a man who identified himself as a physician stepped out. Apparently, St. Clair had sent a messenger on ahead to have him waiting. Before she could ask anyone where her son was, Adrian had already scooped her up and was carrying her into the house. A room had been prepared upstairs, and Adrian had been told in no-nonsense terms by Mrs. Gordon, the housekeeper, that he would need to wait outside.

Kendra fretted while the doctor did his exam. She almost refused the bath that had been brought in, but the housekeeper told her Owen wasn't there. Her husband had taken him for a ride since they didn't know what condition she would be in when she arrived. The thought of hot water soothing her sore muscles was too much to resist. It wouldn't hurt to delay telling Adrian for just a little longer.

Just a few minutes…

****

Adrian paced like a caged bear in St. Clair's receiving room. The physician had departed only minutes ago, with the good news that Kendra would be fine after a day or two of rest. He'd been about to charge into her room when the housekeeper told him, quite firmly, that Kendra was taking a well-deserved bath. He'd started to say he could help her with that, but he didn't think Mrs. Gordon would let him. She was as much a commander in this house as any of Bruce's men in the field.

"Are you the knight who rescued the princess?"

Adrian jerked around at the sound of the young voice. A small child with a headful of black curls held a miniature shield in front of his face and, in the other hand, a little wooden sword. Adrian wasn't sure if the boy was shy or trying to play.

Adrian smiled at the sight. "If you're going to fight, lad, you need to be able to see your opponent."

The shield lowered slowly as the boy's face appeared. Adrian's smile froze. The child had the same uncanny color of gold eyes as he did. In fact...

"How old are you?"

He held up four fingers. "Mama says this old."

Four years. *Mon Dieu.* The night he'd spent making love to Kendra... had she become with child? Adrian hesitated, almost afraid to ask the next question. "And who is your mama?"

"My mama is the princess. I'm Owen."

"Well, Owen, my name is Adrian."

The boy tilted his head slightly like Adrian sometimes did. "Are you a knight?"

"*Oui.* I am a knight."

"The one who rescues the princess?"

Adrian paused again. "I suppose you could say I rescued a princess."

"In the story, Mama says the knight looks like me." He observed Adrian with a look far older than his years. "You look like me too."

Adrian took a deep breath as a strange sensation he couldn't identify coursed through him. He held out his hand. "Perhaps we should find your mama."

****

Kendra had just donned a clean woolen dress when she heard a knock at her chamber. Mrs. Gordon was nothing if not efficient. The housekeeper had hardly left and already the scullery lads had come to take the bath away. She pushed her loose hair back and went to open the door. And nearly fainted.

Adrian stood there with Owen.

"Mama!" Owen flung his arms around her waist. "Mama! I brought you the knight from the story."

Kendra stole a glance at Adrian and then smiled at her son. "It seems you did."

"I found him downstairs." Owen looked up at her. "Will he stay with us? In the story, you always say he will."

Kendra looked up at Adrian, but before she could answer, he did.

"I am going to stay, Owen. A knight must take care of his princess." He gazed at Kendra over his son's head. "I suspect your mama and I have much to talk about."

"Yes, we do." She ruffled Owen's curls. "Would you go tell Mrs. Gordon that I'm starving?"

He nodded. "I'm hungry too!"

Adrian stepped inside her room and closed the door as soon as Owen had scampered off. "When were you going to tell me?"

"I…I tried…" Kendra paused. "You told me not to talk."

"Remind me never to do that again."

"Are you…" She stopped, then continued. "Are you pleased?"

His eyes widened in surprise. "Of course I am. Why wouldn't I be?"

She felt her face heat and looked down. "You…the night we made love…nothing was said about the future—"

"I'll say it now, then." He put his hand under her chin and lifted it. "I want you and I want Owen in my life forever. Not just as my woman, but as my wife."

"And I want to be both your wife and your woman, Templar."

He glanced toward the bed. "Perhaps we should

somehow bind this agreement."

Kendra took his palm and kissed it. "I find myself suddenly starving for something other than food."

"So do I," he said as he picked her up and carried her to the bed. "So do I."

A word about the author...

Cynthia Breeding lives on the Gulf Coast of Texas with a very non-spoiled poodle-mix and enjoys walking and horseback riding on the beach, as well as sailing.
Visit with her at:
www.cynthiabreeding.com

Thank you for purchasing
this publication of The Wild Rose Press, Inc.

For questions or more information
contact us at
info@thewildrosepress.com.

The Wild Rose Press, Inc.